WINTER WHIMSY

WINTER WHIMSY

ELEVEN TALES OF CHILDLIKE WONDER

Balance of Seven

Winter Whimsy
Eleven Tales of Childlike Wonder

Copyright © 2018 by Balance of Seven
All rights reserved. Printed in the United States.

All stories are copyrighted to their respective authors and used here
with their permission.
"Missing in a Yuletide Blizzard" by K. N. Gemme was originally
published in *Snowflakes from Heaven* and is reprinted by permission of
K. N. Gemme.

For information, contact:

Balance of Seven
www.balanceofseven.com
Publisher: ymalakova@balanceofseven.com
Managing Editor: dtinker@balanceofseven.com

Cover Design: Seventh Star Art
www.seventhstarart.com

Copyediting and Formatting: D Tinker Editing
www.balanceofseven.com/d-tinker-editing

French Language Consultant: C. M. Lander

ISBN: 978-1-947012-96-7

Library of Congress Control Number: 2018963652

24 23 22 21 20 19 18   1 2 3 4 5

To the child

within each of us:

You were forged

from magic and dreams.

May you burn bright in every season.

CONTENTS

INTRODUCTION

Dear Reader,

I remember that winter . . . maybe you do too . . .

The epic snowfall.

School closed for days.

Your body bundled up in so many sweaters, coats, and gloves that you almost couldn't move.

And freedom.

Glorious. Magical. Limitless freedom.

A time of exploration and imagination, when front yards turned into far-away places through the magic of wet snow and a little bit of sweat that sometimes lead to igloo villages at the North Pole or racecar races at the Indie 500.

That year, we sculpted a pirate ship in the middle of a boring front lawn. Looking back with adult eyes, I'm sure it looked like shapeless piles of snow, but to my child self, it was the exact replica of One-Eyed Willie's ship, which I *knew* could take me anywhere I wanted to go!

I can still feel the pride of showing it off to our parents and the tummy tingles of anticipation that I got every time I walked its decks, sailing the seas with my brothers as we created our own adventures and steered toward new horizons.

Introduction

Life filled with the awe that only childlike wonder can bring!

That's the gift the authors of *Winter Whimsy* want to give you here within the pages of this anthology. From enchanted objects to mystical creatures, let them remind you of the magic, whimsy, and childlike wonder of days past when all it took was a little snow and a powerful imagination to transform your world into almost anything you wanted it to be.

Enjoy! And remember: the magic doesn't have to stay on the page. We hope you'll take some of it with you when you return to the "real" world.

Loves & hugs,
>Debbie Burns
>Founder of Fiction Expedition

THE SNOW DEMON

M. ROSE CALLAHAN

The winter here holds unexpected secrets, and those hidden deep beneath crisp, pristine snow can be deadly. Near the safety of a glowing hearth, I clack knitting needles together with each stitch, wishing the noise would muffle my internal whisper: *I should have known.*

Across from me, Nana rocks in her chair, creating an even rhythm of creaks and groans against the floorboards. At my feet is her cat, Oscar, swatting at the yarn dangling from my needles.

I take a deep breath. "Have you ever seen a snow demon?"

The creaking stops. Nana's gaze is fixed on the fire. Smoke swirls from her lips and nose as she puffs at the stem of a slender white pipe. Moments pass before she replies. "Such tales, my Kata. It's a story made to scare children, or on which misfortunes can be blamed."

Without moving her eyes from the fire, she adds, "You dropped a stitch. Undo what you've done and make it right."

The wayward stitch is down several rows, all tight and bunched. My fingers fumble to capture the loop and work it back to the active line on the needle, which proves to be more trouble than necessary. I rip the knitting loose and start over.

"Were there snow demons when you were a girl—I mean, were stories told about them?"

"Since the beginning of time." She winks at me. "If you believe the stories."

My hands lower to the pile of bent yarn on my lap, and I lean closer to her.

"Very well." She removes the pipe from her mouth. "It's said the demons are born from a goddess's tears. When she cries tears of sorrow, the ground is gently nourished with her love. When her tears turn to anger, each falls hard and with such force, they burn through snow and ice, pierce through rock and soil, and seal her hate into the frozen earth."

"Then they're around all the time?" With my head down, I return my focus to the yarn work. "According to the stories, I mean."

"Of course. Yet these are things you need not worry about. Yes?"

"But *if* they are around all the time, why aren't little devils running around the village or in people's houses?"

"Is it not so that all make-believe creatures must be invited into one's home to do harm?"

"Like when someone knocks on the door? You open it and say, 'Come in'? Then it's invited in? That makes no sense. If I see a devil at my door, I know not to let it in."

Nana glances at me through narrowed eyes. "Or window. You could argue one could knock on a window."

A window? My jaw hangs slack.

Nana cackles. "You worry so much about nothing." She pushes herself up from the chair in stages and taps the bowl of her pipe on the mantle. Delicate ashes float into the firebox. "Besides, the only way to summon a demon is to make a snow angel at dusk."

A knitting needle slips from my fingers and bounces on the stone hearth near my feet. Tingles shoot through me, knotting in the pit of my stomach.

"Why the long face, Kata? Are you missing your home?"

The mud and rocks of my home never saw snow. My vision blurs and I bow my head. You can't make angels in mud.

"It must be the cold. You'll get used to it, my sweet one." She cups my chin in her hand. "And your blood will be as thick as a woodsman's soon enough, I promise. For now, I go to bed."

Her bedroom is separated from the main room by a single sheet hanging from the ceiling. On her way, she stops by the front door to let Oscar outside. "Please. Will you let the cat in before you sleep? More snow is coming."

The handle jingles as the door is shut. Next to the door on a frayed piece of rope hangs an iron circle, twisting near its bottom curve, from which two tail-like vines dangle, swirling into opposing scrolls. Nana touches her fingertips to her lips, presses the kiss onto the ornament, and then disappears behind the sheet.

Left alone to study the embers pulsing in the firebox, I can't help but see the similarity between them and the misshapen pinpoints of memory buried within the ash of my own regret. One such pinpoint flares as the recollection of what I did only hours earlier sweeps over me.

If only it had been bright enough. If only the sun had shone a few minutes longer. If only I had known.

A scratch at the door pulls me from my thoughts. "Oscar. I nearly forgot you were out there." I make my way to the door.

The view into the night leaves me breathless. The forever-greens balance snow pillows on outstretched limbs. A few bare branches, encased in ice, poke through like boney fingers clawing at thick snowflakes gliding from a night sky the color of the apricot tea roses that will be in bloom back home.

But no cat.

"Oscar," I call. "Come in." The snow softens my voice to a whisper.

A red shawl hangs on a nail close by, so I grab it and wrap it around my shoulders, leaning beyond the threshold. A gust affronts me, pelting my face with snow and sleet. Cold stings my lungs, freezing the breath in my chest. I stumble back into the hut, where the warmth gives me strength to call out from inside the shack. "Come in already. If you don't come now, I'll leave you out there to fend for yourself."

With the handle still firmly in hand, I close the door, much to the protest of the hinges. A second gust attempts to rip the door from my grip, but I slam it shut with the full of my weight. The latch clicks into place.

A shiver slides down my spine. Grabbing my bed—two old curtains sewn at the edges and stuffed with feathers and horse hair—I toss it near the hearth. Changing into a nightdress and socks made of wool gives me comfort, as do the fur pelts. Until I remember Oscar in the snow. "You should have come when I called, you old cat."

I lie for a few minutes in darkness, sleep keeping its distance. Outside, the wind howls. Between gales, a tap-tap-tap strikes the window.

Kicking the blankets onto the floor, I bolt upright. A long, thin shape is silhouetted against the window pane. My shaking hands grasp a candle, knuckles turning white. Held to a dying ember, the candle ignites, yet the flame's aura casts more shadows than light. Attempts to moisten my lips are useless. I must press my face against the glass to see clearly.

What if?

In my chest, my heart pounds. I forgot to ask Nana what a snow demon looks like.

Tap, tap, tap, tap . . . meow.

My muscles relax as I pull the window open. A streak of marmalade fur hops in and dashes toward Nana's bed. "Oscar. You are a handful."

I flop down onto my pad. With the furs spread over me, my eyelids grow heavy. Somewhere in the haze of awake and asleep, I imagine Oscar hissing but pay it no mind.

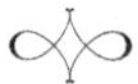

Bitter cold comes with the morning light. Nana yanks the furs off me. I scramble to a simple wooden chair next to the hearth. A blaze crackles in the firebox. I push the chair aside and stand close to the flames. On the uneven stones separating the wooden floor planks and the fireplace is the needle I dropped the night before. A rush of guilt washes over me.

I haven't felt the pang of such guilt since I was six, when I covered broken eggs with straw in the chicken coop back home. I blamed the farm dog, as any child would, right? The disappointment in my father's eyes was almost unbearable.

The needle is warm as I lift it to my chest. It is shorter than the whip was, though the same thickness. My free hand subconsciously drifts to the back of my thigh. Nana would never have whipped me for such a mistake. But would she be disappointed?

It is a secret best kept to myself.

In this moment, I tell myself yesterday's snow angel was made after classes, or before dinner, or even before breakfast. The earlier the better. I'll tell myself anything to make it so.

"Snow demons are only tales," I whisper.

The kettle wobbles in my grip when I remove it from the swing crane to pour into a large metal bowl. I remove my nightdress and rush to wipe away yesterday's grime. Steam rises from the washcloth that I pull from the bottom of the basin and wipe across my skin to erase the cold-bumps.

Because it is a school day, I dress in a smock of boiled wool, a fur-lined vest, and thick stockings to guard my legs from the chill. It never seems enough. I finish dressing by twisting my thick coal-black hair into braids and pinning them in a low bun.

Nana hums as she ladles porridge into shallow wooden bowls set on the table. "Eat before it gets cold, my Kata." For me, she scoops a bit more. "A little sugar for you? A splash of milk?"

"Only milk, please."

Nana nods, pours the milk for me, and lifts the sugar bowl, tipping it before spooning what remains into her cup of tea.

"I've wrapped cheese and bread for your meal today. Don't feed the squirrels. Yes?"

"You make too much fuss over me." Fourteen years old, and I feel like I am too old for school. "What do you think the others will say when they find my grandmother makes my midday meals . . . and at my age?"

"They will say, 'Our friend Kata has the best cheese and bread in the village.'" She places her soft, wrinkled hand on my cheek. "They will say, 'It will make her a smart midwife like her nana.' Yes?"

It's been three months since my arrival in Adjensen, and this topic is mentioned every day. I know nothing about being an apprentice. I know of farm life, not medicinal herbs and babies. And she needn't worry about who will replace her when the time comes. I've seen calves and kids born abundantly, all without the help of people. Babies can birth themselves . . . for the most part.

Her brow is as soft as her hands when I kiss it.

"One more thing, child, before you leave me for the day. Wipe the snow from your boots when you come inside. I had a terrible time this morning mopping up the mess you made last night." She walks me to the door and opens it. "Why did you go outside to get Oscar? Just call him. He will come."

"But I didn't go outside last night. It was too cold."

"Maybe you sleep too soundly. You forgot, yes? We will tie you to your bed tonight." The pale folds on her face shroud her eye as she winks.

"Yes, Nana." I want to believe that I sleepwalked.

She tucks my food into my bag and hands it to me. Oscar scampers from beneath grandmother's bed and rubs against my legs. I resist playing with him. "Shoo, cat. I'm late for school." As I reach to push him away, his hisses, swiping sharp claws at me.

"Bad cat!" I shout. "You'll get none of my dinner tonight."

Something unseen, a bug perhaps, catches his attention and he dashes off to chase it.

Snowfall from the night before softens the sharp edges of the shops along the square, creating the illusion that everything in the village is velvet and curves. The schoolhouse at the end of the main road is centered in an open field of white, with a dense line of forever-greens beyond it and the mountain range farther away still. On either side are small hills, perfect for making snow angels. The angels made yesterday are filled in with a lush blanket of powder, shimmering in the sunlight.

Except for mine. The form remains, but I'm not worried. Even though Nana said it is just a story, I take a moment to thank the saints that the imprint didn't walk off the slope like I'd imagined.

A squirrel dashes in front of me, skittering across the gentle indentations of the other children's angels, each buried peacefully beneath the fresh snow, until it reaches mine. It stops, sending a cloud of powder up around it. Rearing on its hind legs, it chitters and barks but does not move forward.

Nothing is there but the barren hill. Shadows of the forest trees stretch across the land, dipping into my angel's grooves with strips of darkness that accentuate what I did.

A wind brushes past me, carrying with it the laughter of classmates playing on the opposite side of the schoolyard. Carried on the joyful breeze, a child's song floats by.

Wings at dawn, Angels appear,
Wings at dusk, Demons to fear.
Clean the water, make it clear,
With a glowing witch's spear.

All sensation within me rushes to the pit of my stomach, and breath escapes my parted lips as a moan.

"It's only a story," I say to the wind.

"What is?"

My insides jerk. I fall half a step forward.

Sven Ogden walks toward me, his boots kicking up powder with each step. Despite being the smithy's son, he is thin, with a pair of spectacles perched on his nose and his long blond hair tied back with a leather strip. When he turns his head, I see a clasp securing it, like the buckle of the book strap slung over his shoulder.

I don't know what caught his attention, but I exhale and fan the fingers of one hand over my chest. I glance back to my snow angel.

"I see." He pulls an object from his pocket. "You know hate is blind? Through her demons, the goddess seeks to spread the misery and pain she felt."

He opens his hand to display two iron discs the size of crackers and a third no larger than a bean. "These are iron. Some creatures are said to be weakened by it."

Sven hands the two larger pieces to me. Both have open wirework, one the shape of a fish, the other a star. "The images mean nothing . . . they are only a design. I like them."

My face is tight with worry and my heart pounds against my chest, but I smile. "Me too. Thank you." I point to the smaller one still in his hand. "Does that have a design too?"

He holds it up for me to see a small eye etched on its surface. Then, without explanation, he stuffs it into his pocket.

Over his shoulder, I notice his twin sister, Skadi, trodding toward us. Twice his size, she is the image of a blacksmith's child. In the foundry, she's the one who works the forge with their father.

"Brother," she bellows, holding up a metal item. "Look what I did this morning."

"You spend too much time with the hammer," he replies. "You've almost missed the school bell. I can't cover for you every day."

"You'll forgive me when you see what I have." Skadi pushes the object, a box, at her brother.

"The eternity box! You've made the adjustments." He moves in close to her and takes the box. Holding it at eye level, he examines it. "Oh, it's wonderful. I can hardly see the hinges." He presses its sides. The center of the lid opens like a blossom. Sven hands it to me. As he releases it, the petals close.

The etching on the top is a circle sliced into a dozen sections, all curving into a center point. I press on its sides. Nothing happens. I shake it. "How does it . . . ?"

Skadi takes it from me. "Like this." Within her grip, it opens. As she hands it back, the petals fold close.

I squeeze it.

Sven placed his hands over mine. "It works with an internal mechanism. When you press against the clips on the sides, levers are released, and . . ." He pushes my fingers over two thread-thin bars under the surface edges and a small vibration tickles my fingertips.

"Whoa!"

"All the gear work is within the sides of the opening. When the levers are triggered, all the sections"—he points his pinky at the surface—"that make up the opening pull in, and the sides pull up."

Keeping the clips engaged, I hold the box for a closer look. The design isn't an etching as I first believed, but the edges of a dozen seams. The clips are tiny. I release them, awestruck by the graceful metallic twist as it closes. Wanting to repeat the movement again and again, I press the clips repeatedly. The faintest clicks sound prior to the top opening, until after one such click, the petals crunch to a stop and remain open.

I drop it. It falls to the snow with a hush. "I-I'm, sorry. I don't know what happened. I promise." My gaze darts from one twin to the other.

Sven picks it up, wiping it on his pants. "It's only meant to open a few times. It's been catching. The edges need tapping, is all—"

"Which I will not do again," Skadi interrupts. She slaps her brother's back, knocking Sven off-balance. "I do the heavy work. Sven's good at the details."

"If it's only meant to open a few times, what's it for?"

Sven takes a handkerchief from his pocket and wraps it around the box. "To keep things safe."

The bell clangs. From the opposite side of the yard, children race toward the schoolhouse. As we near the building, a girl bumps me, knocking the book bag from my shoulder. The lunch Nana made me spills onto the ground.

"Hey!" I cry out.

She inhales a quick, deep breath. Her eyes widen. Realizing what I've done, I bend my knees a few inches and touch her sleeve. "Hey, why is everyone playing over there today?"

A frown distorts her face, furrowing her brow. She twists her head toward the hillside where we played the day before. "The angels won't play there no more."

Snowfall caresses the innocent designs of yesterday's childhood games. Amid the delicate bumps and ridges is the shape of my own making, mottled in shades of onyx, rust, and chestnut. What I earlier mistook for the trees' shadows is charred ground, blackening from the inside out, a shape within a shape, eating it away and expelling it as sludge.

And it is growing.

Today's lessons are blurring. The click and crunch of Sven's eternity box is a musical worm in my brain, with images of snow demons jigging to its haunting beat.

Two iron discs jingle in my coat pocket. They're warm to the touch, and I grip them in my fist, then let them tumble through my fingers. How could I have been so childish? I'm almost an adult as my fifteenth birthday approaches, and I went and did something so stupid, so dangerous. It's not hard to imagine what harm can be brought to the village, to me—to Nana.

Cursed daydreams occupy my thoughts. I am so distracted by them that a squirrel steals my bread at lunch and would have gotten my cheese if not for the Ogden twins. I had the bread set on a fence rail, and a squirrel snuck by unnoticed and grabbed it. I simply didn't know any better, just like last night.

Last night, I watched the younger children making snow angels and thought it looked fun. When they had left the schoolyard, I dropped my bag and fell back into the powder-covered hill, delighting in the sensation of snow giving way to my body. Large flakes drifted down from the early evening sky. The clouds, once gray and bleak, brightened to a dark salmon as the sun slipped below the horizon—an indication that heavy snowfall was coming.

At first, I struggled to move my arms at the same time as my legs. Once I was able to move them in unison, my arms made wings, my legs a bell skirt. Lying with my eyes closed, the wisps and sighs of snow being pushed charmed me into pretending I had taken flight.

A kick to my foot brought me back to earth.

Sven blocked what little sunlight was left as he reached down to me. "It's too late to play. Time to go home."

My cheeks flamed for a brief second, though I felt its burn for several minutes longer. I clasped his outstretched hand. He pulled me up to standing with much more force than I thought necessary.

"Why not stay a few minutes more. Playing in the snow—" I shook my head. "I know. I'm too old."

"Fourteen is not old."

I lifted my chin. "I'll be fifteen soon enough."

"Fifteen. Doesn't matter."

But it does matter. To me. Back home, fifteen is a grown woman, either starting an apprenticeship, going off to university, or newly married and starting a family.

"It doesn't matter how old you are; it's too late to play out here."

Though I hadn't noticed Skadi walk up to us, she appeared. Lifting my bag from where it had fallen, she said, "Snow demons." She left it at that.

It wasn't until that evening, in the safety of my grandmother's cottage, that I realized what I'd done.

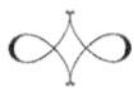

Nana lives in a small structure outside Adjensen. In a faraway clearing deep in the Norlandic forest, it is a small village in the Valley of Giants, nestled along the edge of forever-green borders, whose towering trees isolate the hamlet from the rest of the world. Nana's cottage is farthest from the village. As she tells it, her home was built when the trees were saplings and the mountains were hills. It is a single-room house under a roof of turf that, should winter ever pass,

I'm certain would sprout delicate flowers and lush ferns. But now, it is buried under inches of fine white powder and trimmed in icicles.

I rest my hand on the door handle, a flat wooden arm on the outside that, when pushed down, disengages the latch. When it's pulled up, the door locks. Inside, the handle and all its parts are rusted metal, no doubt crafted by the smithy generations ago. This afternoon, I press the handle down and it detaches, falling off in my hand. Inside the hut, the iron mechanism rattles to the floor. The door creaks open.

"For the love of Fryyah!" Nana curses.

I stand frozen, clutching the broken handle.

"Don't stand there like a hemp fish. Come in." Nana rocks forcefully in her chair made from bent limbs and twigs. Smoke puffs from the brown pipe clenched between her teeth and drifts toward the ceiling. Next to her on the floor is a blob of partially churned butter.

The tense atmosphere warns me to tread with caution. I close the door, cringing with each screech and pop the hinges make.

"I am not mad at you, my Kata. I am glad you are home."

My bag slinks to the floor as I sit by the table.

"What a miserable day." She puffs on the pipe, which I don't recall seeing before today. "This morning, I set to churn butter and the lid pops off, sending the crank across the floor, spilling cream all over the room, me, and Oscar."

"Oscar? Where is he? Is he okay?"

"Oh, of course. Worry about the cat. He loved it. Licked himself all day. Begged for more." With her tongue on her arm, she mimics him cleaning cream from his fur. "Then, the stem of my favorite pipe snaps when I start to clean the spilled churn."

"How did cleaning the churn break your pipe?"

She purses her lips and snorts. "I stepped on it." Her rocking stops. "I am done for the day. Here I sit thinking how I will feed us tonight. I have nothing but smoked fish and pickled cabbage." She walks to a nearby shelf and brings down an old tin. "I was going to trade butter for flour and winter skoord. Such a shame. I had my heart set on fresh bread and roasted skoord."

The door creaks open again with a burst of wind.

"And now, the door is broken. What next? Please, push the churn against the door. It is of no other use today."

I set the handle inside the churn and drag it over to its new position. Water puddles to the left of the door and against the wall.

"Clean the water, yes? I have been mopping it up all day. Heavens to Fryyah. The roof leaks too."

The puddle is made up of something other than water. It's tackier, though not sticky. It also crackles when I touch it. Cleaning it is fast since it clings to the rag. When I twist the last of the liquid into the bucket, more water bubbles up through the floorboards. I toss the rag over it.

"Today at school we talked about Adjen folklore." It's a lie, but I want to distract Nana from the puddle.

"What things they teach in school—how will that help you become a responsible woman? Learning stories will not put food on the table."

"I learned about snow demons."

Nana stops, her spoon hovering over a bowl. She faces me, hands now on hips, the spoon dripping crimson juice down her apron. "They have nothing better to teach you? Sit down and eat. I will teach you things." The thump of the spoon she bangs on the lip of the bowl is loud, hollow. "You will become a good midwife, like me. This spring. Lots of babies to be born. I will teach. You will learn. Now eat."

"Do you ever make mistakes?"

"Usch. Yes. When I first started." She blesses herself. "Thankfully, the babies do most of the work on their own."

"Have you ever been yelled at because of a mistake?"

"Babies are a very stressful thing, and sometimes words are said that are not meant. I understand the yelling." She smiles at me, displaying a chipped tooth. "This interests you? Good. The decision is made. We'll begin in the spring. The blacksmith's baby is due first. Perfect lesson in birthing large babies." She nibbles on a piece of dried fish. "Ack. I want skoord."

We eat in silence until I gain the courage to ask, "How do you stop a snow demon? The story was never finished in school. Do you remember how to stop one?"

"You will not let go of this. Why does it scare you?"

"I'm not scared. I only want to hear the end of the story." It is difficult to keep my voice from catching.

"If I tell you, will you stop with the fairytales?"

I nod.

"Very well. It's not easy, I should think. The demon, it is said, is not snow but water, like the goddess's tears. Because snow is water, as is ice, it can move as different forms. To stop one?" She pauses for effect. "It can be burned, but not with flame. Now, no more talk of snow demons. Ever."

At the hearth, Nana busies herself pushing scorched logs over dying embers in the ash pile. "I've struggled with this fire all day." She pokes the pile with an iron rod. One overly aggressive jab sends the heap to the side of the firebox, knocking the kettle to swing and send water sizzling onto the logs and embers. Smoke billows into the room.

I jump from the table. The fire, I realize, must keep burning. Flame cannot burn water, but the heat can make it disappear. With the two of us here, I'm certain we can boil the puddle down to nothing. Behind me, the puddle spreads to the door and inches its way toward us. What we need is the biggest fire we can make.

"I'll gather more logs and kindling." Before I can reach the door, a knock pushes it open. Wind blasts in, bringing with it swirls of falling snow. Skadi enters, sidestepping the churn but nearly landing in the puddle.

"Nana Heldatter." Her breaths are deep, but quick. "The baby's coming."

"Are you certain? It is too soon. Winter is no good time for a baby."

"Pop asked me to bring you back. I rode the cart over."

Nana blesses herself and pulls on her red cape. "We come right away. Kata, get my birthing kit and we go."

"Only you, Nana," Skadi says. "There's only room for one more in the cart." She shuffles her feet. "I didn't have time to unload it before Pop sent me."

"It's all right. I'll work with the fire, and the house will be warm when you return. I'll join you the next time. In the spring. I promise." That's what I say, but in my heart I'm not so sure.

Nana gives me a quick nod. A single stroke with a glove-covered hand on my cheek leaves me with a scent of smoke, fish, and cabbage.

She and Skadi ride out into the snow, until neither the rattle of the cart can be heard nor the red of Nana's cape can be seen. I am alone in the house with a cat too frightened to come out of hiding—and a demon.

I gather as much wood and tinder as possible and place the driest pieces close to the embers. The skirt of the apron I'm wearing is the perfect fan to ignite the kindling into flame. Once the hearth glows dragon-breath red, I move the rocker next to the blaze. I pull a long piece of yarn from the middle of a newly wound skein and bite it off. The string serves to create a necklace loop for Sven's iron discs. I knot the yarn around my neck and tuck the amulets beneath the neckline of my bodice.

Knits and purls are a great distraction, so I set to keep my hands busy. The comforting sway of the rocker, the light clacking of the needles, and the warmth of the fire soon put me to sleep.

When I wake, my breath is vapor, the fire is a faint glow, and the poignant odor of burnt wood and cool ash hang heavy in the room. I rub the sleep from my eyes. The puddle near the door has vanished. Perhaps, I wish, it was all a bad dream and Nana is asleep on her featherbed with Oscar curled tightly at her feet—and the story of snow demons is merely a fanciful imagining.

The chill I try to shiver away freezes my core. A snowstorm whistles against the window, pounding the walls like phantom footsteps. Since the fire poker is out of my reach and the knitting still lies in my lap, I take a needle and stoke the fire until the embers throb again in bright tones of citrine, amber, and ruby.

"Please come home soon, Nana." I clasp a hand around the material of my bodice, clutching the amulets that rest over my collarbone. The metal is icy, and the sensation seeps through the fabric, awakening the skin of my fist, jolting me into reluctant memories of my father. Among the cinder coals drift visions of him, one memory like another, with only a small detail divergent between them—a switch, a leather strap, the back of his hand—grinning before each blow.

A series of crackles ripple through the cottage. It doesn't come from the fireplace, but from above me. Hanging from the wooden planks of the ceiling is a silvery splotch thicker than water, like a clear gelatin not yet set. Within its center, a dark mass pulsates.

The fine hairs on my neck, arms, and legs prickle—a sense of dread simmers.

Without taking my eyes from it, I bury the pointed end of one knitting needle into the firebox and stir the embers. As I do, the blob stretches toward me, every movement the sound of splintering glass. My muscles become icicles frozen to my bones as intensely frigid air replaces what waning warmth surrounds me. Impressions of glaciers within mountains, open and barren as the empty arms of a grieving mother, flash in my head. In the moments that follow, sorrow and distress replace the fear gripping me.

How long has this creature lain beneath rock and dirt, waiting to be released from its earthen prison? Images of my own crying, my own abandonment—my own anger—flood me. This demon is not so different from me. I release the needle.

In a flash, the blob stretches and folds upon itself, molding into a likeness of horrific familiarity. From a shapeless puddle to a solid form, it becomes the face of my father.

It grins. I stagger back.

"Papa? I'm s-sorry. It's not my fault." I can't take my eyes from him. I breathe my plea. "I didn't know."

The smile on the creature's face goes slack, its pupils cold, black. It lurches at me with unnatural speed but misses by hairs.

I snatch the needle from the fire, iron searing into my palm, and stab it.

The demon reels back, shrieking a screech that hardens the blood in my veins. I drop the needle and clutch my ears. The creature falls to the floor, bubbles sizzling at its wound. No longer a semisolid mass but pure liquid, it drains through the cracks of the floorboards near Nana's bed and disappears.

The sheet creating the space for my grandmother's bedroom billows. A shadow low to the ground creeps along its edge. I hurry to swirl the needle in the embers. Soft steps on the floor patter my way. Pulling the needle from the cinders and praying it's hot enough to injure the creature once more, I scream.

"G-go away! Leave us alone!"

My arms shake, and the needle slips from my hand. Clanging as it hits the floor, it bounces under Nana's rocker.

"Purr-reow."

For the first time in two days, I laugh.

"Oscar!" I scoop the tabby up and kiss him between his ears. His marmalade fur smells of dust and feathers. I kiss him again. "You have no idea how close you came to being skewered. Come along. You must be hungry." As if whispering a secret from one coconspirator to another, I speak my next words tenderly. "I know where Nana hides the dried fish."

Oscar warms himself next to me by the hearth as I knit. Dawn's light shines through the window, washing the room with goldenrod rays, by the time Nana arrives home.

Skadi helps her in, pushing the churn to one side. Her arm is threaded through the straps of a large muslin bag. "Sven and I will be back later to fix the door. Until then, Pop would like you to accept these gifts from our family." Before she leaves, she gives both Nana and me awkward hugs.

While Nana rests near the fire, I empty the sack. It is packed with flour, honey cubes, root vegetables, and a large winter skoord, its white feathers unplucked.

"The baby is a boy. Midwifery pays well for the boys." She hums a tune as she rocks in her chair. "Tong Ogden breeds 'em big, that one does. Well, she bred two of three big."

At the bottom of the bag, my fingers skim a metal object— Sven's box!

"Ah. The older boy might not be hefty, but there's none who can match his detail work. It's a wonder he can bend iron so fine." She turns toward the fire. "He called it an eternity box. Said it's for you and that you would know what to do with it."

I rub the two amulets through my collar. Sven gave me two gifts yesterday, and I thanked him by dropping his box and breaking it. So he gives it to me? A third gift? Or a reminder of what I've done? I shake my head. At least he got the lid to shut. But what will I do with a busted box?

Carefully, I take it to Nana's bedside table for safekeeping. When I return, my grandmother is up from her chair, pulling the kettle from its swing crane in the firebox.

"You will be a good midwife, I have no doubt. More babies come in the spring. You will get practice, much practice."

Oh. My promise. I rub my forehead. I can't bear to disappoint her if I make another mistake.

Nana pulls open the door, kettle in hand.

I reach for it. "I'll get that for you. The well might be frozen, so I can run down to the stream, if needed."

She gives me the kettle and a kiss for my efforts. "Oscar and I will enjoy the nice fire you have built."

I walk through the door, glancing back around the room for any sign of the snow demon.

Nothing.

The remainder of the day is uneventful. The Ogden twins arrive in the afternoon to fix the broken handle. The interior and exterior are both iron, decorated with ornate flourishes designed by Sven. It is too fancy for our little cottage, but it makes Nana happy.

I serve them root tea, fresh bread with the flour their family gave us, and violet codberry jam from the cupboard before they head home.

In the evening, I resume my knitting while Nana tends the fire from her rocker with a poker in one hand and a pipe in the other, the delicate scent of mountain moss tobacco filling the room. She is content with living in this shack, petting her cat, smoking her pipe, and delivering babies. How many babies has she delivered over the years? I can't imagine what this village would do without her. What would I do without her? My heart feels the heaviest it has in some time.

"I am going to sleep." She pats my head as she passes me. Oscar follows close behind.

I lie in my bed next to the warm fire. Through the window, if I want to count a thousand stars on such a clear night, I can. The sky balancing on the horizon of the snow-covered window sash is a peaceful sight to behold. I snuggle under my furs and fall asleep.

◦◊◦

Gurgling and banging wake me. The fire is out. I shiver under my blankets but force myself to investigate. Nana is sitting up on her bed, her back against the wall, scratching at her throat. She kicks her own fur blankets to the floor, and her night table is tipped on its side. Her eyes are bulging, and her face is the deep hue of codberries. Oscar is hunched in the corner—hissing.

It takes time for my eyes to adjust to the darkness in this part of the cottage. When they do, I see a swirling vapor, a black mass in its center, hovering over my grandmother.

"Leave her alone!"

The vapor slows its whirl for a moment. In response, it makes a deafening noise, a series of cries like ice-covered branches snapping from bare trees.

I cover my ears. Instantly, my mind is muddled, and my body stiffens. I will myself to break free from its control and dig for the amulets under the collar of my night dress. Not knowing what drives me to do so, I throw the necklace at the creature. It recoils, releasing its invisible grip on Nana.

She wheezes. Before she can take a good breath, the demon attacks again. As if in a funnel wind, the blankets, the shawl, the hanging sheet, and my hair all whip around, making it difficult to see clearly.

I hurry toward the two of them, charging the vapor. I pass through it, and icy crystal-sharp shards pierce my skin, causing beads of blood to surface. I tumble against the far wall, nearly landing on the cat. Oscar is crouched low, his ears back, his eyes black, his tail the thickness of his body. He charges the demon, stops short of it, and backs away.

Lifting myself for a second advance, I catch a moonlit glint sparkling under the bed. Sven's box fell to the floor when Nana's nightstand toppled. I grab it and press the side clips. It blossoms open. Glowing inside is the bean-sized disc etched with an eye that Sven had stuffed in his pocket.

I scream, louder than before, "Leave her alone!" I thrust the open box into the demonic mist. The skin on my hands hardens in the cold, pain shooting through my arms, my flesh freezing. The box glimmers, illuminating the demon inside and out with rays of light. The creature fights an invisible pull, elongating its form away from the box shaking in my hand. I clutch it until my knuckles pale. Slowly, the gaseous mass of rotating light and dark dissolves into the case. I release the levers.

The top remains open.

The vapor stretches beyond the lid of the box and begins forming ice crystals in a shape larger than the container. It grows, and the crackling sounds grow with it. As it lifts itself from the box, I see visions of my grandmother's death, my friends' misery, and my village in ruins in the reflections of its faceted form. With all my strength, I press the edges of the box together, but my grasp slips.

Now it is my turn to fight. To hold on. To not give up. I slam the box against the floor. In a burst of light, the creature is sucked into the case. Gears click. The top snaps shut.

Nana lies across her bed, coughing.

I cry out, "Tell me you're all right!"

She nods. Her eyes seem to search me for an answer.

I can no longer hide from what I've done wrong. Words spill from my mouth. "That was a snow demon. I made it. In the snow. At dusk. I made that demon. I made that . . . mistake." The stinging pressure behind my eyes releases as a torrent of regret.

"There, my Kata. It is my fault too for not speaking the truth of things. Do you forgive this old woman?"

Tears fall on my nightdress as I bend my head.

"Sven made you a good box, yes? Tomorrow, I think you and he will bury it . . . for safekeeping."

I press my face to her shoulder.

"The biggest mistake you made was not trusting your nana. Together, we can fix anything. Yes?"

I hug her tightly and wish for tomorrow to come.

Amautalik and the Wolf

Kimberly Gail

The harsh Arctic wind whistled through the cracks in the ramshackle walls of Amautalik's cabin. Grabbing a fistful of furs in her gnarled fingers, she pulled them over her head to block out the noise. Satisfied with her cleverness, she settled back in to sleep. Her eyes were closed for only a moment before a great howling added itself to the wind's whistle and wrenched her from the brink of her much-coveted sleep.

Snarling a string of curses, the ogress struggled out of bed and fumbled in the darkness for something to stuff into the cracks of the walls. As she blindly searched, the howl sounded again, louder this time. Cocking her oversized head, she listened more closely to the wailing lament. She recognized that sound. It was not the wind. This was a sound she knew quite well. It was the sound of a frightened child.

She shuffled her way toward the front of her shanty. The howl grew louder as she approached the door. *Has some unfortunate child wandered away from home and ended up on my stoop?* Fortune did not shine upon Amautalik often, but when it did, she was not so foolish as to be unaccepting. The old woman lifted the latch and threw open the door.

On her stoop was a large basket. It was not a driftwood basket like the ones she made and decorated with small white bones and other treasures. This was a simple basket, of the kind the people in the fishing village near the base of the mountain made. But like her own baskets, it was the perfect size for hauling a child across the tundra. She lifted one dry, cracked foot toward the basket and poked at it with a crusty, yellowed toenail. At her touch, a wonderfully awful howl rose up from the basket.

She cackled. "Someone has delivered breakfast!"

Heaving the basket up into her arms, she brought it inside and set it upon the table. Licking her lips with anticipation, she raised the lid. Inside, wrapped in furs, lay a small child who looked to be no more than two. The boy stared up at her. His perfect pink lips pulled apart to form a pouty O, while his eyes, as blue as the ice of the Arctic sea, widened.

"Don't you look the tasty treat," the ogress cooed at the child. "Let's get you out of those furs and see how well old Amautalik will eat today."

Her gnarled hands felt for an opening in the furs but failed to find one. She poked all around but could find neither flap nor button nor string. Frustrated, she yanked the boy from the basket and gave him a good shake. The furs held tightly to the child.

She placed him upon the table. He watched her with wide eyes as she grabbed an arm and ran her fingers along its fur. The child had not been wrapped in furs, but instead he had his very own growing right out of his skin. Amautalik traced the fur down his small arm, where it stopped at his wrist. There, she encountered chunky pink hands and fingers like those of any child. She grabbed his small legs from where they dangled off the end of the table and did the same as she'd done with his arm. At the ends, she found tiny pink feet with one, two, three, four, five toes counted on each.

Ankle to neck, wrist to shoulder, the boy was covered in gray and white fur. His hands, feet, and head looked like any other child's she had ever seen. Atop his head was a thick patch of straight black hair, the same as any of the Inuit people in the village. She grabbed a lock of the boy's hair between her brittle yellow fingernails and lifted it.

She jumped back with a gasp. Below the hair, she had discovered pointed fur-covered ears. "You've the eyes and ears of the wolf Amaruq! You are surely his child." The hag gulped. "What sort of games is that old trickster up to?"

Not many things brought terror to Amautalik. After all, what could be more frightening than herself? An ogress of exceptional strength, speed, and stealth had little to fear.

Little, but not nothing. For Amaruq, the demon wolf, could snatch one's very soul from the waters of his lake, causing any who crossed him to drop dead in an instant. Amautalik was not eager to meet that fate herself.

"Your father will come for you, little one," she told the wide-eyed boy. "And when he does, he will find you alive and well."

She scooped up the child, carried him to the corner, and placed him into one of her finest baskets, where he immediately began to wail. "What is wrong with you, boy? That basket is made of the best driftwood and tied with the strongest bits of sinew. And see here," she said, as she rattled a small cluster of bones and teeth tied onto one side, "such pretty things for you to play with."

The boy stopped his crying and watched as the hag rattled the bones about. But as soon as she stood to walk away, he began to cry once more. Bending her bulging body down toward the basket, she poked a finger down into the bottom and asked, "Do you not find this to be the softest seaweed you've ever laid upon, child?"

He lifted one small hand covered in rancid seaweed ooze and grunted. "Ugh."

"Well, it's not to everyone's taste, I suppose," she said. "I would guess you are more used to furs, Amaruq's son." The old woman liked the sound of that so much that she decided to call the boy Amaruqson. After all, she had to call him something while she waited for his father to come for him. With a great sigh, she strode to her bed and grabbed her finest fur. She lifted the child out of the cage and set him down upon the fur on the floor. The boy looked up at the ogress and smiled.

Having decided child was not on the menu for breakfast, Amautalik went outside to fetch some fish from her icy cellar. Her arms loaded with fish, she sat with a heavy plop onto a stump she used as a chair. It and her bed were the only items in her cabin sturdy enough to hold her bulk. She had just bitten into a fish head when she felt a small hand on her thigh. She looked down to see Amaruqson standing there, rubbing at his tummy.

"I've already given you my best fur. I hardly think I should have to share my food with you as well."

At that moment, the boy's stomach let out such a growl that Amautalik thought for certain it was the growl of a wolf. She quickly handed the child a fish, which he carried back to the fur on the floor and tore into.

"You certainly eat like a wolf, Amaruqson."

For three days, the old ogress waited for Amaruq to come claim his son. She had nearly given in and eaten the child at least once on each of those days. By the fourth day, she had grown weary of caring for the wolf's pup and even more so of fighting her urge to eat the boy. She packed the boy up into a new cage she had made for him—this one lined with fur and decorated with shiny rocks and animals carved of wood—and set out to return him to his father.

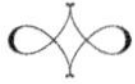

Fresh snow fell in a gentle cascade as the ogress made her way across the tundra. The small wolf-boy was secured away in the basket designed to fit perfectly over the bulging contours of her hunched back. Crystalline fractals landed on the matted tangles of Amautalik's unkempt hair. She did her best to ignore the accumulating crystals at first. But as the flakes increased in size, they drew the attention of Amaruqson. The soft coo of his oohs and aahs blew to her ear with the warmth of his breath. In it, she could smell this morning's breakfast of Arctic cod and seaweed. But it was not the boy's sounds or his breath that agitated the old woman, rather his attempts at capturing the ice crystals.

Amaruqson's fascination with the large, intricately designed bits of ice led him to try capturing one for himself. Since Amautalik had covered his basket with whale hide—she did not dare deliver a soaked and sickly pup to Amaruq—no snow fell within the basket. He could, however, both see and reach the crystals that landed in the disheveled mess of the ogress's tresses. Each attempt he made to get a flake within his grasp resulted in him successfully grabbing and pulling a clump of her hair.

From deep within her chest, the hag built a menacing growl before huffing it out in a puff of smoke created by the frosty air. She had spent many years developing this sound that had terrified many a child and reduced them to frightened whimpers. But the small boy upon her back merely barked out an attempt at emulating the sound. Amautalik's irritation at his lack of proper fear and respect for her was almost great enough for her to resist the urge to laugh at his efforts.

Almost, but not quite. A snort escaped her as the young pup spit forth another growl.

In this land of rock and ice, there was little entertainment to be had. The mimicking behavior of the small boy broke up the monotony of the full day's walk through the frozen wastes. And so Amautalik occupied their time with teaching her tiny captive to growl, snarl, and even hum an eerie tune she'd composed to frighten the village children.

It was late afternoon when they reached a great frozen lake. The resounding reverberation of feral growls now emanated from their stomachs as much as from their mouths. Amautalik whisked the basket from her back and placed it upon the ground before plopping her heavy frame onto a nearby boulder.

She looked at the tiny pink hands wrapped around the bars of the cage and imagined how scrumptious they would taste in a nice stew. The appearance of the boy's face between those hands arrested such thoughts. More specifically, the glacial blue of his eyes, so very much like his father's, reminded her of whom the boy belonged to. With a regretful sigh, the ogress pulled two hunks of seal meat from the pockets of her whale-skin coat. She tossed one to Amaruqson before biting into the other.

Her belly full, the old woman slipped to the ground, leaned back against the boulder, and closed her eyes. Sleep had claimed her for no more than a few minutes when a fright-filled howl ripped her from her dreams. The driftwood cage before her sat empty, its top thrown open. The latch had proven too simple for the dexterous fingers of the Trickster's clever son. A forlorn cry rang out once again, and Amautalik turned toward it.

Out on the frozen surface of the lake sat Amaruqson. She watched as the boy tried to stand. His bare feet found no purchase on the slippery surface and went skidding out behind him. His tiny frame fell straight forward, his chin slamming into the hard ice. His wail was now more human than wolf, and the familiar sound spurred Amautalik into action. She grabbed her basket and rushed out onto the lake to retrieve the boy.

Instinct caused her to approach slowly so as not to frighten the child further. But when the wolf-boy caught sight of the ogress, he did not shrink away. Rather, the child reached out to her, crying for her help. The boy's cries stirred a natural instinct within her, a desire to feed. Luckily for him, her sense of self-preservation from Amaruq and her full belly were enough for her to fight the urge. Instead, she pulled the child to her and comforted away his fears.

When his cries had stopped and his trembling had settled, the old woman stood the boy back upon the ice. Immediately, he began to wail and hop about. Amautalik turned her eyes to the boy's tiny feet and saw they were turning from pink to red—and in some spots, a rather worrisome shade of blue. Her coat hit the ice as she quickly peeled it off and began to remove the second layer of skins she wore beneath it. With her excessive strength, she was able to tear the seal skin into strips, which she then wrapped around Amaruqson's feet.

Sitting on his furry rump, the boy stared at his newly dressed feet in awe. He wiggled them back and forth, watching them with his lips once more parted in an O of wonderment. With a cackle, the old hag pulled the boy onto his feet and gave him a small push to urge him forward. With a tentative step, Amaruqson began to make his way across the ice.

Once he had become comfortable with walking on the ice, the boy began to run. He soon discovered that if he ran several paces and then stopped, his momentum would cause him to slide across the slippery surface. If he fell, he would simply giggle and get right back up. Once again, the old woman let the boy's merriment entertain her as they carried along on their journey.

At one point, she decided to see what he could possibly find so fun about ice gliding. She ran alongside Amaruqson and slid with him. The force of her running being far greater than his, the ogress slid well beyond where he stopped. Behind her, she heard a hearty "Ooh!" and grinned at the boy's obvious reverence of her superior gliding skills. With his finger pointed toward her, he gave a small grunt.

"What? You want me to do that again, Amaruqson?" she asked and received another grunt in reply. Looking to really impress the boy, Amautalik ran as fast as she could before stopping and sending herself into a wild glide. She soon found herself out of control. Her arms windmilled as she tried to gain control, but it was a useless effort. The old woman's feet went sailing out from under her, sending her flying up into the air before she landed on her back with a hard *thwack* on the ice. The wolf-boy ran toward her before gracefully sliding to a stop by her side, where he dropped onto his rear end and howled with laughter.

With a growl, the ogress scooped up the boy and plopped him into his basket before slamming the lid shut. With a snarl on her face and a grunt in her throat, she set off across the ice toward Amaruq's mountain. From inside the basket upon her back, she heard the giggles of the overly amused pup.

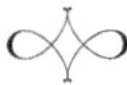

They made the long climb up the mountain to meet the demon wolf in near silence. The only sounds were the whistle of the Arctic wind and the soft snores of the child in the basket. Thanks to decades of carrying children away to her lair, Amautalik was accustomed to the difficult task. Despite the distance and the sharp slope of the mountain, she ascended quickly. Her strength and stamina were greater than those of most men half her age. But even the great ogress of the tundra grows weary. After a long day's journey, she needed rest before facing Amaruq.

Having placed the basket aside, she plopped a rock atop the lid to keep young Amaruqson from escaping again. Then she settled down to sleep among some dwarf shrubs that had sprouted up through the snow along the mountainside.

Hours later, the old woman woke from her much needed slumber and rubbed the sleep from her rheumy eyes.

When she turned toward her basket, she was startled to see a man standing there. He wore a thin coat of gray and white fur, with darker fur leggings beneath. She could see only his profile, which revealed high cheekbones, a strong chin, and a sleek nose that was long, but not too long. He looked far younger than his gray hair implied. Although on closer inspection, she decided it more of a remarkable silver than gray. It reached his shoulders, and the loose tendrils blew about in the wind. He was a handsome and alluring creature, even to her old eyes. She sat captivated by his exquisite good looks, unable to look away, until she was distracted by the slight whimper of Amaruqson.

Somehow, the fact that the boy was being held aloft by the handsome stranger had escaped Amautalik's notice. But there he was, held in one strong hand by the scruff of his neck. The boy whimpered as the strange man turned him this way and that as if in appraisal. She could only assume he meant to spirit the child away while she slept. Offended by the audacity of anyone who would dare attempt to steal from her, she rose to her feet with a contemptuous growl.

The stranger turned to her with a lackadaisical grace. The

knowing stare of his glacial blue eyes told her he had known she was awake and watching him and he could not have cared less.

But why should he? Amaruq feared no one.

One side of his mouth lifted, and she thought him about to snarl. Instead, he graced her with a sensuous smile. "Amautalik, mighty ogress of the tundra," he said. "What brings you to my mountain?"

"I've come to return what is yours," the ogress answered, indicating the boy he held in his grasp.

"Why would you believe this to be mine?" The Trickster turned his icy blue stare back to the child, whose eyes were a mirror of his own.

Amautalik had held little doubt of the boy being a son of Amaruq, and seeing them together now, even that little bit vanished. Aside from the rarity of their extraordinary eyes, there was a resemblance that was undeniable. Knowing that Amaruq's clothing was merely a manipulation of his own fur, she could see how exactly it matched the boy's. And while the child was young and still held the rounded features of a toddler, it was evident his chin and nose would someday match those of his father's human form. Despite these overwhelming similarities, the demon wolf seemed ready to deny the child.

In her experience, flattery was the way to win any man over, even when that man was really a wolf. "He is such a beautiful child. And no one but you has eyes so dazzling." At that moment, her stomach growled, as if questioning why she tried so hard to convince Amaruq of his paternity. If he denied the boy, she would be free to feast, and yet she continued. "Surely he must be yours."

"Perhaps," he remarked absently as he dropped the boy back into the cage and slammed the lid closed. "Follow me to my cave, dear old Amautalik, and we will visit over breakfast." With that, his form shifted into a wolf, and he cantered up the trail. The ogress could do nothing more than hastily throw Amaruqson's cage upon her back and follow the Trickster home.

A low, narrow opening in the mountain's side stood barely

visible before them. Twisted jumbles of vine, along with the rotted wood of fallen logs, were strategically strewn about the opening. Amautalik wondered how she would fit her bulky form through such a space. To do so while also carrying the burden of the basket would be an impossibility.

Having noticed her distress, Amaruq regained his human form. She found herself once again caught off guard by his uncommonly good looks. She began to understand his ability to enamor the village girls. This power was even more evidenced when his sultry voice invited her in. "You are welcome in my home, Amautalik." With those words, the apparent difficulties of his den's entrance vanished. Gone was the illusion, and in its place stood a tall, wide doorway free of debris. The Trickster smiled at the cleverness of his deception.

Nests of dirt and straw lay alongside beautifully carved furniture, fulfilling the needs of both wolf and man. Amautalik released the pup from his basket and dropped herself into a chair, marveling at its exquisite softness. Amaruq presented her with a breakfast of rabbit and sat himself in the chair adjacent to her own. He tore into a rabbit shank and eyed the young boy, who came sniffing his way. The child was obviously hungry, yet his father continued eating with no regard for the boy. With an annoyed grunt, the ogress tossed the boy a chunk of her own meal. Amaruq merely snorted at the gesture.

"Tell me, ogress," the demon wolf drawled, "how did you come to be in possession of this boy?"

The question did not take her as off guard as it would have just a few hours before. In her short time with the Trickster, she had gleaned enough to realize her assumption that he had placed the child upon her stoop had been incorrect. "The child was left outside my door. When I saw his lovely coat and brilliant eyes, I assumed him yours. Of course, my first thought was to bring him to you."

"Of course." The wolf's sly smile and condescending tone implied he knew what her first thought truly was. "I suppose it was a wise decision to bring him here. Yet I am afraid you have made the journey for nothing."

"He is not yours?"

"It is quite possible that he is mine. He is, after all, a remarkably beautiful child. His age would be in alignment with a dalliance I had with a village girl. She too was incredibly beautiful." With a wistful look in his eye, Amaruq let out a longing sigh and told the ogress the tale of the romantic encounter. "When her father learned of our love," he said as he finished the story, "he made her choose between me and her family. As she is not by my side now, you can guess which she chose."

"She never told you about the child?"

"No. I am sure the child brought her great shame. Why else would she dump him on the stoop of a child-eater?"

"Perhaps her father forced her to make that decision as well."

"Perhaps," Amaruq mused. He watched the boy for a moment as he toddled about the den. "I can see her in him." There was a note of pain in his voice that Amautalik would have never guessed possible from the demon wolf. It felt wrong somehow, and she sensed it was a bad sign for poor Amaruqson's fate.

"That child is more man than beast." Both Amaruq's tone and countenance had changed. An air of resentment now surrounded the wolf in human form. "I have no use for such a creature. Take it away and do as you will with it, ogress."

⚬⟩⟨⚬

Amautalik stood staring down the mountain, dreading the long voyage home. She had not anticipated having to carry Amaruqson in the basket strapped to her back on this leg of the journey. She was strong, but she was old and weary. Looking about, she spied a pile of wood and considered lighting a fire. It would be a long walk. A nice meal before such a trek would provide much-needed energy.

She set the basket down and eyed the boy within. Amaruq's rejection of his son meant there was no longer any reason she could not eat the child. "You would make a fine meal, but I think perhaps you would taste much better slow roasted with some of my finest spices."

The boy looked at the old woman with a serious expression. He then pointed a finger at her and shouted something that sounded a lot like "Salt!"

"Yes, yes. That's just the thing. I shall have to wait until we are home to eat you, Amaruqson." Having lived alone for so long, Amautalik was typically a woman of few words. She had done more talking in the past few days than she had in some months prior. Now, even her voice felt weary.

"Your name is a mouthful, Amaruqson," she declared. "And since that old wolf takes no claim of you, there is no sense in honoring him. I believe I will call you Ruqson now, instead." The small boy rewarded her decision with a large smile.

Satisfied that the dropping of a few letters would ease the work of her mouth, she puzzled out what to do about the work of her body. Ruqson pounded on the slats of his basket. As she watched him pound away, she got a wonderful idea. She decided to strip down the basket and fashion it into a sled. Then she and Ruqson could simply slide down the slope and be halfway home.

Once the old woman had situated herself on the sled, there was no room for the boy. She had to place him upon her lap, which had ample room for the small child. Wrapping her arms around him, she leaned forward, using her significant weight to tip them over the crest of the hill and start their descent. The small mountain had a slight decline at the top, but it became much steeper a few meters down. The driftwood basket turned sled gained momentum with the sharper angle and quickly picked up speed. Amautalik struggled to keep control.

She had rigged the sinew ropes in such a way that she could use them to steer, but to do so properly, she had to release her grip on Ruqson. She could feel the boy slipping off the side of the sled. Grabbing the child and pulling him tight against her meant she had to let go of the rope. With no one at the reigns, the sled slipped out of control, hurtling them straight for a tree. A quick pull of the rope by the hag saved them from the tree but caused the sled to skid sideways. Such strong momentum at that awkward angle flipped the sled and sent its riders flying.

Amautalik's weight kept her from flying too high or too far, but she lost her grip on Ruqson. The child flew from her arms and landed headfirst in the snow. She looked to where he had landed and saw his furry body sticking straight up, his small cloth-wrapped feet flailing in the air. He stayed that way for only a moment before his body tipped down toward the ground. He rolled in such a way, with his head buried in the snow, that Amautalik was certain the child's neck had snapped. She supposed she would now be eating the boy sooner than expected.

She began to crawl to where he lay in the snow, expecting to find a lifeless body. Instead, she saw his small body shaking uncontrollably. She reasoned he must be suffering in horrific pain, until she heard his howling laughter. She sat next to him and waited for his mirth to subside.

"Liked that, did you?" she asked as she rubbed at her own aching hip. In answer, the boy hopped up and ran to the sled. Grabbing hold of the rope, he pointed a small finger back up the mountain and grunted.

"What?" she asked. "You want to do that again?"

A small pink tongue burst through his lips and hung loosely from his wide-open mouth as he made a loud panting sound. The sight of a small boy panting like a happy wolf made Amautalik laugh aloud. "Well, if you feel that strongly about it, I suppose we could try it again."

With the boy tucked under one arm and the ropes of the sled gripped firmly in her opposite hand, Amautalik made her way back up the mountain. The climb was awkward, but thanks to her exceptional strength, it was still not too difficult. Once they had reached the top, she decided on a better way to arrange their bodies on the sled. This time, she wrapped the front of her coat around the boy and tied it tight. It was not until she was certain he was securely in place that she grabbed the reins and sent them downward once more.

Ruqson's laughter was immediate. Soon, the old hag joined him in his merriment as she steered them down the mountainside. This time, they managed to reach the bottom without incident. She untied the boy from her coat and placed him on the snowy ground. He bent himself low and somersaulted his way the last few feet down the slope. A snort escaped the ogress at his antics. After their initial tumble, he had apparently decided sledding was supposed to end with him going head over heels.

With a pointed finger and a grunt, he indicated his desire to do it all over again. "No, no, Ruqson. This grunting will not do. If you want old Amautalik to take you back up the hill, you are going to have to use words." With a heavy sigh, she stretched out her legs and waited.

"Ugh!" came a second grunt, accompanied by the jabbing point of a finger.

"Do you want to go again?"

"Ugh!"

"No, Ruqson. If you want to go again, you will have to tell me." At this, the boy gave a frustrated howl. It earned him nothing more than a scowl from the ogress. "Even that rotten trickster of a father of yours can do more than howl."

Dropping his furry bottom to the snow, he stared at her with his icy-blue eyes. A whimper escaped him as he stuck out his lower lip. "Don't try your wolf cub trickery on me. I told you, if you want to go again, you will have to tell me so with your words."

For a moment, the small boy merely sat staring at the ogress with his pouty lips. Finally, he pointed up the mountain and shouted, "Again." Cracked lips smiled around sharp gray teeth as the ogress enjoyed her victory. Then she scooped him up and carried boy and sled up the mountain once more. And then "Again!" And "Again!" And "Again!"

On their sixth run down the mountain, Amautalik steered them toward a snow-covered boulder that launched them skyward. Howls of laughter mixed with great cackles as they flew through the air. Strong arms wrapped around the child as they came down toward the snow. Warm and safe in the old woman's embrace, Ruqson squealed with delight as she took the brunt of the impact when the sled touched down upon the snow. It was not the most graceful of landings, but they managed to stay upright and coast to a stop at the bottom.

Rubbing at her aching spine, the ogress climbed from the sled. This time, when Ruqson asked to go again, she firmly told him no. Even her tough old body had its limits. Continuing his cry of "Again," the boy tugged at the reins of the sled. Both wolf cubs and small children have difficulty walking away from fun; it was no different for small wolf-boys. But an ogress never loses in a battle of wills. Amautalik was far too clever for most adults. A small child did not stand a chance.

She reached down and grabbed two big handfuls of snow, which she formed into an enormous ball. Her arm reared back before she pitched it as far as she could. Ruqson's eyes grew wide, and his lips formed their customary O of wonder. Soon, he had begun creating his own snowballs and flinging them as far as he could. He would then chase after them and throw them again. If one had fallen apart when he got to it, he simply made a new one. With this new game, they made their way back toward Amautalik's shack.

Amautalik felt weariness stronger than she had ever known in her life by the time the pair reached her unkempt property. She felt an aching deep within her bones. In a faint daze, she somehow managed to stagger to her bed and collapse. Overtaken by exhaustion, the ogress fell into a deep sleep.

The harsh Arctic wind whistled through the cracks in the ramshackle walls of Amautalik's cabin. Grabbing a fistful of furs in her gnarled fingers, she pulled them over her head to block out the noise and settled back in to sleep. She dozed for only a moment before a great howling added itself to the wind's whistle and wrenched her from her slumber. Blinking, she pondered the familiarity of the situation. The howl sounded again, louder this time, and her heart tapped out a frantic rhythm.

Ruqson!

Her mind raced through the events of the past two days. Most of it she remembered clearly, but the particulars of her return home were blurred in her mind. It struck her like a vicious slap to the face as she realized what had happened. A few miles from home, the boy had fallen asleep, and she had placed him upon the sled, pulling it behind her for the remainder of the journey. Once home, in a complete state of exhaustion, she had managed to get herself to bed but had forgotten the child asleep on the sled. He had spent the night outside in the harsh cold. In a panicked rush, the old woman flew to the door and threw it open.

On her stoop sat the small boy. Ice clung to his fur and to the skins she had thankfully thought to wrap around his feet and hands. He looked cold and miserable, but it appeared he would survive his night in the cold. At the sight of her, the boy's howls ceased. "Mo!" he exclaimed as he looked up at her with his wide blue eyes. He reached out for her, and the old woman scooped the child into her arms and held him close.

"You will be fine, Ruqson. You're a strong, tough boy." He gave a soft rumble of agreement as he nuzzled closer into the fatty folds of her neck. "Your name still feels like a mouthful, child. From now on, I think I will just call you Son."

Placing a kiss upon his head, she turned and walked back into their home.

The Cold Truth

LOGOS PEREGRIN

The truth can be cruel.

So can ice faeries. I'm not talking about the little creatures whose dance heralded winter in that one musical film I loved as a kid.

For one thing, those don't actually exist.

No, when I say ice faeries, I mean something much worse. I mean tiny, brutish beings that live in the high mountains north of the human kingdom of Calonai. They're spiteful creatures who encase themselves in needle-thin icicles and swarm anyone who comes within sight. Outrunning them is impossible, unless you have the speed of a vampire or a half-dragon—yeah, thanks, guys—and even hiding from them is nigh unimaginable.

Not that that kept me from trying on the last job my friends and I accepted.

And now I'm just getting ahead of myself.

The name's Vita. Well, that's what people call me, anyway. Here in Calonai, where anyone can alter the world itself with just a couple of well-spoken words in the Language of Truth, nobody uses their True Names. Not necessarily a law, so much as an ingrained way of life.

As a Royal Namer, I'm one of the few people legally allowed to use the Language of Truth—a magic we call Naming. As both the youngest Royal Namer in the history of Calonai and a traveler from another world, I also have a certain . . . freedom to roam that most Royal Namers don't.

Which is how my friends and I wound up fleeing from a swarm of enraged ice faeries. And how I found myself squeezing in between two icy boulders deep in the high mountains in an attempt to hide from them.

"'It'll be easy,' he said," I muttered as I twisted to get my hips through the jagged freezing opening. "'A simple task for a Namer like you.' Blasted troll. I should have—"

I yelped as tiny pinpricks of pain besieged the backs of my knees and prickled the skin beneath my boots. With my hands shaped like claws, I dragged myself fully through the opening and threw myself back against it, hoping to block it with the broad side of my pack.

"This," I gasped out, though I really should have tried to regain my breath so I could Name myself a more long-term sanctuary, "is what I get for not doing background checks on the jobs I take."

Altius keeps saying I act naive for someone who's been through as much as I have, but I usually retort that I'm just optimistic. When something like this happens, though, I kind of have to agree with him.

A soft chatter, oddly innocent, echoed in my ear. I jerked my head around to face it, automatically pulling back at the same time to focus on the sound.

Big mistake.

The swarm poured in along my right side, and needle pricks of pain blossomed along my arm and up to my shoulder. Cursing, I threw myself forward, away from the opening. All I could think then was that maybe I could find a way to evade them farther into the cave I'd now trapped myself within.

Anything had to be better than sitting still and just accepting the faeries' abuse—though looking back, I admit that doing so might have given me the time and breath to Name myself some protection.

As I scrambled away, the chatter grew louder behind me. Unlike other times I've dealt with faeries, I couldn't understand a single word these faeries were saying.

Which should have been my first clue that something was horribly wrong.

"A simple task for a Namer," I repeated scathingly as I ran toward a blue-green opening at the back of the cave. "They don't even speak a lick of the Language of Truth. How—"

I yelped and cursed as my legs slid out from under me. I landed on my back with a groan, the lumps of my pack digging into my spine and ribs. I blinked and tried to make sense of the wavering blue, green, and white that filled my vision. That is, until the chatter filled my ears again like a swarm of bees.

"Darn it!" I tried to roll over, but they'd flown above me and were hovering there as though to taunt me for my inability to run. I groaned. **"Just leave me alone!"**

As soon as the words were past my lips, the world went sideways.

The blue, green, and white that had filled my vision before shifted to a rainbow of jewel tones. Purple crystals, deeper and more vibrant than any amethyst I'd ever seen, hung heavy from the ceiling. Green spikes, beyond the color of emeralds, rose around me. Flittering red specks, like undying sparks released from a raging fire, swirled just above me, their movements slow as I watched them.

Even the very air shifted. It fractured, like multiple panes of colored glass sliding away from and turning perpendicular to each other. Yet they never seemed to run parallel to any of the others, and there were too many angles and too many colors for me to even begin to understand.

When I began to spot planes of color that I don't think I could ever find names for—at least, none that would make any sense beyond how I felt viewing them—I closed my eyes and rolled onto my side, shifting my pack out from under me. Unfortunately, cutting off my awareness of the bizarre visions only opened my mind to another aspect of the sideways shift.

Silence.

Gone was the wind that I hadn't even realized was howling outside. Gone was the whistling of air rushing between the two boulders I'd shimmied past earlier. Gone, even, was the disturbingly unintelligible chatter of the ice faeries.

In their place was a void, an emptiness that couldn't be filled by the buzz and whine my ears seemed to produce in automatic response.

"Great," I said, just to fill the void. The word echoed and warped until nothing was left of it but haunting dreams.

I shuddered. I wasn't sure in that moment which would be worse: opening my eyes to the madness of angles and colors or leaving myself shut within the insanity of broken words and silence. Hoping for a compromise, I kept my eyes squeezed shut and spoke aloud again, though I tried to keep the words soft.

"I need to find the others." Even soft, the words were torn open into broken consonants and dying syllables. "I need to figure out what happened."

"What happened?"

I grimaced as my words were twisted and echoed back to me from the deep silence. "Great. Well . . . at least I've now got echoes to keep me company in the silence."

"What happened?"

I huffed as the echo repeated and shook my head against the cool ground beneath my cheek. "Okay, so I must have said something to get myself into this. Unless . . ."

I briefly considered the possibility that the ice faeries could have done this to me, but I've spent years studying the Language of Truth and speaking with other faerie swarms. If these creatures had been capable of doing something like this to me, I would have been able to speak with them, at the very least.

"What happened?"

I grunted and stuck my tongue out at the echoing silence. "Fine," I muttered. "So obviously I had to have done this to myself. But how? What did I say?"

"What did I say?"

I did my best to ignore the echo of my words and thought back to the moment the world shifted. Thinking about it, I could remember the roll of words off my tongue that were definitely not English.

"But heck if I can remember what they were."

"What they were?"

I groaned and risked peeling open one eye. Colors I could barely comprehend assaulted my vision, along with shapes and angles that I still don't want to wrap my brain around. Shaking my head again, I squeezed my eyes closed once more.

"Nope. Not doing that."

"Doing that?"

"Stop it!" I snapped. I knew it was pointless, but I felt like the repetition of my own words would drive me mad faster than the bizarre visuals and ear-blistering silence.

"Stop it?"

I growled. "Leave me alone!"

"Alone?" The word echoed back piteously, but I was already gasping with realization and cursing myself furiously.

"I was trying to get the ice faeries to leave me alone," I muttered. "I was so desperate to get away from them, I must have slipped into the Language of Truth without thinking. Even if they couldn't understand it, it still should have hindered them, maybe enough for them to leave me alone."

I squinted open one eye for a second before slamming it shut again and groaning. "And they did leave me alone." I cursed and shook my head hard, scraping my cheek against the ground beneath me. "The whole cursed world left me alone."

That's the one pitfall of being fluent in a language as dangerous as the Language of Truth. No matter what you mean, if you don't specify who or what you are addressing, the world will take your words to mean the whole of itself.

"Stupid Vita," I muttered to myself. "You just had to be thoughtless and speak the Language of Truth, and now you're stuck here alone—wherever here is—with nothing but your own voice to keep you company."

"*Nothing!*"

I yelped and threw open my eyes, though I quickly closed them again. So far, the silence had been echoing back the last words I'd said, but that last one wasn't even close.

"*Nothing!*"

I frowned. Taking the time to consider the strange echo, I had the odd thought that it sounded awfully enthusiastic, like a child proud of recognizing a word.

"*Nothing!*"

"Nothing?" I asked tentatively. Following a sudden impulse, I added, "Is that . . . is that your name?"

"*Name.*"

I took a shaky breath. All right, so maybe telling the world to leave me alone wasn't as simple as I'd thought. "Not that there's anything simple about what I'm seeing or hearing."

"*Hearing. Seeing?*"

The rearrangement of my words startled me, and I chuckled. "Smart, aren't you?" I muttered. I ignored the responding echo as I considered the implications.

"So the world interpreted my command to leave me alone as a command to . . . what? Surround me with nothing? That doesn't exactly explain the bizarre sights I see when I open my eyes."

"*Sights? Eyes?*"

I lifted my head from the ground thoughtfully, though I was careful not to open my eyes. "You wouldn't know what those are, would you? I mean, you understand hearing because you can hear me, but you don't have eyes."

"*Hear. Eyes?*"

I shook my head. "But you wouldn't have ears, either, not if you're nothing. So how can you hear me?"

"*Me!*"

I blinked. "What?"

"*Me!*"

I sighed and let my head drop back down to the ground beneath my shoulder. "I don't know what you're saying."

"Nothing. Me."

I nodded, though I had to hold back a sudden flash of impatience. "Yeah, you're nothing. Or at least, it sounds like that's your name." I frowned. I was starting to get the uncomfortable sense that that distinction might be important.

"Your name, Nothing. Name, me?"

The echoing words roused me from the realization brewing deep within my mind. I blinked and mouthed the words that had echoed back to me.

When I'd worked out their meaning, I laughed.

"No, no, no. Me isn't my name, it's just a pro—a, uh, way for a person to refer to oneself." I shook my head, chuckling. I suddenly felt like I was back in high school with Logos and Rapier, helping people learn foreign languages. "When I talk to you, I say, 'Your name is Nothing.' But you would say, 'My name is Nothing.'"

"Nothing. My name is Nothing."

I grinned. I couldn't help it. Even with the strange colors and angles that threatened my vision when I opened my eyes and the strange, breaking silence beating against my ears, I could feel warmth spreading through my chest.

"Your name?" suddenly echoed around me.

I let my grin soften into a smile. "I'm Vitamare. Most people just call me Vita, though."

"Vita."

I nodded, but my smile was slipping. No longer fully focused on Nothing, my mind was sliding back to the problem of my presence in that strange place. "How am I going to get myself out of this one?"

"This one?" Nothing asked.

"Yeah. I told the world to leave me alone; that's how I ended up with you. I can't stay here, but I don't know how to reverse what I did."

"Can't stay here?" The words held such sorrow that my chest ached even as I shook my head.

"I don't belong here, Nothing. I'm human, and humans are social beings, and—"

"Social. I don't belong here."

I snapped my mouth shut. The urge to open my eyes and peer around again was strong, but I'd seen enough of what surrounded me to know better. I considered Nothing's words. Minutes before, I would have put it down to Nothing's tendency to repeat my words, but I'd already praised it—her?—for being smart.

"Nothing . . ." I spoke the name slowly. Maybe it was my imagination, but the air around me seemed to come to attention. "You said your name is Nothing, right?"

"Right."

I nodded as the idea that had been percolating in my mind earlier slowly took shape. "But you aren't nothing, are you?"

Silence answered me for a long moment. Then a soft *"Social. I don't belong here"* reached my ears, as if from a distance.

I nodded. The idea from before was solidifying, and I found my breath speeding up unexpectedly. "Do you know what you're supposed to be? Angel? Daeva?" The memory of chattering nonsense and pricks along my skin flushed through my mind, and I caught my breath. "Ice faerie?"

My words disappeared into the deep silence around me, torn apart and echoing oddly the way they had when this first began. Impatience nipped at my mind, but I kept it still. If Nothing had been that way for long enough, she—somehow, I was almost certain Nothing was female—probably wouldn't remember her original life well. That she had been learning language from me was enough for me to realize that.

"Faerie?" Nothing finally responded, long after anything she said could possibly be mistaken as just an echo. *"I . . . don't . . . know . . ."*

I nodded. Nothing might not have been certain, but the twist in my gut and the prickling along my nape were enough for me to be. Her name might have been Nothing—or more than likely, **Nothing**, as it would be in the Language of Truth—but I doubted she was created as nothing.

Which gave me an idea of how I might be able to get myself free from my own predicament.

"Nothing," I said, and that sense of awareness I had felt earlier tightened. "If I can get you free of being nothing . . . if I can get you your original form back . . . would you like that?"

The silence seemed to thrum before a sharp *"Like!"* echoed around me. I bit my lip. Perhaps I should have used the word *love*. Even now, I think it would have fit her enthusiasm better.

"Good," I whispered. I took a deep breath and forced myself to relax, and I could practically feel the curiosity rising around me. "I need to think carefully about the words I speak," I told Nothing. "I need to figure out just how I can get us both free from this place and back with the rest of the world."

"Free . . . how?"

I smiled but didn't answer her words. Instead, I settled my awareness within my own mind and focused on the languages that filled it. Using the Language of Truth correctly is about precision in language, and that had never been truer than it was right then.

I don't know how long I spent playing with the language before I nodded and opened my eyes. The colors and angles had deepened and multiplied, but I settled my gaze on a point where several angles met and formed a color that glowed like summer rain. Taking a deep breath, I began to speak.

"As the world has left me alone, so have I found my place with nothing. But the nothing I have found my place with is only Nothing in name. Nothing might be the name of this being, but nothing is not the nature to which this being was meant to be born. The being Nothing is not, in existence, nothing, and so Nothing, with whom I have found my place, must be returned to the nature to which it was meant to live. Return Nothing, with whom I have found my place, to the nature to which it was meant to live. Return . . ."

I repeated the last sentence over and over, uncertain how many times it would be necessary. I knew I'd chosen the right words—the warmth in my chest and the strength in my veins were a familiar reassurance—but undoing a Naming so ingrained was bound to take time and power.

Thank goodness I had both in abundance.

I felt like I was starting the sentence for the twentieth time when a distantly shouted "Vita!" broke upon my ears. My tongue and lips faltered, and I choked on the words as I let my awareness expand away from them.

The first thing I noticed was the difference in the colors around me. Where I had been seeing bizarre angles and colors, I saw only the blue, green, and white of the ice cave I'd slipped into earlier when the ice faeries were chasing me.

Then I noticed the roar and whistle of the wind, and a smile curled my lips. By all the moralities, I was back!

A heavy buzz soon joined the roar of the wind, though, and my smile quickly disappeared. Cursing, I scrambled to my feet. I may have gotten myself out of the predicament I'd Named myself into, but there were still ice faeries to deal with.

And I still had no idea how I was going to handle them.

I made it to my feet with surprisingly little slippage and turned toward what I thought was the entrance I'd come through. I wanted to get out of there, but I could already see the dancing pale spots of the ice faeries, like snow that refused to fall, gathering in the small tunnel. I gritted my teeth but stood my ground.

I should have done this to begin with.

Focusing on my own body, I Named the air dancing just over my skin into a rock-like nature. I didn't dare Name it into rock itself, not if I wanted to continue moving quickly, but the Naming I did would be enough to keep the ice faeries from reaching my skin and hurting me the way they had earlier.

With that done, I looked around the cave, seeking the creature whose very existence had helped save me. All I could see was the ice that lined the cave, sourceless lights distorting its color and image. Worry chilled my skin as the buzz of the ice faeries grew cautiously closer, but I shrugged, shaking off the sensation.

If Nothing was what I thought she was, her presence wouldn't have been obvious anyway.

Then the ice faerie swarm was upon me, though their nonsensical chatter was nothing against the silence that had threatened to rip apart my sanity earlier. They pressed against my arms and neck and chest, and I winced despite the protections I'd spoken into being.

Come on, Vita. You can do this.

I think I heard someone call my name then, but I was too focused on the ice faeries to worry about it. Lifting my hands palm up in front of me, I allowed myself to slip into the Language of Truth.

"Who among these ice faeries is queen?"

The faerie swarm stilled and pulled back from its attempted assault. They milled about before me, and I silently berated myself for giving up on the Language of Truth so quickly before. Sure, they had surprised my friends and me and we had all scattered when they started attacking us, but my friends and I have been attending to these kinds of jobs for years now. We really should have reacted better.

After a couple of minutes, one of the pale lights bobbing before me floated forward and settled on the fingertips of my right hand. As the light grew still, I could make out the tiny humanoid figure standing there, long, thin wings folding down along her back. Another faerie quickly followed the first's lead and settled in a crouch upon the pad of my thumb. From previous experience with other faerie swarms, I knew the second faerie was the queen's attendant.

I lifted my hands up and bowed my head. **"Good day, Your Majesty. I've been hoping you might speak with me."**

Silence answered me for so long that I began to worry these faeries really were incapable of understanding the Language of Truth—even though I'd never heard of such a faerie. I was just opening my mouth to try again when a quiet, tinkling voice finally reached my ears.

"Who . . . are you?"

I lifted my head and blinked at the faerie queen. I hadn't felt it, but she'd moved up to stand on the heel of my right hand. She leaned forward slightly, leading with her chin, but what caught my eye most was the way she cradled her belly with her hands—her heavily swollen belly.

"Well?" the queen pressed. I ducked my head and closed my mouth as I realized I was staring.

"A friend, Your Majesty, if you'll allow me to be."

"And what name should I call such a friend by?" she added with a touch of annoyance. I grimaced; annoyed faeries are the ones that tend to hurt people most.

"Vita," I answered. Not my True Name, of course, but I'd be a fool to tell that to even the faeries I do trust.

"Vita," the faerie queen said thoughtfully. She nodded, the motion only noticeable because I was focused so tightly on her. **"And what, may I ask, did you do?"**

I blinked again. **"Er . . . what do you mean?"**

She dipped her head and rubbed her swollen belly. When she spoke again, awe tinged her words.

"For weeks, I have mourned the loss of the child in my belly because of the scornful words of a hateful rival. My mourning scarred my people, to the point that we were too maddened with the loss to even speak properly."

My mouth dropped open slightly. **"You mean . . . is that why you attacked my friends and me?"** Remembering the original reason we'd come, I added, **"Is that why a mountain troll sought us out?"**

The tiny figure in my hands hunched her shoulders. **"It is not something I am proud of. Our grief led us to anger that I fear has damaged relationships we've held for years with the mountain trolls who have lived alongside us."**

I shook my head. **"No. No, it hasn't."** I grinned as I remembered the troll's wide, earnest eyes as he asked me for help reclaiming his home. **"The troll who came to us was insistent that I only needed to talk to you. I don't think he wanted you hurt."**

In fact, with the ice faeries no longer trying to hurt me, I could remember the troll's dogged insistence. *"No hurt. Just words."* (Mountain trolls aren't exactly known for their eloquence.)

The ice faerie queen trembled, her wings fluttering slightly. **"Thank you,"** she whispered. **"I don't know how you managed to return my child to my womb, but . . ."**

By the soft tinkling that followed, I suspected tears must have been pouring down her cheeks. Lifting my hands closer to my face, I tried to catch her gaze.

"Your Majesty." Her body gave a great shake, and she lifted her head. I offered her a smile. **"Your child saved me as much as I saved her."**

The queen's small eyes widened, and her hands once more framed her belly. **"Her?"**

I winced. If Nothing hadn't already been female, she had to be after that slipup. Silently apologizing to the unborn faerie, I nodded to her mother.

"When I was running from your people, I mistakenly removed myself from the world. It was only because your child was there too that I was able to bring myself back along with her."

The faerie queen shook her head. **"But how? My rival . . ."** She paused, deliberating for a moment before she seemed to find the words that were safest for her to use. **"My rival told me that my pregnancy would bring nothing but despair. How could you have found my child after that?"**

I grimaced. I had to wonder if even the rival realized how much damage they had done. **"I'm sorry, Your Majesty. I don't know what wording your rival might have used, but they gave your child a True Name."** I winced as I spoke the words. To give a child a True Name—only a parent should have such a right.

The pregnant faerie fell back a step. She caught herself quickly, though, and stood straight, lifting her chin. **"What name?"**

I glanced at the swarm still hovering in front of me. They pulled back. Nodding, I brought my hands closer to my mouth to whisper

Nothing's name as softly as I could to the queen. When I pulled back, she looked resigned but nodded.

"Thank you, Vita, for saving my child and sharing with me her name." She smiled brightly then and flew up off my hand. Her attendant quickly followed, hovering behind her as she hung before my eyes. **"It is unfortunate, but that she is no longer such a thing in essence only proves that the truth can set us free as easily as it can harm us."** Her smile grew brighter, and she gazed down at her belly. **"I will make sure it's a lesson she understands well . . . and that she knows who reminded me of it."**

A brief, barely there touch graced my cheek before the queen pulled away, bowed her head, and flew off. The swarm quickly followed her, and I was soon left staring at nothing but blue, green, and white ice.

"Vita!"

I blinked and glanced around. That call had been closer than the previous one, which I still barely remember. It sounded like . . .

"Arden?" I called back.

Minutes later, fiery light filled the small cave as a young man appeared in the tunnel entrance. In one hand, he cupped a ball of fire; in the other, he gripped what looked like a small pane of ice. "Vita!" He halted and tossed a shout over his shoulder. "She's back here!"

As I was ushered out of the cave, down the mountain, and back toward the comfort of home, I shared my tale with my friends, who offered gaped mouths and shaking heads at the appropriate moments. I know they believe me, no matter how strange the tale might sound. They know I would never lie to them. After all, this wasn't our first experience with the lesson the ice faerie queen spoke of.

No matter how cruel the truth can be, only truth can fight it back.

—From the journal of Vitamare Peregrin
    First Earthborn citizen of Calonai

ORPHAN TRAIN

K.A. FOX

I don't like the dark, Evie." Tiny, cold toes pressed against my bare legs, but I didn't move away. Winter had found its way here, and we were all feeling its teeth. Even in the convent's orphanage, with kids packed two or three to a cot, we had to huddle close together to stay warm. But we didn't complain. None of us had anywhere else to go. Inside and cold was better than outside and freezing.

I rested my hand on her head, petting her hair the way my mama used to do mine when I was scared or lonely or sad. "I know, Sarah. But we're not alone, so it's not too bad. Just go to sleep now." I kept my fingers moving, playing with her curls, soft and slow, until she stopped whispering and I knew she was finally asleep.

I rolled over onto my side, face to the door. I would keep my eyes open as long as I could. I didn't know how many days I'd been there, but it was still hard to sleep with my back to the door. I'd been asleep when they'd carried me away from home. There'd been a haze of soft voices saying prayers and last rites. That was all I remembered. I hadn't gotten to say goodbye to anyone who had loved me then. Not Mama, or Joshua, my bigger, stronger brother. Not my baby sister.

Something in me knew that it was because I'd fallen asleep on the night my family died, the coughs and fevers costing them too much. If I'd stayed awake, maybe they would have lived. Maybe I would have seen the people coming to take me away and refused to go with them. We could have still been a family. So I watched the door every night, telling quiet stories in the dark of the ward, until sleep won again.

The swishing sound of footsteps startled me awake. Eyes blinking, I peered into the darkness until a gentle hand glided over my forehead. The touch left warmth behind on my skin.

"Shh, Evie. It's all right. I'm just here with extra blankets. The Society Ladies had them sent over from their ball tonight. Collected them for us. You doing okay?" Miss Anna's voice was soft and cozy, the kind of voice that made you want to curl up beside her when she told stories. She wasn't a nun, but she wasn't one of us orphans neither.

She just made things better.

"I'm good. Sarah was cold earlier, but she's better now. Not shivering anymore. Them kids by the windows could use what you have, I bet. Has to be colder over there."

"I'll start with them, then. Check on you in just a bit." I could make out the shape of her sliding away in the dark. Miss Anna always managed to find her way, even when it was dark as caves. She told me it was a trick her own mama had taught her. But I guessed it had to be the light that followed her, little bits of darting flashes, red and gold and yellow moving together like a fire. That's what showed her where to go.

She moved back and forth, laying blankets over sleeping children, calming the ones that stirred. She stopped at my cot when she was done, one last blanket draped over her arm. "This is for you and sweet little Sarah," she said, covering me and my sleeping partner. She slid down to the floor beside me and leaned her head back against the wall. "Want me to stay for a little while?"

I nodded, knowing she'd see me like she saw everything. "Your colors are so pretty, Miss Anna. They follow you everywhere." The words were said before I could think about them, and I wondered if she would understand.

Her hand dropped onto my head, my hair sliding through her fingers with every soothing stroke. "Thank you, Evie. Yours are too. But let's make this our little secret." Warmth spread through me, working its magic until I fell fully asleep for the first time since I'd come to this place.

The air felt different the next day. Buzzing and busy. There were people everywhere. Ladies in fine hats and men in their suits and sour expressions. They whispered in corners, watching us as we were led through the halls, from Mass to classroom to meals and back again. My skin itched every time I felt eyes on me, and I was tempted to find a place to hide.

That night, as we filed onto our floor to change for bed, I realized that some of us were missing. There were gaps in the line, places that a familiar face had filled just that morning. I looked around for stragglers rushing in late, but there was no one. And the spot next to me stood empty as well. Sarah wasn't here.

Sister Mary walked in, her dark habit brushing across the wood with each step. Miss Anna followed her, but she didn't look at any of us. Her colors were different, like sparks rising from a fire and popping in the air. Angry. She kept her hands twisted together in front of her, the knuckles standing out stark white.

"Children!" Sister Mary's voice carried through the whole room, and scattered conversations fell silent. "Children, you'll notice that some of our wards are not here tonight."

"Did they die?" The words shook, and I could feel the fear in the air spike as every one of us remembered what had brought us here. The question came from one of the smaller girls down the line, and someone urged her to be quiet, but she asked again. Her voice was stronger this time. "Did they die? Are they sick now too?"

"No, child, they did not die." Sister Mary tried for a smile, but it didn't rest comfortably on her face. "They have found families to live with. People who will love them."

The statement hung in the air, vibrating through each of us.

They had been chosen. We had not. I remembered just the night before, crowding onto my cot with Sarah and the feel of her cold toes as she curled closer to get warm. Now the bed seemed too big for me alone. I swallowed as the sting of tears began, and I ducked my head to hide the wet shine covering my eyes.

Sister Mary continued. "Tomorrow, there is a train that will be going West. Some of you will be on it." There was a sob down the line, muffled behind a hand, but Sister Mary continued anyway. "If selected, you will be going to join your new families. Good homes. You will be cared for. And this will allow us to help other children here in our city as well."

She gestured to her left, her hand waving awkwardly in the air like the bird with a broken wing that my brother had tried to save two summers ago. I'd found him hiding in the corner, tears wet on his cheeks when that bird had died.

Miss Anna stepped up beside Sister Mary, her eyes sad even though she smiled.

"Naturally, we will not send you on this journey alone. Miss Anna has agreed to chaperone the girls who are chosen on the way to their new homes."

My heart fell, my stomach already aching at the loss of another person from my life.

Sister Mary turned to the door, her black habit swirling around her feet as she spun. As she stepped out into the hallway, she called back over her shoulder, "Say your prayers, girls." Then she was gone.

Silence hung heavy around us all as we looked from one to another. Who would still be here tomorrow night?

Miss Anna broke the spell holding us in place. "I know this is a shock. And I wish there had been a chance for everyone to say their goodbyes." She walked down the line of girls, gifting each of us with a calming touch as she passed by. The colors around her looked furious still, but I was the only one who noticed that. Even her voice was soothing.

"Tomorrow will be here quickly. I know that every one of you has something special you wouldn't want left behind. We have a little time before bed. Find whatever it is you'll want to have if you're called to go, so it doesn't get forgotten." Her hand lingered over the pocket of her skirt for the barest moment before she smoothed down the dark fabric, as if she were wiping away a wrinkle that didn't exist.

I sat at the edge of my cot, pulling out the small basket of possessions I kept just below it. I didn't have much. Most of the things in our home had been burned for fear of spreading the sickness. But I had been wearing a clip in my hair that last night, one that my mama had worn when she was a girl. It was the only thing I had left of her. I carefully slid it under the heavy weight of my hair, clipping it tight against my scalp so it was covered and would go unnoticed.

The other girls were doing the same, staring at their feet as they made their choices. Some of the little ones cried, silent tears rolling down their cheeks. I wondered which was more frightening for each of us. Being chosen and sent away to live in a place we'd never seen with people we didn't know? Or to be left behind, in this place of unchanging familiarity, with no one to claim us as family?

Once we were all ready for bed, Miss Anna methodically turned down the lamps scattered throughout the room and watched as we all climbed under our blankets. The wind felt even colder tonight, blowing loud and angry.

When we were safely in our beds, she said softly, "Good night, girls."

"Miss Anna, don't we need to say our prayers?"

She shook her head. "Not tonight. For now, we'll sleep." She whispered something after that, words I didn't quite catch, and I saw the colors swirl around her once and then spread out to blanket the room in a warm glow. It faded quickly, but I was already giving in to the heaviness of my eyelids and didn't see it disappear.

Two nights in a row I had slept now. A heavy sleep, unhaunted by dreams of people I'd lost. When I woke in the morning, there was an aching spot on the back of my head, where the clip hidden under my hair had marked my skin. Instead of being bothered by it, I was reassured. This last piece of my mama was still with me. And no one would see it with the thick brown fall of hair acting as a shield to keep it safe from discovery. I wouldn't risk someone taking it from me.

We were seated in Mass, girls on one side of the chapel, the boys we seldom saw sitting together on the other side. As the Benediction ended and we gathered ourselves to go, we were told to stay in our seats. Sister Mary came to the front, a piece of paper in her hands.

"As I read your name, please stand and step to the center aisle, forming a neat line. We don't have a lot of time before you'll need to leave for the station. Your belongings have already been packed and will be waiting for you in the back."

I heard a gasp from one of the girls seated behind me, a muffled sob escaping from someone I couldn't see. A boy I didn't know started to say something but was hushed up by the priest beside him.

Sister Mary, her voice strong and echoing, began to read the list of names she held out in front of her.

"Meghan O'Malley.

"Connor Reilly.

"Katherine Sheehan.

I stopped listening, my eyes cast down at my feet. I held my hands together so tightly in my lap that my nails dug into the skin of my palms, tiny half-moon bits of pain marking me.

"Evelyn Kelly."

I jerked my head up, not sure I'd heard correctly. The older girl next to me patted me on the shoulder. Whether it was meant as congratulations or condolences, I wasn't sure. My knees were weak as I stood, each step I took wooden as my feet guided me automatically to the line of children grouped in the center aisle.

"Please proceed to the back of the chapel at this time. You will each find a bag with your possessions and a coat to wear. There are numbers pinned to each coat. Please do not remove them. This is how your new families will claim you."

A boy seated in the pew to my left started to cry, and one of the small boys ahead of me stepped out of line and rushed to him. He threw his arms around the crying child, and their tight embrace drew my attention to their identical honey-colored curls. I looked at the group of children in line with me. So many bore shining eyes as we watched the final remnants of a family being separated.

Miss Anna appeared in the aisle, moving over to the pair of boys. She knelt next to them, a hand resting on each boy's shoulder. She leaned her head in toward them, and from the side, I could see her lips move. The colors around her spun, then moved away from her to douse the boys in rosy light. The three of them stayed like that, almost frozen, for a long moment, the sound of sobs fading away.

When they pulled away from each other, the fear and grief had eased from their faces. This time, when Miss Anna spoke to them, I could hear her words. "You will both remember."

She took the little boy by the hand and brought him over to where I stood. She pressed his hand into mine as she said, "Jack, this is Evie. She'll be your friend on our trip."

Then we were walking way, the last ones in the line of children as we were handed all we owned in the world and shuffled into coats marked by numbers to identify us. They led us out of the chapel and through the heavy carved doors into harsh sunlight. The wind blew hard, biting through our clothes as we followed the priest leading us away from our temporary home. None of us tried to argue or plead for a chance to stay. Even though we were children, we knew that would be futile. The decision had been made. We were going West.

We stood on the station's platform, grateful for the momentary shelter from the wind. The train pulled in, steam rushing out from below as it plowed to a stop, the sound of it making the little ones flinch away. As the conductor stepped toward our group, his hand out, the priest intercepted him. He handed our tickets over, gesturing at all of us and giving instructions, his words lost in the noise from the train. The conductor nodded, then turned and waved us to come forward.

We filed toward the door of the train car that stood open for us. Some of the children were excited, exclaiming over the brass hardware that reflected the cold light. Others were nervous, looking over their shoulders. Jack stood close beside me, his hand squeezing mine tightly. I smiled at him, hoping I appeared confident. I did what I could to keep him moving, one foot in front of the other, pointing out the beautiful letters on the side of the car and reminding him it would be warmer inside.

One of the girls slipped as she stepped up into the car, falling backward. Miss Anna tried to reach for her, her reaction slowed by the children that hung onto her. Someone brushed past me, colors of blue and silver blurring by with a chill that stung. Strong hands grabbed the child and swung her up into a man's arms.

With a laugh, the girl's rescuer said, "Now there, be careful, little miss. No sense gettin' hurt before your adventure even begins." He set her gently on the ground and tipped his hat. "Go on. You can do it."

She giggled, jumping up into the train car without a mistake this time. The rest of us followed her, our group shrinking steadily as each child disappeared into the darkness of the car. Miss Anna was directly behind me, her presence a warm comfort at my back. I heard her thank the man for acting so quickly that one of her charges wasn't hurt.

The light inside was dim, but my eyes quickly adjusted, and we were all able to find spots on the padded benches. Miss Anna surveyed us, her lips moving as she silently counted heads. A shadow rose up behind her, the form of a man blocking the light from outside.

Miss Anna turned, the red and gold sparks around her swirling with surprise.

"What are you doing?" she asked as the rescuer from the platform stepped into the train car.

The man smiled at her, his lips a little crooked, higher on the right side than the left. The blues and silvers that surrounded him glowed brighter as he said, "I'm to get these boys to their new families. Thought I'd see a little more of this country when I'm done."

I turned my attention to the window, drawing aside the shade that blocked the wintry light. The priest that had led us to the station was shaking the conductor's hand, clasping him on the shoulder before stepping down from the platform and walking away.

Behind me, Miss Anna said, "They told me there would be a chaperone for the boys. I just assumed it would be Father Mark accompanying us."

The man shook his head, his smile still in place. "I'm Malcolm. And you're Miss Anna. We met once before."

I watched Miss Anna, her eyes searching over Mr. Malcolm's handsome features. She gasped as recognition lit her face. "Your family," she whispered, reaching out to him and laying her graceful fingers against his wrist. "How are they?"

His smile shifted, turning a little sad. "My ma died and so did my little brother, William. But my sister and I made it through. She's married now. Happened two weeks ago. She's got a good chance because of what you and your mother did." He leaned in, the distance between him and Miss Anna almost too small now. But there were no nuns about to object. "Thank you for that, how you helped us. I heard you lost your mother too, in the end."

Miss Anna looked away from him, her eyes lit with tears. She opened her mouth to speak, but the train vibrated beneath our feet, the floor shuddering. Miss Anna staggered, losing her balance, but Mr. Malcolm steadied her with a hand on her elbow and helped her to a seat. The colors that swirled around them were dizzying, twining together before separating again. It looked like they were dancing together.

I looked back out the window to where crowds of people stood, calling out goodbyes to their friends and family, the people they loved. A sudden sadness swept over me, weighing me down as I realized there was no one out there who cared to wait, to see us off. No one to watch the train disappear and miss us as we faded from sight.

The train lurched forward, causing laughter and shrieks to ring out. My heart lunged in my chest with the motion of the car, excitement taking the place of loneliness. Jack pressed close next to me, a small smile spreading across his face, and I felt lighter at the simple sight of it.

On the other side of the car, one of the littler boys started to cry. He might have been four years old; the coat he wore was too big for his frail frame. "I want to go home," he said, pointing his finger to the window as the station began to slide by.

Mr. Malcolm went to him and slid onto the bench beside him. "No worries now. We're all going home. We just haven't seen exactly what it looks like yet. That's why this is an adventure." He gave the boy a wink, and with a quick twist of his fingers, a glistening star made of ice appeared. The little boy laughed and clapped, his worry instantly replaced by awe as he reached out to the touch the shining crystal.

Malcolm offered it to him, and the little boy snatched it, turning to show his new treasure to the other children around him.

Miss Anna laughed. "Now that's a handy trick to have."

"Cold comes easy to me." Mr. Malcom tilted his head to the right, considering her. "But you . . . I think heat is your talent. Fire lives inside you. It's why you're so good at healing."

Miss Anna looked away, catching me as I watched their interaction, fascinated. Mr. Malcolm followed her gaze to me, nodding his head as he looked me over. "Oh. I hadn't noticed before. She's got the gift as well."

I sat up straighter. "What do you mean, the gift?"

The two adults regarded me silently for a moment, then Miss Anna leaned across the space between our benches. She took my hand, leaving Jack sandwiched between us. "I was going to tell you when we had a little more time together. To help you understand. There's magic in you. Just beginning to show."

Joy and astonishment swelled within me. "Really?" I barely breathed the word.

She nodded. Keeping her voice quiet, she said, "It's a wonderful thing. But it can frighten some people, so we have to be careful who sees the things we can do. Frightened people can do terrible things."

I considered her words. They made sense, in a way. But I wasn't afraid. Instead, I wanted to know more. "Will I be able to do the things that you can do?"

Miss Anna gave me a smile, one that made her face glow. "With time. And practice."

"What about hiding from people?" I looked to Jack, whose head twisted back and forth between us as we spoke.

Mr. Malcolm gave a laugh. "Children aren't who we have to hide from, love." He reached around to ruffle Jack's hair. "Little ones are made of magic. They don't get scared so easy when they see it happen right in front of them. Some lose their magic as they grow up. Others have so much that it never dies."

Jack giggled and snuggled into my side. A wide smile on my face, I asked, "Like me?"

Mr. Malcolm nodded. "Like you, love."

✧

The rest of our trip was spent with Miss Anna showing me things she knew how to do. Things her mama had taught her when she was first beginning to grow into her magic. Mr. Malcolm entertained the other children with games and his own tricks. He made snow fall around us inside the train car, until Miss Anna gave him her one of her looks and, with a snap of her own fingers, it was warm as high summer around us. The snow was instantly gone, the moisture in the air frizzing our hair before it faded away.

After what felt like a thousand tries, I managed to coax a small flame to life. Jack crowded me, reaching out a chubby finger to poke at the ribbon of fire dancing in the center of my palm. He hissed at the heat pouring from it and snatched his hand back before it could burn him.

Miss Anna whispered into my ear, "Try to pull that heat back into you now, Evie. Let it soak into your skin. It can't hurt you."

I concentrated, the high heat of the flame calling to me. I

opened myself up, no longer afraid of being burned, and felt the warmth dissolve into me. I gasped. The fire was still there, flickering in my hand, but there was no longer any heat radiating from it.

"Come here, Jack." Miss Anna waved him into place next to me. "You can touch it now. Evie made sure it won't hurt you."

Jack looked at me questioningly, and I nodded, reassuring him. The heat coursed through me, filling me from within. It was still safe. Jack took a deep breath and then closed his eyes, putting his hand into the center of the flame I held. When nothing happened, he opened his eyes. The flame licked up between his spread fingers, tinting his skin a rosy gold. But there was no sign it hurt him.

He laughed, jumping up and down next to me before throwing his arms around my waist. My hands fell and wrapped around him, holding him close. The fire was gone, snuffed out before I touched him.

"This will be your secret now. The two of you. Okay, Jack?" Miss Anna asked him, wanting to make sure he understood. "You have to be careful, to keep each other safe."

Jack nodded, and his grip on me tightened a fraction. The weight of responsibility settled on me a little more heavily.

The train horn startled us, and we broke apart. The light-hearted chatter from the other children faded away as the car shuddered around us. The train rumbled gradually to a stop, and the sight of a station drifted into view through our windows.

We all looked at each other. The fun and laughter we'd been enjoying disappeared as we realized our time was up. We were here.

Miss Anna helped the girls change into our best dresses, moving between each of us with quick, careful movements. She brushed out our hair and then braided it up, deft hands making quick work. She made sure we all remembered to eat some food. She coaxed smiles from those of us who were nervous or afraid. She made sure we were all scrubbed shiny and that the numbers assigned to each one of us were easy to see.

When it was time, we were led up to the front of the town's gathering hall, climbing up the few steps to the stage so everyone could see us. We were lined up in number order. Jack clung to my hand, his sweaty palm in mine a comforting feeling.

Names were called, and people would rise, walking to where we stood, examining us all before moving to take charge of the child sent all this way to become part of their family. Jack was shaking. I could feel the tremors of his muscles as they traveled from his skin to mine.

Miss Anna met an older couple as they walked up to where we stood and shook their hands. She whispered something I couldn't hear, and they nodded, their eyes flicking over me. They stepped toward us, and my fingers tightened around Jack's. He gave a pained sound, and I relaxed my hold on him, suddenly afraid they would take him from me.

"Evie, this is Mr. and Mrs. Fraser. They're your new parents."

I swallowed, unsure what to do. I couldn't leave Jack behind. My fingers wouldn't uncurl from his. It felt like abandonment.

Mrs. Fraser looked to Miss Anna. "And the boy. You're sure we can take him too? We can have them both?" I could hear hope in her voice, the sound tenuous and unsure, as though she was afraid something she desperately wanted was about to be snatched away.

Miss Anna nodded as Mr. Malcolm joined our group. Glancing around, I saw that we were the last children; all the rest were moving toward the door. No time for any of us to say goodbye.

"He was meant to go with a family from the next town over. But the husband passed suddenly, and his wife is going to join her family back East." Miss Anna looked to where Jack and I waited, giving me a smile. "They're both yours now."

Mrs. Fraser grasped her husband's arm, and he gave it a gentle pat. "Just like you always wanted, my dear. A girl and a boy."

Mr. Malcolm lifted me down from the stage, setting me carefully down before turning to do the same for Jack.

I looked to Miss Anna, a question forming on my lips, but she stopped me before I could say anything. "Malcolm and I will be

staying here for a while. Just to make sure everyone gets settled.
You'll see us again."

She dropped a kiss onto my forehead and ruffled Jack's curls.
Then we were walking away from her, led out of the building into a
blindingly bright day. And even though it was still winter here, it
didn't feel nearly as cold as it had before.

I sit in my parlor, rocking back and forth, with a grandchild of my
own cuddled in my lap. It's winter again, but we're warm inside.
Embers glow in the fireplace, flaring up as I whisper to them, the
room comfortable and cozy.

"Was that really how you and Uncle Jack came here?" asks Rose,
my towheaded granddaughter. She sits on the floor, her legs crossed
under her. Her elbows rest on her knees as she props her chin on her
hand. "On a train made of magic?"

I grin at her, nodding as I gently pat the sleeping baby I hold.
"That's exactly the truth. A train made of magic."

She bites her lip, tiny white teeth leaving a dent behind. "Were
you scared?"

I think back to that time, fifty-three years now gone. To the little
girl who was alone in the world, with only a hair clip and some
donated clothes to call her own. To the adventure of that journey, the
excitement of learning how to call a flame to life and watching it
dance in the palm of my hand. I remember the awe of the other
children, the happiness we had on that trip even though none of us
knew what might be waiting for us at the end.

"Grandma?" Rose prompts me, wanting an answer.

"I was a little afraid. But it had a good ending. Things usually do,
I've found, if we don't get in the way too much."

The baby stirs in my arms, and I run my hand over his soft hair,
petting it the way I did to Sarah's once, so she could fall asleep. The
way my mama had when I was tiny and needed comfort. I look back
at Rose, to the colors that are already starting to halo her form, tiny

sparks that match the embers in the grate. Made of magic, through and through.

"I found my family at the end of that journey. A home." Rose leans in toward me, her eyes bright and her hair lit rosy gold from the fire as she listens. "I found love. And that's the real magic, my girl."

The Trapped Spirits of Yekaterin

Kelly Lynn Colby

The winter wind raked Yuliya's back as the whipping flames of a modest fire toasted her hands and feet. She'd brought the pocket of heat to life with a bit of cold tinder and a spark from her own finger. She should've been proud of her accomplishment, yet anyone could light a fire with a few basic tools. This particular skill brought her no closer to her goal of being a healer.

She rotated on the log, giving her backside a turn at warmth. Tucking her feet beneath her and her hands into her lap, Yuliya hoped the residual heat would last long enough for her back to thaw. Squinting at the wagon in the dimming light, she shivered as she caught sight of the frozen cape that hung stiff in the biting wind. Icicles hung along the bottom of the wool like decorative tassels. Yuliya would have to wear the ice shroud to mask as much of her body heat as possible when they entered the Yekaterin Forest. She wondered if she'd ever be truly warm again.

Yuliya startled at a sizzling hiss behind her and tumbled off her log, face first into the snow. Rolling to free her limbs, she crouched in a defensive stance. Smoke rose from the charred remains of the fire. The burning wood smell intensified at the same rate as the warmth faded.

The last bit of the dying sun cast a long shadow over Vladlena, her witch mentor. Yuliya didn't have to see her features to predict her mood. She never held anything but a scowl on her face anyway.

"You clumsy oaf! You better get it together before we fill the buckets with spirit water." Vladlena kicked another clump of snow over the red embers. "A drop of that is worth more than three of you."

"I understand, Vl—" Yuliya blushed as she almost used her mentor's first name instead of her honorarium. "Tyotya."

Vladlena kicked snow off the top of her boot as she squinted at her apprentice. When the witch turned toward the wagon instead of reprimanding her for the slip, Yuliya sighed in relief and brushed white flakes from her face. The snow stole any warmth she'd gleamed from the fire. She'd never be warm again.

Though she'd been apprenticed with the witch doctor for four months now, Yuliya had questioned her decision to volunteer after only a few hours. The Tyotya only accepted apprentices who could read and write, which meant Vladlena had to pull from the wealthier of her clientele. After the witch had saved Yuliya's father from a devastating illness, the noblewoman had offered her youthful strength and writing hand to learn the ancient skill of healing.

Beyond the weak fire spell, Yuliya had learned how to properly scrub a cauldron to prevent cross contamination, how to prepare the perfect mutton stew, and how to dry herbs without promoting mold growth. At this rate, she would never learn enough to make a decent hair-growth potion. True healing seemed completely out of reach.

"Tie up the beast and ready the wheelbarrow. It's almost time to head in." Vladlena gestured to the Yekaterin Forest without lifting her eyes.

Yuliya mirrored the usually steady woman's reluctance by averting her own eyes from the forest. Even when the sun shone directly overhead, the Yekaterin remained pitch black, as if it absorbed all the light offered by the weak winter globe.

Throwing a wool cover over her thin robe, she stuck her arms out the holes and knotted the innermost ties before securing the outer layer. She would throw a shawl over her shoulders to protect her arms, but first she untacked Malcolm and guided the mule to a tree. Not wanting Malcolm to escape before they returned, Yuliya dumped a healthy pile of hay in front of the mule. Hauling the heavy buckets of spirit water out of the forest would be tough enough. Yuliya had no desire to drag them all the way back to town without the aid of the pack animal.

The rattle of buckets hitting the wheelbarrow hurried her back to Vladlena's side. Whenever the witch had to perform physical labor herself, her mood fell from annoyed to angry as quickly as an infant moved from laughing to screaming.

Vladlena jumped from the wagon like a woman half her age. "You better have properly waxed the insides of these buckets. Not a drop of spirit water better soak into the wood."

"I thoroughly waxed them, Tyotya." Yuliya set the six buckets upside down in the wheelbarrow. She didn't want to stack them together and risk scratching the protective layer.

Vladlena harrumphed and tossed a coiled length of rope on top of the buckets. "Help me with this cursed thing." She slid her frozen cloak from the pole it was slung over.

"Yes, Tyotya." Yuliya climbed onto the back wheel of the wagon and wrapped a leg around the railing for balance.

The two women lifted the cloak, much heavier with its coating of ice, above Vladlena so she could snake underneath. As the witch forced her head through the opening, the collar crackled as little pieces broke off.

Yuliya grabbed her thick shawl from her bag in the wagon and tied it around her shoulders. Her mentor helped toss her own ice shroud over the insulation of the rest of her clothing. Taking an extra breath as she learned to maneuver with the massive weight, Yuliya grabbed the small wheelbarrow's handles with her gloved hands.

Oddly, she felt warmer under her layer of ice. Fear sliced through her moment of comfort. "Are you sure, Tyotya, that these will protect us from . . . them?"

Vladlena tutted at her apprentice's fear. "Of course, child. I have completed this journey every year the conditions have been conducive. This is the third snow of the second month of winter. Anything that could produce heat is hibernating. The sun stays in the sky for such a short period, the bare branches high up in the canopy don't have time to thaw before it falls below the horizon again. The spirits are powerless."

She pulled the straight pole, from which the cloaks had hung, from the spokes of the wheel. Sparkles of purple and green glittered along its surface as it transformed into a twisted wooden staff with a clear crystal globe mounted on the top. Vladlena claimed that each witch had to craft her own magical staff and the closer to home she could source the materials, the more powerful it would be. Yuliya had spent more than one night asking the staff to reveal its origin, but it refused to tell her anything.

As Vladlena marched through the snow to the tree line, she flicked the crystal, causing a blue-tinted light to emanate from its depths.

"Tyotya, will that not alert the spirits to our presence?" Yuliya pushed the wheelbarrow through the snow after her mentor, the frozen ground making the vehicle easy to manage. Which was a good thing since her whole body trembled with a mix of fear and excitement.

Vladlena pivoted to face her apprentice. Her usual angry spin lost some of its drama when the frozen cloak refused to flare in a swirling circle around her body. Instead, it hung stiffly and lifelessly at her side. "Yuli, are you ever going to trust me? The spirits need heat to manipulate objects in this world, not light. And though many times the two are united . . ."

The witch swung the crystal at Yuliya. Shocked, she dropped the wheelbarrow handles and rushed to cover her face, too late. The blue light blocked all other sensation as the crystal pressed against her nose. Her heart beat so hard, she swore the ice cracked over her chest. She calmed as she realized no heat radiated from the staff.

Vladlena pulled it back. "In this case, we have light without heat. Until you trust that I know what I'm doing, I won't be able to teach you anything of substance." The witch harrumphed in perceived superiority as she continued toward the forest.

Yuliya appreciated the temporary blindness caused by the sudden removal of the bright crystal. If she had been able to see clearly, she might have rammed into the old bat and watched her haughty face roll in the snow. With her hands still shaking, though from anger instead of fear, Yuliya pushed the wheelbarrow over the small embankment surrounding the Yekaterin.

The Great Queen Mother had saved Plotavka from the plague of evil spirits by trapping the whole lot of them in the forest on the edge of the kingdom. Never wanting a single citizen to face such torment again, she had had her army build an artificial bank around the perimeter to mark its borders. Yuliya tightened her hold on the wagon as she imagined apprenticing under the Great Queen Mother instead of the second-rate Vladlena.

A booming voice shook Yuliya out of her daydream. "Any who cross the border of the Yekaterin puts their life and their sanity in the hands of the mad spirits who live here. If you value either, turn around and never return."

She swore her heart stopped as her entire body froze. "We woke one up," she whispered so softly, she wasn't sure if a sound escaped her lips or if it remained in her mind.

"You can't wake up a spirit. They don't sleep," Vladlena boomed almost as loudly as the warning had. She waved her hands in dismissal. "It's an automatic enchantment for the cold-brained fools who don't heed the warning signs and have no idea of the barrier they've crossed."

If the old witch could speak up, then so could Yuliya. "What signs?"

She flinched as Vladlena pivoted again, brandishing her glowing staff. The witch aimed its light toward a large rectangular plaque that Yuliya had to have passed on her way through the ditch. She hadn't noticed it.

"Ah," she said, feeling a fool. With her head down and

determined not to ask another stupid question, she followed Vladlena deeper into the Yekaterin.

The witch's confident pace showed she knew exactly where she was going. Having come here every couple of winters must have anchored the route in her memory, for Yuliya could see no sign of a trail, either natural or engineered. She supposed ghosts didn't need footpaths, considering they never touched the ground.

For a while—Yuliya couldn't tell how long—the only sound she could hear came from her and Vladlena's padded feet crunching on top of the snow. She had expected a quiet forest in the middle of winter. The woods right outside her family manor stayed peaceful from winter snowfall until spring rain.

The Yekaterin was different. The stillness transformed from peace into oppression. Yuliya kept glancing over her shoulder, expecting to see someone following her. The feeling of being observed overwhelmed any sense of serenity. Vladlena had assured her apprentice that gathering a few buckets of spirit water was completely safe as long as they took the proper precautions. Yuliya's skin prickled the farther they traveled, but it wasn't the cold that was getting to her.

Unable to handle the quiet any longer, Yuliya asked another question. "And this spirit water does what, exactly?"

"The water has been stuck here in an ancient well with the dead. Over the years, it has picked up some of the otherworldly qualities of its neighbors." Vladlena seemed just as relieved as Yuliya to interrupt the cold silence. "With only a few expensive drops, a person can see into the future or into the past or far away or within themselves, for spirits are connected to this world and the next."

Yuliya thought about the moans and screams rumored to echo from Yekaterin during the warm summer months. "Does it hurt?"

"Does what hurt?" Annoyance returned to the witch's voice.

Clearing her throat, the apprentice gathered her courage to continue. She had to know. "Does it hurt to be a spirit, to be stuck between this world and the next?"

"Of course it does, child. That is why there are so few ghosts." Vladlena made a quick right turn around a fused pine and oak.

Yuliya's pace slowed as she stared at the bare, dead-looking branches of the oak twisted around deep green pine needles. She cornered the awkward wheelbarrow around them. Their grim embrace morphed into a grotesque image of the dead eating the living as the soft light of the crystal faded.

Tyotya Vladlena continued. "Don't feel sorry for them, though. The dead choose to move on or to stay. If they choose to be torn asunder by the constant pull of two worlds, that's their free will. But if they wait too long, they go mad and forget why they were holding on in the first place."

Yuliya jogged to catch up with Vladlena, her breath filling her hood with steam at her exertion. The ice above her eyebrows crackled, and a single piece fell off and shattered on the packed snow.

"No, no, no."

She forced her breathing to slow to a more measured pace. Her lungs ached from the dry, bitterly cold air, but she ignored the pain to decrease the amount of heat her body released. If a spirit sensed her warmth, it could siphon every bit from her body until she froze. The ice coat kept her almost invisible. She needed to maintain its integrity until they could make it out of the Yekaterin.

"Tyotya," she called to her mentor. "Please. I can't . . . keep . . . up." Her head felt light and the world spun. Yuliya leaned on the wheelbarrow, trying to stay upright as she fought the disorientation.

"You are blue, child." Vladlena sighed and shook her head. "You can breathe normally. The spirits are so weak this time of winter, it would take an abundant supply of heat to attract their attention."

An orange sparkle danced in Yuliya's vision. At first, she thought she was going to faint. Then she heard the distinct crackle of firewood and caught a whiff of smoke. She pointed to the anomaly that seemed to grow larger by the moment. "You mean, like a fire?"

"No one would be that—" Vladlena sniffed the air, like a dog when salted pig hit the frying pan. Her face scrunched so tight, every line was magnified under the shadow of her hood.

If Yuliya didn't know any better, she would have mistaken the expression for fear.

The witch squinted in the direction of what was quickly becoming a bonfire. The light soon overwhelmed the dim blue of Vladlena's crystal-topped staff. Yuliya could clearly see a stone circle raised from the ground of a clearing. That had to be the well.

Yuliya had never seen her mentor hesitate. "Should we leave before the spirits reawaken?"

Her voice set something off in Vladlena, who tossed her staff in the wheelbarrow and shoved the much smaller Yuliya to the side. "No. I've traveled this far."

"Tyotya, is it worth the risk?" Yuliya got her answer as the witch pushed the cart at a sprint toward the well.

Looking back the way they'd come, she considered returning on her own. Her family would take her back. The wealthy Lebedevs had questioned their daughter's decision to apprentice with the Tyotya anyway. Her mother would be relieved to see Yuliya at her doorstep again.

The sound of the buckets being flung from the wheelbarrow came a moment before Vladlena's yelling. "What sort of fool are you to tempt the spirits on this night?" A flash of blue light fell across the clearing, and the bonfire dimmed to meager embers.

Yuliya chewed on her lower lip, which was already slightly cracked from the dry air. She had pledged an oath to obey and assist and defend Tyotya Vladlena for the duration of her apprenticeship. If she ran away at the first sign of danger, what kind of healer would she be? After one more glance toward safety, Yuliya jogged toward the old witch.

Forgetting that her outer cloak was frozen solid, Yuliya leapt over a bucket in her path. Her knee hit the stiff cloth and bounced off. She tumbled over the wood and smacked her head on the ground.

An unfamiliar quavering voice addressed her. "You've arrived just in time. My father will be here any second."

Ice crystals fell from her cloak like water droplets as she found her footing. She sighed at the most recent destruction to her protection.

"Ignore the crazy old man. He must have sipped some of the spirit water without properly preparing for its effects." Vladlena motioned to her apprentice as she raised her staff overhead, aiming its base at the frozen surface of the raised well. "Grab the bucket and bring it here."

Yuliya jumped as sparks shot up from her right at the same time as the witch shattered the barrier over the well. An old man wearing no more than a wool coat and slippers tossed another branch on the embers. Flames crawled across the dry wood, even as the lower level of embers steamed in the melting snow. His cracked smile was highlighted as the new light reflected off his broken teeth and brightened his face until the ancient wrinkles faded. Yuliya couldn't decide if he really was a crazy old man or if he was one of the spirits made solid by the heat of the fire.

Pain ripped through her shoulder. "Ow!" Yuliya glared at Vladlena, who picked up another shard of ice to toss at her.

"Hurry up!" The witch picked up one of the buckets close to her and dipped it into the crystal-clear water. "We must finish before the spirits find this old fool."

Yuliya set the empty bucket at Vladlena's feet and accepted the full one. "Are we to leave the old man to his fate? What if we were meant to save him?" She grunted as she lifted the heavy load into the wheelbarrow.

"There is no 'meant to,' only 'choose to.'" The witch dipped another bucketful out of the well. "I choose to live."

Yuliya walked with heavy steps to the wheelbarrow, her hands aching from the pressure of the bucket handle. She inhaled a lungful of icy air, then hauled the full load into the vehicle. A bit of liquid sloshed over the side and flowed along the cracks in the ice on the front of her cloak, like a vertical river through a barren landscape.

A strong gust of air howled through the trees, fanning the flames of the growing fire. Until that moment, Yuliya hadn't notice the absence of the constant winter wind among the trees.

"Hurry, hurry. We've no time for your hesitation and constant questioning. Just keep moving." Vladlena tied the rope to the next bucket to get it deeper into the well. "The spirits awaken. I wish not to face them."

Yuliya jogged to the well, trying not to concentrate too much on what her mentor had just said.

The old man threw a few more logs onto the fire and jumped up and down, clapping his hands. "I am here, Father. I have come to free you."

The image of her father sweating and moaning, looking years older, washed over Yuliya, almost more real than when she had stood beside his bed. She had joined this woman to help people. How could she abandon a man who was obviously in need? Biting her lip, she abandoned the bucket and joined the old man.

"I am Yuliya."

The old man leaned over and hugged her. He was no thicker than a twig, and Yuliya didn't know how he hadn't frozen already. "I am Iosif Morozov, and I am here to free my father."

A touch of warmth toasted Yuliya's cheek from the growing fire. She could only hope the spirits would be attracted to the more tempting fire first and allow the living to escape. She held the old man's shoulders, trying to get him to look in her eyes. "Please, come with us. If your father is here, he is no longer who you remember."

Vladlena scoffed at her apprentice. "Quit wasting your breath and come help me."

"We can't leave him."

"I can, and I will." No sympathy echoed in her words or her movements as she hauled another full bucket from the well. "The spirits will come and consume all his warmth, however little resides in his shriveled form. Then he will join his father, for no spirit can escape the borders of Yekaterin, regardless of its choice."

Yuliya's face flushed. "I thought you said it was the choice of the dead to remain or move on?"

Vladlena remained unmoved by her apprentice's hurt feelings. Her breath came in huffs as she deposited a full bucket into the wheelbarrow beside the first. "Anywhere else, that is true. Within Yekaterin, no spirit can escape. The Great Queen Mother gathered all the ghosts from the entire Poltavka kingdom, all the dead who refused to move on, and trapped them here. If anyone dies within its borders, he will suffer the same fate."

"Lies!" the old man yelled. "My father was a great general in the war. He fought for Srubna and almost won."

"I don't have time for you, old man." Vladlena grasped one wheelbarrow handle. "Yuliya, come. We need to go."

"The war between Poltavka and Srubna was eighty years ago. And we won." Yuliya couldn't shake the feeling she was missing something. She took Iosif's hand and guided him to the wheelbarrow.

"You only won because your witch queen cheated." Yanking his hand from Yuliya's grip, the old man ran into the woods, mumbling about more firewood.

"How dare he speak of the Great Queen Mother that way!" Yuliya questioned why she was driven to helping the old man.

Another violent wind whipped the branches around the clearing. Fear drove Yuliya to aid Vladlena with the wheelbarrow. If Iosif chose to join his father in permanent torment, who was she to argue?

Iosif appeared on the other side of the glade. He dumped more wood onto the fire. The howling wind morphed into a terrorized scream. Yuliya's insides heated as adrenaline pumped through her veins. Her instinct to run was beginning to outweigh her need to please her mentor.

Vladlena tossed another bucket into the well and manipulated the rope until the wood tilted enough to fill with water instead of floating impotently on the surface. The witch's robe dripped. Yuliya focused on her own protective layer and realized the heat of the fire was liquifying the ice.

"Leave the bucket, Tyotya." She rushed to the witch's side and held up the now pliable fabric. "We have no warding left."

Staring down at the sinking bucket in disgust, Vladlena nodded at her apprentice. "Help me with the one I've already filled."

The two women walked in synchrony as they hauled the last full bucket of the season up into the wheelbarrow. Some of the water sloshed over the side, but the witch said nothing.

Yuliya startled when the old man grabbed her elbow. She took a deep breath and gave it one more try. "Come with us, Iosif. We—" Vladlena shook her head, dismissing her inclusion. "I will help you find your father."

Iosif bounced on his toes with the energy of a five-year-old, rather than that of a man approaching a hundred. "I knew you were the one. But first, you must understand."

With surprising speed, Iosif dipped a cupped hand into one of the buckets and dumped the lot on Yuliya's face. Most of the liquid flowed into her mouth, and she swallowed to avoid choking on the shockingly cold water.

The renewed wind morphed from a howl to a scream. Yuliya fell to her knees and covered her ears. Nausea replaced all other feeling as her mind swirled with colors, an odd contrast to the blacks and whites of the nighttime forest.

"Curse you, old man. I am responsible for the girl." Vladlena's voice floated above the noise of the battle scene forming inside Yuliya's head.

Or was she being transported to another time? The images felt so real. She heard iron clanging off armor. A horse galloped by in a sheer panic. Its rider hung off the side of the saddle at an awkward angle, a gaping hole in his neck leaking deep red. The copper smell of fresh blood mingled with the acrid smell of clay and the stench of human filth.

A horn blasted to her right, followed by the roar of a rushing line of soldiers. The bright green and yellow of the Srubna banner waved as the battalion cleared the hill and clashed with the much smaller army on the other side. The orange of a setting sun fluttered in the air, the banner of her home kingdom, Poltavka. The bearer retreated as the enemy soldiers slaughtered the defenders. The proud men fell, screaming in pain and anger and fear.

Yuliya knew what she witnessed: the Great War. Her history books said Poltavka had easily routed the barbarian Srubna in the final battle, ending the ten years' war. Something must have happened later, because her kingdom was getting slaughtered at the moment.

The bloody scene swirled around her until her head throbbed and she forced her eyes shut. Her knee hit a solid object, and she threw her arms out to stop herself from tumbling forward. They hit the surface of a table covered with a map and a few rolled scrolls. Tent sides flapped in the wind, but an overwhelming scent of honeysuckle wiped out any hint of the battle raging beyond its confines. The vines sprung from pots and grew along trellises surrounding the tent, which was packed full of officers in armor, half deep orange and half green and yellow.

Yuliya stood in the middle of a negotiation. This must have been the surrender of Srubna.

"Come, Queen Oksana of Poltavka, I have men to tend to." A large man with general stripes on his pauldron dropped a scroll onto the map. Two of his men unrolled it and placed rocks on either end to keep it flat. "The surrender is as our ambassadors discussed and we both agreed. Now come and sign so we can end this bloodshed and begin a new era as one united kingdom: Srubna."

Gasping out loud, Yuliya flung a hand over her mouth, but no one seemed to notice her there. The queen stepped around a honeysuckle-laden divider. The apprentice had seen portraits of the Great Queen Mother in her youth, but nothing prepared her for the grace and confidence of the beautiful woman. She walked as if she ruled the world, even though she approached defeat.

"Why the rush, General Morozov? Would you like some refreshments?" She gestured to a side buffet overflowing with ripe fruit, a variety of cheeses, and loaves of fresh bread.

Morozov? Yuliya dug in her brain, searching for the familiarity of that name. *Iosif's last name! Is this his father? Can it be . . . ?*

"Stop wasting time." The general flung his gauntlets at his second and picked up a quill. "Are you ready?"

Queen Oksana leaned across the negotiating table. "If we are going through with this, why do you still hide behind your military title? Ashamed of your true responsibility as King Rodion of Srubna?"

His men grumbled, while the Poltavka officers gasped in shock. General Morozov, who was apparently also King Rodion, slammed his fists on the table. The inkwell tipped over and threatened the document. The queen scooted the scroll out of harm's way in an elegant flip that rolled it up.

King Rodion scowled. "If you already know who I am, it should give you even more reason to sign." He dipped the quill in the ink that had spewed across the map and offered it to her.

Queen Oksana refused the quill and produced a small dagger from her belt. The king's guards formed a barrier in front of him with their hands on their sword hilts. The queen's guards did the same.

Frowning at her people, she shooed them off. "I need no protection." She held up the tiny dagger. "Do you?" she taunted the much larger, armored man opposite her.

Predictably, he waved his men back. Yuliya's respect for the Great Queen Mother grew. She knew how to work a room. She couldn't wait to see what the queen did to turn the negotiations in her favor.

"In Poltavka, blood reigns over all. Without a sample, the signature would be worthless." She unrolled the parchment, pricked her finger with the dagger, and pushed the wound to the bottom of the document. As her blood soaked into the fiber, the contract flashed, so subtly that Yuliya suspected she had imagined it.

King Rodion didn't seem to notice anything. He rolled his eyes but held his hand out for a dagger from one of his guards. "Your ways are barbaric, but I don't want the Poltavka people to rebel before they've been converted to true civilization." He pricked his finger and placed his blood beside the queen's.

She laughed, a high-pitched, gleeful sound of triumph. "You might see us as barbaric, but we know who the true barbarians are . . . or, should I say, were."

The king's eyes narrowed. He tried to remove his finger from the document, but it wouldn't budge. His entire hand flattened against the table, secured by some magical force. His face morphed from anger to fear. "What have you done?"

"What I had to do to protect my people." Queen Oksana sat on her makeshift throne and pulled another scroll from her robe. She smirked as she tore it to pieces.

By the Great Queen Mother, she switched the scrolls!

The men in green and yellow collapsed, one by one, around their king. Outside, the sounds of battle ceased, and cheers rang through the valley.

A tear fell from King Rodion's cheek. "I don't understand." He collapsed onto the table, his hand still attached to the spell scroll.

Yuliya wanted to be proud of the Great Queen Mother's triumph, but something disturbed her. Something was wrong.

"Come, come. I thought you were in such a hurry to get this over with."

Yuliya backed up against a honeysuckle vine, afraid that Queen Oksana had addressed her. A pop echoed through the tent, followed by the rise of a white shadow from the fallen king. His spirit hovered above his still warm body. Soon, the ghosts of his men joined the king's, hovering above their corpses like single branches from tree trunks.

King Rodion spoke, his voice just as deep as it had been in life but with less forcefulness and confidence. "You've killed them all and . . ." He struggled for a moment, then stared at the queen in horror. "We can't leave."

"I did what you forced me to do. Every man, woman, and child who swore fealty to you, King Rodion of Srubna, is dead." Queen

Oksana leaned forward. "But don't worry, you will be together for eternity in the grand Yekaterin Forest for as long as the trees stand."

Yuliya wept. How could anyone misuse their power so grotesquely? She couldn't believe she'd admired the Great Queen Mother.

"You are truly evil," King Rodion's spirit accused.

The queen waved away his words. "Evil is a term used by weak people to demonize what they fear. The people of Poltavka will worship me as their savior for generations."

The spirits spoke in unison then. "Free us. You have the power."

The queen laughed. "Of course I have the power. But why would I undo what I've so carefully orchestrated?"

"Free us. You have the power." A chorus of voices repeated the phrase from across the battlefield. "Free us. You have the power."

"That's enough." The queen snapped her fingers, and the spirits faded with screams of agony.

Before completely disappearing, King Rodion focused on Yuliya, who cowered against the sickeningly sweet-smelling vine. "Free us. You have the power."

His head flung to the heavens, he released a cry of agony and defeat.

Yuliya's head spun, and she fell to her knees. She shot her head up at the crunch of snow. She was back in the clearing by the well, and she knew what she had to do.

"I understand!" she yelled into the Yekaterin. She hoped King Rodion could hear her.

To kill one's enemies to defend one's kingdom was one thing. To trap their spirits, as well as those of all citizens, went too far. Yuliya aimed to be a healer. She would start today.

"What did you see?" Vladlena tried to grab her elbow, but Yuliya dodged the grasp.

"Queen Oksana tricked the Srubna king in the Great War and murdered every citizen. Those are the spirits who are trapped here. They didn't ask for it, and they didn't deserve it."

Vladlena's face paled. "The spirit water showed you this?"

Yuliya nodded. "You can leave if you wish, or you can help me." She snapped her fingers to produce a small flame. "I'm freeing the spirits."

Iosif clapped his hands and kicked a burning log from his fire. "Yes, yes! I knew you were the one. Father said you were." He brandished the burning log over his head.

Yuliya raised an eyebrow at Vladlena.

The old witch sighed and crossed to Iosif, who was attempting in vain to light a tree on fire. "That will never work, old man. The tree is too cold. Why don't you come over here and watch my apprentice work?" She winked at Yuliya. "She's gotten quite good with fire."

With the vote of confidence and Vladlena and Iosif safely by the well, Yuliya snapped the fingers of both hands, producing a modest flame. She balled the dancing fire into a bigger circle. Balancing the ball just above her left hand, she produced more small bits with snaps of her right and added them to her growing ball of heat and light. Warmth slid through her body.

Her ice sheet had melted some time ago. Now the extra heat dried the fibers, so they blew in the increased wind and howling of the surrounding forest. She no longer feared the noise, knowing the spirits' only desire was to be set free.

The burning flames multiplied until the ball became too hot. Yuliya waved her arms, sending the wagon-sized fire to the top of the trees. With a mini-sun in the sky lighting up the shadows of the forest, Yuliya picked out white shadows, trapped spirits at the base of the trees.

They picked up the chorus they'd started in Yuliya's vision. "Free us. You have the power."

The hope-laced desperation energized Yuliya to bring peace to these people. She whispered the words of lifting that she had tried on the laundry one day. Instead of rising from the floor and falling at once into the basin, the pieces had flung themselves all over the cabin. This time, she knew she could do it.

Yuliya used her left hand to maintain the ball while weaving the lifting spell with her right. The specific hand gestures came with a natural ease as she raised the bonfire of her own creation and doubled its size. The chanting in the trees intensified until the trunks themselves vibrated with the noise.

Soaking up their belief, Yuliya clasped her hands together, entwining her fingers. She pictured the ball of fire as her hands, the flames tumbling one over another in a huge mass of heat energy. She ripped her hands apart and swung around in a circle. A second later, the ball of fire exploded. The heat ignited the canopy and spread from tree to tree with maddening speed.

Smoke filled the air. Yuliya threw her cloak off as sweat poured from her overheated body. A white shadow walked to her through the smoke. She could almost hear the clinking of armor as her vision faded from her severe coughing. The general guided her weary body to the well. Vladlena dumped a bucket of cold water over her head, shocking the apprentice back to full awareness.

King Rodion knelt beside her. "You freed us, Great Tyotya Yuliya the Healer. We knew you could."

As the trees burned, spirits rose into the sky, disappearing into the darkness.

"Father, Father, I heard you and I obeyed." Iosif shivered before the spirit, though the forest still burned with radiant heat.

"You did. I am proud of you." King Rodion hugged his son, who was now much older than he had ever lived to be. "You can rest now. Go see your mother."

"Mother. Oh, yes, I want to see my mother." Iosif curled up at the edge of the well. With one last sigh, he stopped fighting death.

His spirit popped out of his body. "Mother!" he cried as he rose with the smoke.

Yuliya asked the king, "Why was your son not cursed with the rest of your people?"

"Queen Oksana specified those who had sworn fealty to me. My son was too young for such a pledge. For that, I am grateful." He sighed as the last of his people disappeared into the dark. "Though other acts deserve avenging." Without another word, he disappeared.

Vladlena harrumphed. "I should be grateful not to be the Great Queen Mother right now."

Yuliya laid back in the snow, exhausted. "He called me 'Great Tyotya Yuliya the Healer.' What does that mean?"

"The inhabitants of the spirit world live in the present and the past and the future." Vladlena squeezed her dripping cloak. "I suppose it means you have a long way to go."

Yuliya rolled her eyes.

"You can start by helping me get this wheelbarrow back to the wagon before that useless mule runs off and we freeze to death."

The apprentice rolled onto all fours to gently get to her feet. "I think it means I don't have to wash dishes anymore."

"Ha!" Vladlena leaned on her staff. "I think it means you can handle more chores than I've been assigning you."

Yuliya groaned, though a smile tugged at the edge of her lips. "Surely we can negotiate."

Vladlena started into the still-smoky forest. "Unlikely. I am the tyotya and you are the apprentice. Those are sacred roles, and we shouldn't mess with them."

Yuliya wrapped her arms around the witch, surprising the old woman.

"Well." Vladlena pushed the girl off a few minutes later. "At least I will be known as the great teacher who raised Yuliya the Healer to be a powerful witch."

"Ha! Unlikely." Yuliya wiped a tear from her cheek and pushed the wheelbarrow along the muddy ground with significantly more effort than before. "History will teach how lucky I was to survive your cruel treatment, Tyotya."

Vladlena lit the crystal of her staff to guide them home. Yuliya snapped her finger to produce some warmth to protect them from the impending cold.

Tomorrow would be another day of training, but today, Yuliya was a hero.

Snow Battle

H. M. Forrest

Keen, gray eyes peeked up over the top of a thick, fluffy
snowbank, perusing the landscape with all the intent of a
predator, the top of the figure's head barely showing. A hood
covered his head, a light brown, sturdy garment that easily blended in
with the dead wood of the nearby trees. A tendril of golden-brown
hair drifted out of the hood, blowing in the gentle wind that was still
swirling light snowflakes around in the air.

After spending several moments assessing every nook and
cranny of the horizon, the figure turned his head back behind him
toward what appeared to be a solid mountain, but at second, more
careful glance contained a slender crevice that was gaping black
nearly from the bottom of the ground up to the height of a small oak
tree. The snow had layered against the mountain wall and crevice
until a solid, several-foot-high wall had built up, leaving just enough
space in between to allow the figure to stand behind the snow and
peer out.

Suddenly, the figure moved, reaching for something behind the
wall of snow, and a second smaller figure was lifted over his head and
plopped down upon the snow with a teasing air, exhilaration and
expectation shining in the gray eyes that carefully watched the small
one. The small figure, obviously a child barely out of toddlerhood,

stood on top of the snow, perfectly still, with eyes wide in shock as it looked around. This figure also wore a light brown cloak and hood, from which ruffled strands of soft blond hair flitted.

The first figure swung himself up on top of the snow with one hand, nearly flying through the air and landing gracefully on his feet beside the small one. Though he did not have special snow shoes attached to his tall, brown boots, he did not sink into the snow like most creatures might. He laid a hand on the small figure's shoulder, gently, as though reminding him where he was and who was with him. Then he waited, watching the smaller one with a look of great delight upon his face.

The small figure turned his head up to watch the sky, a look of great awe upon his tiny and beautiful face. If the tall one was fair, the small one looked like an angel with his delicate, pale features. Large eyes of the lightest blue watched as a light snowflake drifted down and landed upon his small, upturned nose. He gasped, holding himself perfectly still in case any movement might cause the snowflake to disappear. He reached up one small, slender hand and tentatively touched the snowflake, a soft cry of anguish erupting from his small mouth when the snowflake disappeared.

The elder figure chuckled, his light voice ringing musically in the quiet of the winter glade. The branches in the surrounding trees rustled weakly, as though attempting to sway with the musical sound.

The small figure turned his face to look up at the elder, a look of excitement growing on his fair features and his eyes beginning to sparkle in a way that made the other figure yearn for better times. "Is it *real*, Brother?" he whispered, fearing if he spoke too loudly that the magic would disappear.

"Aye, little one. It is very real! It is called winter, and the white stuff that falls is called snow. Come, reach out and touch it. I have left your gloves off for now so that you may see how it feels, but I dare not let you remain without them for long because of the chill in the air." The elder tugged the small one down with him to squat in the snow, pushing his little hand into the soft drifts.

"Ooh!" The little one shivered suddenly. "What is that funny feeling, Brother?" He began to feel around in the snow with growing curiosity, first with one hand, then plunging both hands enthusiastically into the deeper slush.

"That is the cold you are feeling, Amneth," the elder brother said gently, furiously blinking back tears from his gray eyes.

The little one, Amneth, caught the funny tone in his beloved brother's voice, his hands still covered in white drifts. "Why do you cry, Artonian?" he pleaded, beginning to look distraught.

Artonian reached forward, pulling the small figure against his side and tilting his head up with a finger under his chin. "You should have always known what winter was! You should have always felt the snow drifting through your fingers, Little Brother. I wish we did not have to live as we do. I wish we did not have to hide away like cowards in the darkness of the mountains."

Amneth frowned, tilting his head as though trying to understand why his brother was so upset and how he could help him. "I like our home," he said in a slightly confused tone. "Father keeps us hidden because it is safe. He has told me so himself."

Artonian growled, the sound still managing to lighten the clearing despite the intent. He plunged a fist into the snow beside him, inadvertently flinging a few flakes onto his little brother, who widened his eyes and promptly giggled. The branches swayed almost violently in the trees around them, the wind blowing through their bare limbs and hissing angrily in the silence.

The child giggled even more. "The trees think you are funny, Brother!" he managed to gasp through his laughter. "They think you are trying to start a Snow Battle with me!" He managed to stop laughing, remembering belatedly that they were not in the Safe Place and abruptly clamping his snow-covered, reddened hands over his mouth, eyes growing wider in distress.

Artonian pushed his anger aside and gently pulled his brother's hands away from his mouth, covering them firmly in the folds of his large woolen cloak. "I sense no danger today, little one, or I would not have chanced bringing you out. Perhaps I should not have done so at all, but I just could not bear for you to stay away from such beauty for any longer, for it is not right. *This* is where we belong!"

He stopped, not wishing to cause the child more distress. The little one was worried enough about a simple excursion into the snow for the first time, and it should not be necessary.

He smiled down at his brother, patting his thin cheek, then tugging his hood down over his forehead. He pulled a set of small brown gloves from a pocket on the inside of his cloak. Retrieving the little hands from the warmth of the wool lining, he checked them to make sure they had not suffered from the cold. Seeing no damage, he pulled the fur-lined gloves swiftly onto Amneth's hands, trying to hide his amusement at the little pout gathering on his brother's face.

"I wished to still feel the snow!" Amneth protested, and Artonian wondered at the change just one small adventure had wrought in the little being, for Amneth *never* complained *or* whined, as some small children might, *or* even expressed frustration. Artonian enjoyed seeing a little independence straying forth and would not scold the child *now* for finally expressing an interest in something.

"I understand." He nodded gravely. "For I enjoy feeling the snow in my hands as well. But you can still feel it a little through the gloves, and this way your hands shall not fall off from frostbite!"

Amneth's mouth dropped open, and he gaped up at the elder. "Would that really happen?" he breathed, eyes round with horror as he looked down at his gloved hands. He then pulled them swiftly into the safety of his own cloak, as though to keep them firmly attached to his small arms.

"Well, your fingers might . . ." the elder brother amended, snatching Amneth's hands back out and plunging them swiftly back into the snow. "See, it is still cold, is it not?"

Amneth nodded, too intrigued to answer as he once more began to plunge his hands around in the thick layers of white. His expression again changed to fascination and excitement as he watched how the snow drifted through his gloved fingers, the larger clumps slowly falling apart, completely absorbed in his task.

Artonian smiled secretively as he silently gathered together a pile of snow into a tightly packed ball. He then stood just as silently and stepped several paces back, taking aim . . . and fired!

"Ouch!" squealed a little voice into the quiet of the peaceful glade, once more causing the branches of the winter-deadened trees to rustle. Large, blue eyes turned to look around, then landed on the elder brother accusingly. "What was that for?" he exclaimed, clumsily brushing off the spattering of snow from his shoulder, where the snowball had landed.

"The trees think we are having a Snow Battle, Little Brother. We must not disappoint them!"

Artonian began to gather up more snow, going slowly this time so that the curious child could see how he packed it together. Amneth was intelligent and quick to learn, and he swiftly copied his brother. He finished even before Artonian was done and threw his own smaller ball with a *splat* right into Artonian's face.

"Argh!" the elder elf cried, though still in a softened tone, as he swiftly rubbed the snow out of his eyes. "That's it, little one! Let the battle commence!"

There came many small grunts, splats, and thwacks after that to break the silence of the forest, until the elder decided the child had had enough excitement for now—and enough cold! The little one was shivering quite thoroughly from the wet, icy snow running down his face and under the neckline of his tight, thick shirt, and the elder could tell some of the slush had made it under the edge of his shirt sleeves and gloves as well, for his little brother kept rubbing intermittently at his slender wrists. They were already going to be in enough trouble for this little escapade; there was no point in getting the child sick as well! Amneth was frailer than most of the youth of their race, for he had been born in the caverns and, though there was much flora growth and magic in their home, there was not the pure fresh air and sunlight that their race required more than any other.

Artonian threw up his hands after his brother landed another good hit against his shoulder. "I surrender!" he cried laughingly. Then he leaped at his little brother, gathering him into his arms and tossing him up into the gently falling snowflakes.

The little one shrieked happily. "I am flying, Arto!" he exclaimed, and though his voice was still light and soft, the forest around them seemed to awaken, bare limbs and deadened underbrush whistling and shaking as though in celebration. Perhaps they *were* celebrating. It was not often that they had a visit from his race anymore. Artonian smiled at his little brother as he looked up at him, hands held at the ready to catch him. He looked like an angel flying through the drifting snow, with his light hair, huge innocent eyes, and a large smile on his fair tiny face that brightened Artonian's weary heart and the little glade around them.

He caught his brother easily, swinging him around a few times amid many quiet giggles before pulling him tightly against his chest. Amneth leaned back and placed his small gloved hands on either side of Artonian's thin face.

"I wish to stay out here *forever!*" he breathed, his so-pale cheeks finally sprinkled with a touch of healthy coloring.

Artonian sighed, the weariness in his soul growing to sadden the air around them, and Amneth frowned, immediately sensing it. "I wish we *could*, little one; I wish we *could*. You *know* it is not safe, however. Father is not needlessly being cruel to us. It is the world that has been cruel. It is not kind to our people, and the dangers are many and frequent. We would not survive out here for long."

Amneth threw himself forward and hugged his brother tightly, burying his face in the warmth of his elder brother's cloak. "Father will find a way to make it safe again," he said with all the confidence of a small child who thought their parent could accomplish anything in the world. "Then we can come and play in snow all the time!"

Artonian hugged the small figure to himself tightly, frowning as he felt the slight shivers coursing through the tiny frame. "I fear we must go back soon, little one. Come, let us visit the trees with all swiftness, as I promised."

Amneth pulled away, gesturing to be put down, and his brother settled him gently back on the ground. "I wish to take some snow back with us, Arto!" he exclaimed, eyes bright and shining with hopefulness. "I will save it forever in a jar by my bed and always remember our Adventure!"

Artonian chuckled. "I am afraid it does not work that way, Little Brother." He placed a hand against Amneth's chest. "You will always have the memory here and can pull it out whenever you need to. The snow would only melt as soon as we returned to the caves. Such is the manner of snow."

The little one's eyes grew round as he processed this new information. He nodded somewhat glumly. Then he looked around the glade as though memorizing the sight, before prancing lightly over to the great trees guarding the clearing. He stopped beside the large oak at the edge of the glade and placed a gloved hand against the bark. Artonian watched him, curious. He did not think the little one would be able to fully commune with the trees, having forgotten that they had already done so earlier, in a manner, when mentioning the Snow Battle. The trees were in winter and mostly sleeping, they were touched with the darkness, his brother was too young, and he wore gloves on his hands.

Artonian's eyes widened in shock when not only did Amneth start giggling, looking up into the tall branches with glowing eyes, but the large branches began to wiggle and shake, almost as though the tree were dancing. His little brother was powerful indeed, or else the trees were just that eager to converse with one of them again, and more specifically, a child.

After a moment, his small brother looked over at his carefully watching elder brother, eyes wide with delight and gratitude. "Thank you, Arto!" he breathed, awe in his voice and his beautiful tiny features filled with a serene happiness such as Artonian had never before seen in his frail little brother. "They are sleepy, but they bid us well and are happy to see us. Thank you for bringing me out here. Thank you for risking Father's ire to show me these wonders! I will never forget our Adventure!" He turned and looked up high into the branches of the great tree, missing the moisture gathering in his elder brother's eyes.

Artonian quickly rubbed an arm across his eyes, gathering his emotions to keep them in check so that Amneth would not be distressed. His little brother, so small and frail and almost sickly for their kind, never failed to tug at his heartstrings with his mature manner of speech and loving nature. He stepped closer, noticing the gleam in his brother's eyes as he looked up into the branches as though trying to see the sky. He had warned his brother against climbing the tree, for these trees could not presently be completely trusted, and the slushy snow would make the branches slippery and dangerous for small ones, but the child was excited and in a state of euphoria from his Grand Adventure.

Suddenly, the air grew stale, and the clearing seemed to darken ever so slightly. At the same time, he could see Amneth stiffen, and his mischievous gleam changed abruptly to one of fear as he turned to look over at his brother, a hand still placed against the sturdy brown bark of the tree's trunk.

"Arto . . . something is wrong . . . the tree . . ."

Before he could finish the sentence, a darkened shadow crept out from the tree line and snatched up the child, holding him firmly in its grasp, a filthy, mud-encrusted knife placed against the pale, smooth skin of the child's neck.

"My Master will be happy to hear there are still more of you filthy creatures lurking around. He will burn the forests and smoke out the caves." The gravelly voice chortled in a stilted, snarling manner, and Artonian froze at the threat against his brother, his heart beginning to beat too swiftly as fear filled his chest.

The creature looked to be a man, or what used to be a man, the elder brother amended as he assessed this new danger with a warrior's discerning gaze. He was large, larger than most men had been the last time Artonian had seen them. His face was distorted and misshapen; the scars of a sin-filled life were laid bare upon what might have once been rugged features. His hair was tangled and coarse and came barely to his shoulders, and his garments were stained with what appeared to be dried blood and were torn and ragged in many places.

It was his eyes that brought the most fear to the slender creature beholding him, however; they were nearly black and filled with hatred and rage. They held no warmth, and they held no mercy. The very air around the creature crackled with darkness and evil. This was one who would kill easily and without remorse, and Artonian dared not take a wrong step, not with the knife so close to Amneth's small neck.

Artonian almost felt betrayed by the trees of the forest, for they had provided no warning until it was too late. But he had already known the forest was growing dark. He had already known the trees were more asleep than alive. His father had warned him on so many occasions. It was for this reason that he had forbidden Amneth to leave the caverns, and for this reason that he demanded an entourage of at least fifty warriors whenever Artonian left to hunt.

A cold numbness spread slowly over him as he began to realize just what a mistake he had made this day. The absence of enemies these last few weeks during their hunts had given him a state of relaxation that was false, and this small gift he had wished to give his brother might very well have cost Amneth his life instead.

The creature threw his head back and laughed—an ugly jarring sound in the stillness of the winter glade. The branches of the nearest trees creaked and moaned as though in fear and anger, but Artonian could not sympathize with the forest life despite his understanding. They had still betrayed him this day. He slipped a hand beneath his cloak to creep toward the knife fastened securely at his hip. He could not reach for his bow and arrows, the better choice, for the creature would see and react, to the detriment of his little brother. A knife swiftly thrown might unbalance him enough to loosen his hold on the small form in his grip, however.

"Don't even think about it!" the creature barked, all laughter now gone. "I know you nasty creatures have all sorts of tricks up your sleeves, and you won't cheat my Master or *me* out of our fun!"

He pressed the tip of the blade into Amneth's neck, causing a small trickle of blood to flow out and drip to the ground. The snow at the creature's feet melted, and three daisies sprang up and bloomed. The creature snarled and jumped back, the knife digging a little deeper as he squeezed his arm even more tightly around Amneth's small chest. "Stop that!" he growled into Amneth's ear.

To his credit, Amneth hissed out a small breath against the added pain but uttered not another sound.

Artonian—feeling a strange sense of pride at his brother's composure and bravery, even at such an inopportune moment—attempted to reach out mentally toward his little brother to reassure him. The feelings he received from the connection made him realize that Amneth was more in fear for Artonian's life than his own, and Artonian almost smiled as a sense of calm spread over him.

"Here's what's going to happen," the creature said then in a cold voice. "I will be taking this little one along with me so we can all have some fun and the Master will reward me. You can go back and tell your unnatural people that their time is at an end. The Master knows they exist now, and he will purge the earth of your filthy blood. Go back and cower in your home while we enjoy our rare spoils."

He shook Amneth harshly enough to cause his teeth to rattle, and Artonian felt a rush of fear spread through him via their link, though Amneth remained stoically silent against the harsh treatment. He took a step forward once more, not sure what he would do yet but not willing to stand by and see the creature abscond with his beloved brother.

The creature snarled and lifted his knife up in preparation of plunging the knife into Amneth's small chest, his need for control over Artonian stronger than his need to please his Master. Artonian was contemplating just how quickly he could snatch his arm back under his cloak, pull his knife, and throw, or if he should just make a leap for the man, when suddenly the air in the clearing crackled once more as though lightning had flashed nearby, and the sky flickered brightly.

"I think *not!*" came a too-familiar voice that was so musically powerful, it stilled even the wind and falling snowflakes, which halted in the air and lingered, never touching the ground. Before the creature could overcome his surprise and fulfill his purpose, a flying projectile slammed silently into his leg—the only clear target without potentially harming the child—sending the creature flying back against the trunk of the same tree Amneth had earlier greeted and sending the child tumbling onto the ground near the gnarled roots.

Artonian was beside his brother before the child could lift his head and cry out, gathering him carefully into his arms and tucking the folds of his cloak around the child as he clutched him to his shoulder. "I am sorry. I am so *very* sorry!" he muttered over and over as his brother burrowed into the safety of his arms and began to sob finally, the fear and stress too much for his frail system despite his bravery. Artonian pressed a small section of his cloak against his little brother's small neck to stop the bleeding, then he removed it, pressed his fingers to the wound, and closed his eyes, chanting a few words in their lyrical language. Once done, he took his fingers away, happy to see that the bleeding had stopped and the wound was beginning to close.

Artonian then looked up to see a tall, powerful figure stride past him, brown and gray robes flowing in the breeze of his steps. White hair flowing nearly to his waist shimmered behind him, while two lengthy sections that started near his temples shone the color of tree bark and mingled with the snowy white. The contrast lent an almost surreal essence to the being, who carried an unmistakable air of power and royalty. The figure stopped just past Artonian, nearly at the feet of the cringing and sobbing creature, who was holding his skewered leg and muttering insanely to himself.

Clear gray eyes filled with the sky, snow, and forest turned to delve into Artonian's remorseful gaze, but Artonian could not read the emotions lingering in their depths. The moment stretched out into eternity, then the powerful gaze moved to glance over the two brothers, obviously checking for any potential injuries, before flickering back to Artonian.

"Do not let him see." The voice was like fresh water trickling over an aching wound, soothing and healing all at the same time.

Then the piercing gaze was gone as the figure flung his bow back onto the quiver at his back and drew a sword all in one movement. He stepped forward and pointed the blade at the creature rolling on the ground in agony and terror.

"It is *you* who will be cowering in the darkness, I fear, and no message will reach your Master this night. If you think he will even bother to spare a single scout to look for you, you are wrong, for your Master holds no affection for anyone. Had you taken my child, my entire army would have followed you to the ends of the earth and none of your people would have lived past the next dawn. I would let *you* take this message back, but you have seen us and you have threatened my people *and* my sons. It is a shame . . ."

Artonian turned around, hiding his brother's head in his shoulder and covering it with his cloak as he began to sing softly to the trembling child in his arms. He closed his eyes, hearing the unmistakable hiss of a sword being raised through the air, then the soft swish of the blade falling and cutting through flesh, abruptly ending a terrified scream that darkened the lands once more.

Artonian did not look. He could not bear to see what his foolish dismissal of the world's dangers had cost. The land around him seemed to tilt into a buzzing cacophony of wind and softly falling snow as the forest began to return to normal. He could hear the sound of his little brother's heart beating wildly against his chest. He could hear the soft crackle of a branch as it moved in the wind. He could hear the gentle lapping of a nearby lake's water as it tried to dance around the layering of ice barely covering its surface. He could hear the soft steps of the warriors as they slid past him to carry away the creature. It was not a man anymore, he knew, for it had been disfigured by the evil of the lands, but pain still filled his heart at the loss of life, and he clutched his brother to himself even more tightly, unsettling their hoods as he pressed his head into his little brother's neck.

Shining silky hair tumbled from their cloaks, some strands of the purest blond and others of a golden brown. The hair of the two brothers drifted together, then fluttered gently in the breeze, exposing delicate pointed ears to the icy cold of the wind and snow.

A warm hand settled on Artonian's shoulder, and he stilled his fluttering heart, managing to pull his head up and gaze into what he knew would be a condemning look, and quite possibly the last look he would ever receive, considering his crimes.

He was surprised to see forgiveness in the ageless, clouded eyes of his powerful, regal father, though rage toward the surrounding evil still lingered on his fair, pale face.

"I have always loved the snow as well," his father muttered gently into the quiet of the small glade, the tinkling sound of his voice causing the trees to rustle and shake as though attempting to awaken even more. A small bird chirped in the distance, and several strands of green grass edged up through the snow, as though spring were arriving in the little glade. His eyes rested on the small figure clutched in Artonian's embrace.

"Let us hope that this Grand Adventure of his will last him, for it remains unsafe for our people in these lands. Come, elflings. Let us go home now. All is forgiven."

Artonian gaped up at him in shock. He had envisioned many years of captivity in rotting dungeons, cleanup duty for months, or some painful torture—never this!

Amneth had stilled at the sound of his father's voice, beloved among all others, and with a cry of happiness he turned away from his brother and flung himself up into his father's arms with a lightness only their people possessed.

"Father! I knew you would save us! I just knew it! Have you seen the snow? Have you felt its beauty? Will you play Snow Battle with me, Father?"

The small child placed his gloved hands on either side of his father's thin face, beaming at him joyfully and gaining an answering smile in return, shocking Artonian even more on this strange day. It was rare that his father smiled anymore, his days filled with trying to keep his people safe and content.

The powerful ruler held his small son closely to him with one arm and reached out a hand to his elder son to pull him up off the ground. "Perhaps someday soon," he agreed amicably as he led his children, one tiny and one almost grown, back to the hidden entrance of the caverns. "Perhaps soon it will be safe for us once more and we can enjoy the beauty of this earth, for an elf truly needs the fresh air, and an elfling desperately needs his snow!"

Paranormal Polka Dots

Emily Van Engen

A zoo. An absolute zoo, Violeta thinks as she snoozes her blaring alarm. She stuffs her head back under the covers for ten more minutes of peace. Thunder stretches out from behind the bend of her legs and sighs. After last night's events, Violeta knows even the dog is not ready to face this crazy day, either.

❖

The night before . . .

Flash! BOOM!

Violeta shoots off the couch in a panic. Thunder, however, doesn't move an inch from his spot on the ottoman. If a little black schnauzer knows there's nothing to fear, why is Violeta's heart racing? Once she's calmed down, she assumes it was simply her neighbors fighting again. Sharing walls with others isn't ideal, but it's the only option Violeta and her father can afford right now.

Violeta's mother died when she was two, and her father vowed from that day forward that Violeta would be his number one priority. Shortly after her death, they settled down in a small apartment above a flooring business in town. Even though her father makes decent money as a meteorologist, he stows away his earnings in Violeta's

103

college fund. Violeta has always lived a frugal lifestyle, but it doesn't bother her. It has always been just the two of them, and she likes it that way. Thunder was merely a happy edition to the already cozy life she enjoys.

Not long after her irrational outburst, the nightly news reveals the source of the noise: a meteor. A large rock hurtling through space was sucked into the earth's orbit and broke through the atmosphere like an exploding shooting star, causing a 2.0 earthquake. Camera video of the flash-boom and interviews from witnesses flood the next hour of broadcast television. The most important detail of this "paranormal phenomenon" is that the rock broke up over Violeta's small town. She wouldn't call her town superstitious, but she would say the village often gets caught up in the melodrama of things they don't understand.

Violeta studied in astronomy class that meteor impacts are quite common on Earth. She reasons that the piece of asteroid burned up during its entry into the atmosphere and traveled several times the speed of sound, which caused the flash-boom earthquake. Violeta knows deep down, however, that this is a rare incident for her town, which will result in an inflation of unearthly proportion.

Her father rushes through the door, huffing and puffing. His face is lit up with a toothy smile and bright red coloring. Violeta figures her dad must've had an exciting day at work, but the freezing temperature and twenty-five stairs up to their apartment door must also factored into the state of his appearance. He walks into the living room and plops a kiss onto her forehead.

"Hey, little Sonche. I need to go back to work. This is the news story of the *year*!"

The meteorologist takes about five steps, opens the pantry door, and disappears. Rustling sounds echo through the small closet. Violeta continues texting her best friend, Everly, who is also gushing over the strange event. Her father emerges, granola bars in hand, and stuffs them into his briefcase.

"Did you finish all your homework?"

"Nope." Violeta focuses on keeping her face neutral.

"Did you study for your social studies test tomorrow?"

"Nope." A smile threatens to break over her lips.

"That's my girl." Her father rushes a few more feet to his bedroom.

Violeta shakes her head and looks up from her cell phone. "I really think mediocre is the way to go, Dad. Why try hard when others around you are already doing that? I think to be a true leader, you have to make your own path."

"Uh-huh," her father answers as he reappears in new clothing, turns the corner, and adjusts his tie in the bathroom mirror. He returns to the combination living room, dining room, and kitchen, and Violeta shifts her gaze to watch.

Before pulling on the handle of the refrigerator, he pauses. Violeta conceals her smile behind the top of the couch cushion. A 110-percent science test hangs from a magnet next to her semester report card, her 4.0 GPA accented with purple highlighter. He turns toward Violeta and smiles. Chuckling under his breath, he pulls the handle and reaches for a water bottle.

"Great job, little Sonche."

Violeta gets off the couch. Thunder pokes his head up and tilts it as Violeta walks to the kitchen and hugs her dad. The dog leaps off the ottoman and bolts toward them. He paws at Violeta's leg.

As they release the hug, her father glances down at Thunder. "What a jealous little pup."

The dog stops begging and sits, staring into Violeta's eyes.

After a quick moment of staring deeply into Thunder's eyes, Violeta shakes her head and refocuses the conversation.

"Dad, I was worried I would fail the weather unit, but my science teacher told me I have a real knack for it. I wonder why."

"Hmm. I wonder."

The duo laughs, her father squeezing her once more before putting on his puffy winter coat. His hand stops as he grasps the doorknob, and he looks at Violeta. His lips pull tight, hiding under his thick dark mustache. She grows red with embarrassment the longer he stares. Lately, her father has made comments about how grown-up she's getting and about how bad he feels having to work late some nights. Violeta imagines that's what this lingering stare is about.

"Stop it! Go back to work. We'll be fine. It isn't every day a meteor explodes into the atmosphere in *your* town!" She hands him the water bottle he forgot on the counter and shoos him away.

"Te sakam."

"I love you too, Dad." She watches him descend the stairs, careful not to slip on the new piles of glittering snow at the bottom. The crisp air shoots a tingle up Violeta's spine. She shuts the door and picks up her waiting Thunder.

The alarm sounds again, ending her ten-minute escape from what she knows will be an annoyingly crazy day. Violeta throws the covers off her body and on top of her outstretched pup. The lump doesn't move beneath the sheets, expressing his contentment through an audible sigh.

She takes a quick shower and throws on her favorite outfit: a sweatshirt that reads *Everything Is Either Ice Cream or Not Ice Cream*, dark jeans, and high-top tennis shoes. She puts foundation on her olive skin, along with a little eyeliner and mascara, even though her eyelashes are long enough without the aid of makeup. Her wavy brown hair falls past her shoulders in any direction it wants, and her dark eyes dull with dread over having to deal with the chaos that school will bring today.

The kitchen fills with the banging sounds of Violeta making her usual lunch: a turkey sandwich, pretzels, and a few cookies. Thunder gets wrapped up in the blankets and ends up dragging them into the kitchen, the ends still tied around his abdomen. Violeta laughs at the sight with a hint of a snort between breaths. She scoops a cup of lamb-flavored bits and pours them into Thunder's bowl. She unties the sheets from his waist as he inhales the food. Tossing the blankets back onto her bed, she places her lunch into her backpack and kisses her pup goodbye.

"Are you going to be a good boy while I'm at school, Thunder?" He lies on his back, exposing his stomach. Violeta strokes his belly a few times, drawing a kick from Thunder's back leg. "All right. You be good. I'll be back."

She stands up, grabs her backpack and winter coat, and steps out onto the porch. Because she lives so close to the school and would rather sleep in than ride the bus for an hour, Violeta walks to school. With the sky still dark, orange fluorescent streetlamps illuminate her path as she starts her morning walk. The wind blusters, and the snowflakes are so chunky, they hit Violeta in the face at an alarming rate.

She throws her hood on and reaches into her pockets, pulling out a pair of gloves. Polka-dotted gloves. She sighs. Her dad gave her these for Christmas this last year. He was so excited when she opened the box that morning. She hadn't had the heart to tell him that she liked stripes now and not polka dots, so she hugged him and thanked him for the thoughtful gift. She had hoped to stuff them into the closet to "forget" they were there, but her loving dad suggested she put them in the pockets of her winter coat. "Just in case."

Even though they aren't a style she prefers, she puts on the gloves and is thankful for the warmth they provide in this wintry mess. As soon as she pulls on the second glove, the wind calms and the snow stops. Almost abruptly. Violeta notices the sudden change in weather pattern with the rise of a thick dark eyebrow. Stumped, she shrugs and continues her walk to school.

After a few minutes, Violeta removes the hood from her head and sees her shoelaces flailing about as she walks. She stops, takes a knee, and attempts to tie her shoe. The laces stick to her gloves, so she removes them to try again. As soon as the gloves slip off, the wind picks up speed with a gust of snowflakes. Violeta braces herself while tying her soggy wet shoelaces and stands up. The snow builds up in Violeta's hair, and her polka-dotted gloves take flight under the blast of chilly air. She chases them into the front yard of her friend Everly's house and slips them on in a hurry.

The wind calms.

The snow stops.

The sun creeps out over the trees between gray clouds.

Violeta squints deep into her knit-covered palms.

Everly walks from her porch to the yard, joining Violeta in staring at her gloves. After a few moments, Everly coughs, breaking the silence. "Are you okay?"

"Uh, yeah." Violeta stuffs her mitts into her pockets and shakes her head, getting rid of the ridiculous thought in her head regarding the weather and her unfortunately patterned gloves.

"What's with your hair?" Everly points to her own long blonde braid.

Violeta reaches up and feels the thick blanket of snow that weighs down her locks. She gives them a quick shake with her fingers, and the slush plops to the ground.

"Talk about something. Anything."

"So how about that meteor?" Everly jumps up and down with excitement.

Violeta turns around and heads back to the sidewalk. "Anything but that."

Everly slides through the snow and wraps an arm through Violeta's. "Oh, come on! This is like the most exciting thing to ever happen in this town. You know that's all people are going to talk about today."

"Don't remind me," Violeta mutters under her cold breath.

They continue their walk, silent, until Everly bursts again with excitement. "Did you hear they are offering money to people who find a piece of the meteorite?"

Violeta sighs, hangs her head in exasperation, and listens as her best friend rants, again, about where she and all seven of her siblings were when they saw and heard the meteor.

It's almost a relief when the school doors come in sight. Everly is the oldest of her family and doesn't often get a word in edgewise. That means she gets all her words out with Violeta. A blessing and a curse, as Violeta describes it. Being an only child can be lonely sometimes, but Violeta is used to the independence and solitude.

Everly wreaks havoc on her introversion and offers her a sisterly companionship that, while annoying at times, Violeta is grateful for.

The girls walk through the first set of glass doors and stomp their snow-covered feet. Violeta takes her hands out of her pockets and removes the tacky gloves. In that instant, a gale forces the doors closed. Violeta and Everly watch as their classmates attempt to pull open the doors, but the wind outside is too strong to overpower. The wind pins the students up against the doors and windows. Violeta's eyes widen and her heart races. She inspects her gloveless hands, and her face turns red. She shoves the gloves on, and the students who were once pressed against the glass can now open the doors with ease.

"Holy crap on a cracker."

"What is it, Vi?"

"Locker. Now!"

Violeta drags Everly to their shared locker despite Everly's attempts to say hi to their other friends in the commons. Violeta opens their locker and sticks her head in the door. Everly tilts her head like a dog trying to understand, but before she can ask, Violeta grabs her collar and pulls Everly's head into the locker opening.

"This is an interesting way to talk—"

"Shh! I don't want anyone else to hear us!"

"Oh my! What is your problem, Vi?"

"I think I have, um—"

"Yes?"

"Powers."

Everly pulls her head out of the locker and laughs. Loudly. Violeta yanks her back in.

"Focus. I'm serious!"

"Okay. I'll entertain your irrationality. What makes you think you have powers?"

"Didn't you see what just happened?"

"I saw kids pushing on a pull door and getting stuck. Hilarious."

"NO!" Violeta's voice booms, causing Everly's head to shoot out of the locker. Instead of waiting to be pulled back in, Everly rubs her ears and returns to the metal cabinet. "When I took my gloves off, the storm picked up and caused the doors to blow shut. When I put my gloves back on, the storm stopped."

"Completely coincidental." A familiar cracking voice sends a chill down Violeta's spine. She and her best friend remove their heads from the locker to match gazes with *him*. The bane of Violeta's middle-grade existence. Bob Fetore. "The status of gloves residing on your hands would have no effect on the overall weather pattern."

"Do you smell that, Vi?" Everly squints, pinching her nose.

Violeta snorts. "I'm not sure what that is. Do you know, Bobby?"

"My. Name. Is. *Bob*! And I took a shower this morning." Despite the confidence in his voice, he sniffs at his armpit.

"Uh-huh. Sure, sure, Bobby boy." Everly shuts their locker, links arms with Violeta, and turns toward their first-hour class, away from their social adversary.

"I am a *man*, Everly! A *man*!" Bob's adolescent voice whines down the hallway.

Violeta and Everly belly-laugh as they walk to class. Violeta smiles up at her tall, beautiful best friend. She might not be the sharpest tool in the shed, but she is loyal, and Violeta appreciates that.

The warning bell rings as the girls cross the threshold into Mrs. B's social studies class. The girls part ways and head for their assigned seats. Violeta gets out her bell ringer worksheet and reads the day's question: *What did you think of last night's meteor?* She sighs as she wills her pencil to write letters. By the time she's done, the word *meh* resides in the answer box of her worksheet.

The late bell rings, and Mrs. B sits on her stool in front of the class. "Good morning! I know we have a test on ancient India today, and I promise we will get to that. *But* I wanted to give everyone the chance to share their thoughts on last night's phenomenon!"

Violeta sets her head on her hands and watches the students gab on about how they were scared, excited, or asleep when the meteor broke through the atmosphere above them. Their voices blur together in an excited buzz. Violeta waits for the excitement to die down so she can go ahead and pass the test she's been studying for all week long.

". . . oleta?"

Violeta pops up as she realizes Mrs. B is calling on her to share. The class is turned and staring at her, waiting for a response. Having no idea what was asked, Violeta smiles a big fake grin and speaks one word, hoping it is the right one. "Yes!"

The students begin giggling, and Violeta squeezes her eyes shut tight, wishing she had asked what Mrs. B had said instead of trying to guess.

"Class! Everyone, please, calm down." The laughter fizzles out, and the students turn back to the front of the class. "Violeta, you think last night's meteor brought some paranormal activity to our little town?" The class reengages in a low giggle. "I would've figured you for a science girl, seeing how your dad is the county meteorologist."

"Oh, no! I, uh . . . no, I don't think that."

"Yes, she does, Mrs. B!" Everly yells across the room.

Violeta whips her head around and widens her eyes. Everly throws a hand over her mouth, her eyes squinting as she smiles under her palm. Violeta makes a stern face at her, conveying that she needs her to be quiet now. A confused Mrs. B mutters, "Middle schoolers are weird," under her breath, just low enough to sound like a whisper but just loud enough to make her students laugh. She grins and instructs the class to put away all their things except for something to write with.

Violeta stares out the window as she waits for the test to arrive on her desk. The sun beams between streaks of cloud, and a cardinal sits atop the bush outside of the sill. Violeta shifts her fingers and feels the knit against her skin, remembering that she's still wearing her polka-dotted gloves. She looks back out the window, and the cardinal stares back at her. Her thoughts wander to what Bob Fetore said about coincidences.

Mrs. B puts the test down on her desk and whispers, "What's with the gloves?"

Violeta freezes. "Uh . . . new trend?"

Mrs. B shrugs a shoulder. "Whatever floats your goat."

"Isn't it *boat*, Mrs. B?"

"Or is it?" Mrs. B raises her eyebrows in inquisition and then chuckles under her breath as she walks back to her desk.

Violeta glances back toward the window, but the cardinal is gone. It seems calm enough outside, so Violeta decides to chance it and take off the gloves. She's slow and methodical in her movements. She only removes one finger at a time. When the final pinky is uncovered, she checks the window. The sky has darkened, and the bushes whip in the wind. Giant pellets of snow plummet from the clouds, smacking and tacking against the classroom window. The tapping grows louder with each second, threatening to break the glass. Frightened, Violeta shifts her gaze to Everly. Everly motions under her desk for Violeta to put the gloves back on.

"Everly and Violeta. If you talk during the test, I will give you a zero. You know that."

"Yes, ma'am!" Violeta yells out. The class jolts at the volume of her response, but everyone continues marking their packets as the noise outside grows louder by the second.

Violeta slides her fingers back into the still-warm gloves, and as expected, the wind calms and the snow stops. Violeta buries her face into her hands. Maybe she does believe in the potential for powerful phenomena surrounding this crazy meteor? Maybe she's losing her mind? Or still dreaming? Whatever is happening, she needs to start this test, or she'll never get the information she learned about the caste system out of her brain.

The bell rings as Violeta writes the last word of her essay question, her hands sweating beneath the knitted yarn of her embarrassing polka-dotted gloves. She passes her test forward and gathers up her notebooks.

Everly waits for her at the door. "How did you do?"

"Um, okay, I guess."

"Shut up, Violeta. You're like a genius or something. You probably got a one hundred and ten percent even though there was no extra credit."

"Sure."

Everly jumps in front of her, halting their progress down the hallway. "What is *wrong* with you?"

Violeta holds a hand up and wiggles her gloved fingers in a sarcastic demonstration of spirit fingers.

"Oh. That."

Violeta shifts her eyes from side to side suspiciously. "Let's discuss this in the noushnik."

"Why can't you just call it the bathroom?"

"I don't know. That's what my dedo and baba call it."

The girls speed into the restroom and step into a large stall, locking the door behind them.

Everly considers her surroundings. "This is weird. Isn't this weird? This is weird."

"Shut up for once so I can talk to you!" A toilet flushes.

"Vi, I can't believe I'm saying this, but I'm going to have to go with smelly Bobby Fetore on this one."

"It can't be a coincidence! YOU SAW IT HAPPEN!"

"I also believed bunny rabbits laid eggs up until a year ago, so I'm not exactly a reliable source of information and wisdom." The warning bell rings. "I have to go to English. Good luck in science." Everly busts through the stall door, and Violeta follows behind, trying to ignore the confused faces of the girls waiting their turn.

Violeta turns the corner into Ms. Power's room. Violeta adores science class, as well as her quirky teacher. What she doesn't adore is her seat in the back next to her lifelong foe.

"Did you cause that wicked storm in first hour?"

Violeta's eyes widen, and her throat becomes dry. The boy throws his head back in obnoxious laughter at her reaction.

"Bobby, I can hear you across the room. Class has started."

Thank goodness for Ms. Power.

"Sorry."

"All right, class. I want to start things off in science today with a few stories from your supernatural experience with the meteor last night."

Violeta slams her head down onto her arms and sighs, wishing this day was over. A few students share their theories on the meteor's meteorological and mystical capabilities.

"Ms. Power, after the meteor boomed, my little brother started walking! He's only eight months old!"

"I was playing video games with my friends, and as soon as the meteor went by, I earned like a thousand experience points and won the game! It was pretty rad, Ms. Power."

"That's nothing! When the earthquake shook my house, my vision blurred, and I could see through objects for like a millisecond!"

Bob Fetore leans in and whispers, "Don't you want to share your secret glove powers with the class, Violeta?" To Violeta's relief, another student pipes in before Bob can voice his taunts louder.

After indulging her students and their random stories, Ms. Power turns their attention to the laptops in front of them. "I know we've already finished our weather unit, but I thought it would be fun to track the pattern of the meteor today to help us sharpen our mapping skills."

"Great," Violeta mutters.

"That's the spirit, Violeta!" Ms. Power walks around to each group to pass out mapping worksheets of the county. As soon as she steps away from the table, Bob grabs Violeta's computer.

The swift motion causes Violeta to feel nauseated. Her lab partner has gym first hour, and it smells like they ran sprints today. It doesn't help, either, that he apparently tried to cover the smell with that body spray all boys think makes them smell like men. Violeta regains her composure and shouts, "Bobby!"

"It is *Bob*. Not *Bobby*. And I'm trying to show you something." He types a few keys, clicks a few links, and then turns the computer around to Violeta. She squints at the screen in concentration. A map of the county glows before her.

"What am I looking at?"

"Just wait for it. I swear, this school has the worst internet."

After a few seconds, the screen shifts. The map remains in place, but stripes of meteorological patterns float across the screen. Her brow creases as she scowls at her stinky lab partner.

"Don't you see it? In the top right corner? The time shows exactly when the storm squalls hit our village and the school."

Violeta stares at the screen again, this time paying close attention to the times and patterns. She scribbles down the shifts on her map, tracking the storm at every second. Her eyes widen, and she gulps. Words that have never crossed her thoughts or her lips come spewing out with a life of their own. "You're right."

"HA! I told you!"

"Mr. Fetore!"

"Sorry, Ms. Power. This meteor business just gets my juices flowing."

Violeta's lab partner leans in and whispers, "Completely coincidental. You can take off those paranormal polka dots now."

She peers down at her warm hands. The ugly polka dots tease her as she pulls each finger off. She lays the gloves on the table and holds her breath. Bob Fetore stares at her with a playful grin. Violeta can't help herself; she turns to the window to check.

Nothing.

Not even a wisp of wind.

Not a single snowflake.

Violeta stuffs the gloves back into the pockets of her coat and continues with her day as normal. No more violent winds or hail pellets. Just a usual day of angst and awkwardness.

At the end of the day, she meets up with Everly at their locker.

"Did you have any more meteor-power stuff today?"

"No, it's fine. Whatever. I must've stayed up too late last night or something." Violeta laughs it off. She wouldn't admit it out loud, but deep inside she's disappointed.

The girls lock arms and head back outside for their walk home. Everly breaks off and waves goodbye as they near her driveway.

"Don't be too sad, Vi. Maybe something else paranormal happened and you don't even know it yet!"

Despite Violeta's best efforts to hide it, her best friend always knows when something is bothering her. "Ha. Thanks. I'll let you know what I find out."

Violeta climbs the dreaded stairs to her apartment door and stomps the snow off her shoes. She unlocks the door, and Thunder bolts out. He scampers down the stairs, does his business in his usual spot by the lamppost, and shoots back up and into the warm apartment. Violeta laughs at his efforts to pee as quickly and snow-free as possible. She picks him up, removes the snow from his paw pads, and strokes his soft black fur. His tail wags as he squirms in her embrace. When she puts him down, he immediately sits next to his food bowl. Knowing the drill, Violeta scoops out some kibble and pours it for her pup to devour.

She sits on the couch and stares out the window at the white wonderland.

Perhaps I was overreacting today. Maybe I'll laugh about this later.

The front door opens and slams with quick motion. Violeta perks up and watches as her father takes his coat and boots off. He walks over and kisses Violeta on the forehead. "How was school, Violeta?"

"It was just . . . normal."

He flops down on his recliner and loosens his tie. "I figured there would be a lot of buzz surrounding that meteor last night."

"Oh, there was."

"You sound disappointed."

Violeta sighs. "Nope. Just a regular day in our regular, boring town."

Her father stretches. "Well, little Sonche, I've been working for over twenty-four hours straight on this meteor business. Just like the town got last night, I need to take a shower!"

"Ha! Dad jokes." Violeta tries to muffle her laughter with sarcasm; she doesn't want to encourage future corny jokes.

Her father grins wide, pushes himself out of the chair, and drags his feet to the bathroom.

Violeta pulls the latch on the side of the couch, causing the recliner footrest to spring out. Thunder jumps up and stares into Violeta's eyes. After a few seconds, he curls himself into a little ball and closes his eyes.

"I guess nothing paranormal really happened today."

Thunder lifts his head and turns it back toward Violeta. "That's what you think."

GHOST LIGHTS

ALLORIANNA MATSOURANI

It was Friday night, and we were going to the Patapsco Baptist Church's roller-skating party at Derby Hall down in Hampstead. Roger was one of the drivers, and somehow five of us fit into his tiny, ancient, khaki-colored coupe—which he'd nicknamed "Bullheaded Ethel." Susan sat in front with him, and I squeezed into the back with Patty and Ken.

The sky was already dark when we piled into Roger's car. Dusk usually hit around 5 o'clock here in January, which made the nights seem endless. I was looking forward to the skating rink—the smell of stale popcorn lingering in the air, the cheesy organ music that reverberated over the speakers, and even the dilapidated disco ball that threw little spots of spinning, swirling color onto the walls and ceiling during couples' skate.

I liked the crowd at the skating rink. All types of people went there to skate. They came from Carroll County, as well as Baltimore, Harford, and Anne Arundel Counties. The place had a unique vintage vibe that suited me, and I always felt like I blended in. It didn't matter that my skin had color or that my hair was black and straight. No one called me "Indian Princess" here. I was just like anyone else zooming around on the wooden floor.

"You remember how to get there, Roger?" Susan asked as she took off her pink knit hat. "It's out in the boonies. I don't want to get lost again."

"Trust me," he replied. "We just head south on Route 30. How hard can that be?"

"For you, very hard," Ken muttered.

I don't think anyone heard him but me. Yes, Roger did have a reputation for being a bit flaky, but Ken's sarcasm was annoying. He always seemed to be one step away from picking a fight. I didn't understand him. A lot of girls thought he was hot—the brooding bad boy with dark angry eyes and a deep-brown ponytail that hung down to the middle of his back. I thought he was a hotheaded pain, and I wasn't exactly thrilled to be in the car with him.

Roger started up old Ethel and headed out of the parking lot. It lurched a bit as he shifted gears. I wondered if it was the clutch or the driver that was responsible for the less-than-smooth ride. No one else appeared to notice. Susan was quietly talking to Roger—couple stuff, I presumed. Patty's attention was fixed on her cell phone, probably checking her email or Facebook, or surfing the web. Ken was staring out the window.

I was just glad I had something to do. It was winter break and school wouldn't start for another week. Eating burgers at the local hamburger shack was getting tiresome. Hanging out at the mall was boring—I had no money, anyway. And I was running out of library books to read.

We had only gone a few miles when it started to snow—a typical snowfall that comes with a Maryland winter. Between the streetlamps and the car's headlights, the pavement and area directly in front of us was fairly well lit, and from my spot in the middle of the backseat, there was enough light for me to see the big, fat white flakes hitting the windshield. I knew from experience that the snow would start coming down faster and heavier. Roger switched on the windshield wipers, but they could barely keep up with the barrage of flakes striking the glass.

As the snow continued, a crusty ridge of ice formed twin arcs near the top and sides of the windshield, just at the edge of the wipers' reach. All I could see now was a torrent of white, like fast-moving confetti, pelting the windshield and the road beyond.

Roger strained to see the road. I didn't think his face could get any closer to the windshield. Susan was watching as well, her face taut as her eyes stayed riveted to the bit of road illuminated by Ethel's headlights. The snow was accumulating on the pavement, and the mood in the car was getting tense.

"Roger, does this car have snow tires?" Patty asked hesitantly as she briefly looked up from her phone.

"This ol' girl has never had any trouble in the snow before," he said. "God is always with her."

"What does that mean, besides being a load of crap?" Ken asked, still facing the window.

"What do you think it means, Ken? We'll be fine. God is watching over us."

"Freak," Ken grumbled almost inaudibly.

I heard him, though, and I jabbed his side with my elbow, although I doubt he felt it through his heavy leather jacket. "Stop it," I whispered, irritated. "You'll just make him mad, and it's already hard enough to drive in the snow."

"You stop it, Katie," he countered. "Quit trying to be my mom."

I sighed and continued to watch the road through the windshield. It was not worth even trying to respond to him. Ken could be such a jerk.

We drove on, the five of us in that little car. Susan had taken over as navigator, making sure Roger followed the road and didn't miss any turns. Patty had gone back to scrolling on her phone, and Ken was still staring out the window.

"Look," Susan said after about fifteen more minutes had passed. "I see a sign for Route 30. Take this road to the right."

"I thought we were already on Route 30," Roger said. "I don't think we should take that."

"It says Route 30 and that's what we want, Roger. Follow the road to the right."

"But, Suze . . ."

"Do it. Turn now," she demanded.

Roger exhaled and turned the steering wheel toward the Route 30 sign.

"Um . . . this doesn't look familiar," Patty said, looking up from her phone screen to look out the window.

"How could anything look familiar in this snowstorm?" Susan asked, keeping her eyes fixed on the road ahead of us. "Everything looks white and icy. But I did see the road sign."

"Everything looks dark," Patty commented. "Why is the road so dark? What happened to the streetlights?"

"I don't see any, not on this road," Roger answered.

Patty looked back down at her phone and opened the map app. "Guys, I really don't think this is the right road. I'm looking at my map, and Route 30 splits before you get to Hampstead. I think we're on old Route 30."

"We should turn back and call it a night," Ken said, turning from the window. "Weather's getting really bad."

"No way," Roger shot back. "We've come this far. We're almost there. Besides, it'll be fun."

Patty passed her phone over to me and pointed to the pulsing blue target that marked our location. "See what I mean?"

"I think Patty's right," I announced to the group. "It looks like we're on the Hampstead Bypass." I studied the map on her phone. "If we turn left at Route 482, we can get over to Hanover Pike. That's the Route 30 we want."

I handed the phone back to Patty and focused my attention on the view through the windshield. All I could see was a steady cascade of snow that swirled in the glow of the little Beetle's headlights. The windshield wipers flicked back and forth, their rhythm steady and constant as they swept the fat flakes off the glass, only to have more immediately fall right in the spots where the others had been.

It was pretty and peaceful. The snow always seemed to bring an eerie quiet with it as the delicate white crystals blanketed the earth and everything on it—as if they muffled all sound and muted the hustle-bustle of life into a state of stillness that was almost otherworldly.

The snow was beautiful, but I also knew how treacherous it could be.

"Do you think they'll close the skating rink?" I asked.

"Nah," Roger answered. He seemed unfazed by the weather. "This snowfall isn't that bad. There's only a couple of inches on the ground so far."

"We should be coming to the turnoff soon," Susan added. "That road can't be as dark as this one. Why don't they have any streetlights out here?"

"It's the boonies, Susan, remember?" Ken replied. "There's nothing out here. Just woods and farmland. You better pray we don't get stuck, Roger. No one will find us until daylight."

Susan turned around in her seat. "Stop it, Ken."

"Shut up and watch the road, Susan."

"Both of you, stop it," I snapped. I could hear the exasperation in my voice, which was mainly directed at Ken. "We'll be fine. The rink will be open, and I wouldn't be surprised if it stopped snowing by the time we're ready to go home."

"I'm with Katie." Patty looked up for a brief moment from her texting or whatever she was doing. "Let's look for signs for Route 482."

The five of us continued in silence. The VW's windshield wipers tirelessly swiped back and forth, and the headlights illuminated the steady swirl of frozen flakes. We were all immersed in our own thoughts. Susan and Roger were zealously watching the road ahead. Patty was studying her phone, and Ken had gone back to gazing out his window.

I was thinking about couples' skate. People would pair up to glide hand in hand in time with whatever old-fashioned organ ballad was playing as the lights dimmed and the disco ball started to spin. Would anyone ask me to skate? Did I even want to be asked?

I had to admit, if only to myself, that I did.

"Roger! Watch out!"

At the sound of Susan's voice, my attention immediately focused on what was happening to the car. I felt it veer sharply to the right and start bucking as though it was rolling over rocks. Without thinking, I grabbed Ken's arm just as Patty grabbed mine. I looked out the windshield and could still see falling snow. And then I saw a tree coming toward us.

"A tree!" Roger gasped, panicked. Susan screamed.

"Roger! Take your foot off the brake and steer around it," Ken directed with surprising calm and authority in his voice. "The taller grass will slow us down."

From that moment, everything seemed to happen in slow motion. The car bumped along for a few more minutes, but we didn't hit the tree. Finally, Bullheaded Ethel came to a stop, and we all just sat there, silent. The headlights lit the space in front of us, illuminating a landscape of leafless trees and falling snow.

Ken broke the silence. "What happened?"

"It looked like the headlights of a car were coming at us," Roger said. "I swerved to avoid them, but then they just disappeared and I slid right off the road. I never did see a car."

"I saw the lights too," Susan added. "But no car."

"Ghost lights," I said. "I've heard stories about strange lights that move around on this back road. You see them, then they're gone, and then they're back again. People have seen them on the road . . . in the woods . . . in the trees. No one knows what they are or where they come from. Some have described them as looking like giant lightning bugs, but they aren't."

Ken sniggered. "You're kidding us, right, Katie?"

"No, Ken, I'm not." I sighed. "Some people say they're car lights reflecting off some old house in the woods, lights from airplanes heading toward the airport, balls of static electricity, or something like that. But they've been around a long time. My mom told me that both her mother and her grandmother saw them when they were young. And there weren't too many cars or airplanes around here back then. My mom saw them, too, when she was a teenager."

"Ghost lights, ha!" Ken scoffed. "More like ghost stories. You really believe in that garbage, Katie?"

"Maybe. Some things are real, even if they can't be explained."

"Well, we saw them," Susan said. "And whatever they were, they were real."

"They were probably just car lights," Ken stated. "Maybe someone hit a patch of ice and swerved a bit."

Just then, Patty looked back down at her phone. "Oh, great. I don't have any service."

"So, Roger, can you back this car up and get us on the road again?" Ken asked. "Obviously, we won't be able to call a tow truck."

Roger restarted the little car, shifted it into reverse, and stepped on the gas pedal. The engine revved, but Ethel didn't move. He changed gears and tried to go forward. The car still didn't move. I could hear the rear wheels spinning.

"We're stuck," Roger said.

"No kidding, genius," Ken responded. "Try putting it in reverse again and I'll push. The rest of you get out of the car so I can move it."

Patty, Susan, and I climbed out of Ethel and huddled nearby while Roger and Ken worked on getting it out of the rut. Roger sat in the driver's seat and stepped on the gas, while Ken pushed the car from the front. The snow was still falling, but not quite as hard as before. Snowflakes that landed on us melted when they hit our cheeks and noses. I was glad I had worn my hat and gloves. The temperature was dropping, and I was getting cold. Soon, the snow started to accumulate on our coats.

I moved closer to Patty and Susan. "I sure could go for a hot chocolate right now," I whispered. They both nodded in agreement.

Freeing the car was proving to be more difficult than we all thought it would be. Every time Ken pushed it to the edge of the rut, the tires slid back down the snow-covered grass.

"You girls!" Ken shouted. "Don't just stand around watching, for God's sake. Help me push."

Suddenly, Patty tensed and nudged me. "Look."

It was the ghost lights. They were hovering close to a tree next to the car. I could see why Roger and Susan had thought they were headlights. They were bright round orbs that glowed with pulsating pinkish-white light—like oversized glow-in-the-dark softballs. They weren't perfectly still, either; they moved around, independently, like two fidgety creatures observing newcomers. For some reason, though, I didn't feel afraid. Their presence was almost comforting, as though they were guardian angels watching over us.

The boys were focused on getting the car out of the rut, so they didn't see them. But Susan saw them. She pointed a finger at the lights.

"Oh . . . my . . . God. Do you see that?"

"See what?" Ken asked as he pushed Ethel. He looked at the spot that Susan was pointing to and stopped, immobilized. The car once again slid into the rut. Roger stuck his head out of the car window.

"Hey, man, why'd you stop?" Roger followed Ken's gaze, and he also froze, taking his foot off the gas. The engine sputtered and went silent.

"Holy cow! What are those?" Roger asked as he got out of the car.

"Ghost lights," I quipped. "Think I'm kidding now, Ken?"

"Roger," Susan said urgently, panic choking her voice. "What should we do?"

"I don't know . . ."

"Duh. Get back on the road and get out of here," Ken said, commandeering the conversation. "Girls, get over here now and help me push."

As he spoke, one of the lights floated closer to Ethel, then hovered over it, moving from the rear bumper to the top and then to the front bumper, as though it were scanning the entire car. It stopped when it reached Ken. The other light stayed where it was.

"I'm not getting near that thing," Patty said firmly as she took a step back from the car.

"Uh, me neither," said Susan.

Somehow, I knew we weren't in danger. The stories I had heard about the ghost lights were not tragic ones. No one had been killed or hurt by them. They were more of a mystery than a threat. I watched the lights, fascinated, wondering what was going to happen next. Could I get close enough to touch one? Would they disappear or float away?

I walked toward the light that still floated by the tree. Its pulsating glow was mesmerizing, almost hypnotic, and I felt drawn to it—like I was a moth and it was a flame. I was vaguely aware of the falling snow and Susan and Patty trying to pull me back. The light drew me closer, like an elusive living being that rarely ventured out but instead lured others to it like some sort of corporeal beacon.

I felt safe and warm, like a child walking in sunlight toward the outstretched arms of my mother. Although the light was soundless, I could vaguely sense it calling my name and telling me that everything would be okay and I shouldn't worry. I walked closer and closer until the light was just a few inches from my face.

I remember someone shouting at me to stop; it may have been Ken. But then I reached out and touched the glowing orb. At that moment, the light became the only thing I could sense. It was soft yet bright, and I felt as though I were standing on a sunlit beach with my eyes closed.

"Ah, Katherine, daughter of Elizabeth. We thought it was you."

I felt the words rather than heard them—the sensation of a woman speaking to me with a voice that emanated affection.

"The world around us has changed as time has passed, but we felt your thoughts as you traveled through our space . . . much like we feel the thoughts of your mother when she is near, and felt the thoughts of her mother, and her mother's mother many years ago."

Who are you? What do you want? I couldn't really speak the words aloud, but the questions filled my thoughts. I was more curious than afraid, as if this discourse were as normal as talking to my friends in the car.

"We mean you no harm. It was such a surprise to feel your presence that we

were compelled to see you. We didn't intend for the car to leave the road. We will help you and your friends to reach your destination safely."

How do you know me? I asked, completely forgetting that we were standing in the woods in the falling snow.

"It is difficult for us to explain. We are the Custos Angeli, the guardians of this land. We are also charged with protecting those who share its heritage, such as you and your mother, and her mother."

Me and my mother? I didn't understand the heritage of this land or how my mother, grandmother, and I shared it, but I didn't want to disappoint the voice. The sweet, soft, melodious words enveloped me in a blanket of serenity, and I didn't want to leave or be expelled.

"You are Susquehannock. Your people and the Custos Angeli came to this place together. It was long, long ago, and the story is too long to tell you now."

But I want to know. Who are the Custos Angeli?

"The air is cold, snow is falling, and you need warmth and shelter. What was it that you were thinking you wanted? Hot chocolate?

How did you know?

"We can feel your thoughts when you are close by, just as you are able to feel our thoughts through touch."

I had no secrets from the lights. My mind was open to them, but that didn't bother me. More than anything, I wanted to know who they were and what they were. My mother had told me stories about seeing the ghost lights, but she never talked about anything other than the sightings.

Please, I want to know the story. When will you—

In that moment, I felt my hands being torn away from the orb.

"Katie! Katie! Are you okay?"

The light dimmed, and I heard a different voice. It was loud and brash, not soothing at all. As my eyes grew accustomed to the darkness, I saw Ken. He stood in front of me, holding both my hands firmly in his, and yelled my name with an expression of concern and . . . something else.

Fear, maybe?

"You touched that thing and went into some kind of trance for a few moments," Patty said. "It was terrifying."

"Ken ran over and pulled your hands off of it," Susan added. "We thought it was going to kill you."

"I'm fine," I replied.

"What was it?" Roger asked.

"I don't know. But I don't think either of those lights is going to hurt us." I looked around but didn't see them. "Where'd they go?"

"When Ken pulled your hands off that light, they both floated up toward the top of the trees and disappeared," Roger answered. "So, tell us all about it," he continued. "What did it feel like? Was it hot? Were you possessed? Are you glad Ken saved you?"

I looked at Ken, who was still staring at me and holding my hands. Abruptly, he dropped them and walked back to the car.

"Give her a break, man," he said as he positioned himself at the rear of Bullheaded Ethel this time. "Let's get this car on the road. Patty, Susan, come help me."

I walked to the back of the car too, and all four of us pushed. This time, the tires easily rolled out of the rut. Roger was able to turn the car around in a small clearing and then slowly drive forward toward the old bypass. Patty, Susan, Ken, and I walked behind the car in case we needed to push it again.

It didn't take long before we were back on the pavement. I had been right about the snow; it was letting up. As we drove along, fewer and fewer flakes were illuminated by Ethel's headlights. By the time we reached Route 482, the snow had almost stopped falling. Patty's cell phone had service again, and she was once more immersed in whatever site she was scrolling through. Roger and Susan were quietly engaged in their couple chatter. And Ken was looking out his window again. It almost felt as if our encounter in the woods with the ghost lights hadn't happened at all.

I, however, couldn't stop thinking about those lights. I wondered if my mother or her mother had ever touched that orb. I knew our lineage was part Native American and that our ancestors had lived around here, but I didn't know anything about the Susquehannock people or whether I was one of them. Why hadn't my mother or my grandmother ever told me? Were they even aware of our heritage?

More than likely I would never know. I definitely didn't plan on telling my mother about this. At least, not yet. I knew what I wanted to do next, and I was pretty certain she would not approve.

Finally, we made it to Derby Hall and the skating party. The rink was open and everyone else was there. The snow had stopped, and a snowplow had even driven down Route 30—the main route, Hanover Pike.

After we'd been at the rink for a while, the loudspeaker announced couples' skate. The lights dimmed, the disco ball started spinning, and a slow waltz began to play. Everyone paired up and headed out onto the floor.

I felt someone tap my shoulder and turned around to see Ken standing there. "Wanna skate?" he asked.

Ken was so surly that I didn't consider him to be a great partner, but at least I wouldn't be left standing alone by the railing. I swallowed down my disappointment and nodded yes.

We rolled along, holding hands and dodging other couples that skated either better or worse than us. After several laps, Ken guided us over to the line of chairs just beyond the railing. He sat down and pulled me into the chair next to him. I started to complain, but he stopped me.

"Katie," he began, "that incident in the woods this evening was one of the scariest things I've ever seen. When you touched that light, it was like you were totally gone. You were there, but you were empty. Like . . . like . . . a mannequin."

"Ken . . ."

"I want to know what happened," he continued. "Why did you touch it?"

"It's weird, but I felt drawn to it. Like it put a spell on me and pulled me in."

"Weren't you frightened? I mean, did you try to fight it?"

"Fight it? No . . . I didn't try. I wasn't afraid."

Ken nodded slowly, as if thinking to himself. After a few moments, he continued to question me.

"What happened then?"

"Um . . . it talked to me."

He frowned. "The light?"

"Yes."

"How? I didn't hear anything."

"I don't know," I replied, starting to feel annoyed. "Why all the questions, Ken?"

"I'm just curious, that's all. What did it say?"

"Apparently it knew me. And my mother. And my grandmother."

"Really? How?"

"I don't know." My irritation was mounting. "There's a story, but I got the impression it's a long one. And when you grabbed my hands away from the orb, my connection with it broke. That's all I know."

"So what are you going to do?"

"Ken, stop with all the questions already."

"C'mon, Katie. You were lost in thought all the way here. I know you. You're planning something."

"So?"

"So, I want in. Whatever you're going to do, I want to be there."

I turned so I could face Ken. "Why?"

He held my gaze as he answered, his black eyes surprisingly earnest. "You know how you said you felt drawn to it? Like it put a spell on you and pulled you in? Well, I felt it too. Only I felt drawn to the other light, the one by the car. I wanted to do the same thing you did—touch it. But I fought it. And then I watched what happened to you. That could have been me too. And it scared the crap out of me. I don't believe in that stuff. But now . . ."

"Now?"

"That story you talked about? I want to know it. I need to know it. I don't care how long it is. It might be my story too."

"Your story too? How?"

He paused and looked down at the floor, then spoke in a hushed voice. "I was adopted as a baby. I don't know much about my birth mother, just that her family lived somewhere near the woods by old Route 30."

"I didn't know."

"No one knows. It's my family's secret, and I want to keep it that way." He looked back up at me. "But if I can find out more about my past—my roots—I have to try. Maybe I can find out more about my birth mother and her family and about who I really am. Figure out how I fit in . . . what I'm a part of."

Total surprise kept me from responding right away. I would never have guessed how he felt, but it shed some light on his antagonistic demeanor. My annoyance with him faded a bit. I could relate to what he said about understanding where he belonged. I knew my family and I still struggled with finding my place in the world. I couldn't even imagine what Ken must be going through.

"Katie," he said, interrupting my thoughts, "we have to go back and find those lights again and learn the story. Together."

I did want to go back and find the ghost lights and learn about the Custos Angeli. Ken was right about that. There was a hole in my history, one I hadn't even known about until tonight. I had so many questions. Who were the Susquehannock? How was I connected to them . . . and to the ghost lights? Filling in the gaps might help me feel more complete.

It probably would be safer if Ken went back to the woods with me. He could be aggravating and I didn't know if I could put up with his moodiness, but I would just have to try. He wanted to find the Custos Angeli as badly as I did; to me, that meant he was less likely to give up and leave me on my own.

"Yes," I finally replied. "We do. You and me. Together."

PHANTASMAGORIA

YNES MALAKOVA

The Reverend Blackwell arrived late one night;
In the eyes of our town, he was an unwelcome sight.
He stood at his pulpit, hidden like a blight,
Shrouded by a screen, specter-white.

With his back to the crowd, he spoke with his lights:
A *lanterne magique*, he called his device.
It cast shadows and swirls, darkness and smoke;
Through *fantasmagorie*, he claimed spirits awoke.

He was shooed from cathedrals and booed on the streets;
From church to church, he was forced to flee.
And that is the reason, *mon cheri*,
He has returned to Chantilly.

My nanny, Amelia, tells me this story each night before I sleep, and she has done so ever since the reverend came back to live in the city. She reminds me that Reverend Blackwell is not actually a reverend, nor is he truly a Blackwell—at least, not anymore. She calls his house of worship a "traveling circus," and she chews on his name with distaste, acting as if she has bitten into a lemon. She tells me he is a coward; she visited him once, but he remained hidden behind an enormous screen, six feet wide and ten feet tall—never once did he show his face. His wiry frame pitched a long tongue of shadow that cut across nearly the entire height of the screen, and the cast of his gaunt arms spilled to each side.

"I do not know why your mother insists on bringing you to see such nonsense." Amelia huffs and lifts my day shirt off over my head. I raise my arms so she can put my formal shirt on me. "Do not believe a word he says. Do you hear me, Larkin?"

"Yes, *Nounou.*" With my shirt settled, I let her slide my finest vest up over my arms. Then, one leg at a time, I step into my trousers.

"That man kneels at the Devil's left wing. No good can come of this."

Amelia slips my shoes onto my feet, tugging at the laces. I squirm and open my mouth in protest, but Amelia pulls the laces tight, knotting them in place. "Remember my words, Larkin. We can speak no more of this now. Your *maman* returns."

Maman enters the room in a sweeping gown, her dark hair swept back and pinned at the nape of her neck. It is a Saturday night in the summertime, and the lights in my room are bright, too bright for the hour. Most children have already been fed supper and been put to bed by their nannies. I, too, have finished my dinner and afterward moved to my room upstairs to prepare for bed. I expected to find Amelia, as I did each night, laying my nightclothes on my bed, but instead *Maman* was perched on the corner of my bed, frowning and fanning herself, while Amelia pulled my finest garments from my wardrobe and held them up for inspection.

Amelia now sits me in front of the mirror and brushes my hair while *Maman* watches. My reflection furls its brow and twists its lips. I do not understand why *Maman* has come to oversee my appearance. Normally, she spends her evenings locked in her room or otherwise meeting her friends at the café. But tonight, my grooming is of great concern to her. *Maman* intervenes at sudden, abrupt moments to straighten my shirt collar or smooth a lock of my dark hair, and when she is satisfied with my appearance, she waves Amelia away.

"Tonight is a special night, Larkin," *Maman* says to me. "We're going to a show. You like the theater, do you not?"

I nod to her feebly and smile.

"Come now, Larkin. We mustn't keep your *papa* waiting."

Together we descend the stairs, and she gathers her purse. My *papa* stands impatiently in the living room, tapping the polished toe of his shoe against the floor.

"For goodness sake, Helena. How long does it take to get the boy ready? We're going to be late."

Maman utters an apology, and then I am ushered, one hand in hers and one in my *papa's*, down our cobblestone steps. Though carriages pass us on our right, we travel on foot, taking hurried steps down the side of the street. We pass the *Bistro Éclairé*, where once we had dined *en plein air* on spring days: *Mademoiselle* Gertrude had flashed me a smile and a wink as she filled my *papa's* porcelain cup with fresh coffee. She reached into her apron and passed two butterscotch sweets into my hands beneath the table. One for me, the other for . . .

Lucinda.

Tonight, we walk quickly past the *Bistro Éclairé*, and I am glad for it.

My *papa* jerks my hand, and we round the corner and move down the alleyway behind the bistro, pausing in front of a small wooden door at the back. *Maman* knocks three times; the door cracks open, and we are quickly ushered inside.

We enter, and immediately I am met with a white screen at the front of a tiny room. *Maman* said we were going to a theater, but this is like no theater I have ever seen. There are no velvety curtains, no plush chairs for us to sit upon. This space is small and cramped, with crates stacked against the walls. My *papa* pulls on my arm and leads me to a wrought-iron bench at the front of the room—I recognize it as belonging to the bistro—and I am wedged between my parents. My eyes wander around the room; there are only six people in attendance—*Maman*, myself, my *papa*, and two women in fine evening dresses huddled protectively around a third, like a brood of hens.

"I do not know why I let you talk me into this, Helena," my *papa* says. "This *reverend* is the last person we should be looking to for answers."

"He says she came to him in a dream," *Maman* whispers. A tear glistens in the corner of her eye. "She wants to see us."

"Rubbish, Helena, rubbish." My *papa* crosses his arms and sneers.

I squirm; my shoes feel too tight on my toes. I recall Amelia's words. I have heard many rumors of the reverend's services—from more than just my *nounou*. A showman, some call him. A dabbler in the dark arts, a *sorcier*, others say, and still others call him a channeler of other worlds.

"Ladies and gentlemen." The voice rises from behind the screen. "We are gathered here today in remembrance. Every one of us here has lost a loved one due to tragic circumstances. Illness, perhaps . . ." One of the women bursts into tears. I chew my lip, feeling awkward and wishing I were in bed like other children. The reverend continues. "Some of us . . . don't know what happened, or why. But we all have one thread in common. We feel lost. And frightened." I turn to my left and find *Maman* holding her handkerchief to her eyes. I pat her arm, and she smiles wryly at me.

"We are looking for answers. The opportunity . . . to say goodbye."

The other women touch the corners of their handkerchiefs to their eyes as *Maman* does. They nod amid their tears.

"What we are going to see tonight will be harrowing. It may frighten some of you. You'll be seeing your dead. They may not look as you remember. We do not know who and what we are going see tonight. But rest assured, you are safe. They cannot hurt you. It takes a tremendous amount of energy to even be seen in this world. A powerful, driving force to remain. And remember—at any time, you may close your eyes or leave the theater."

The lights dim around us, and the room grows quiet. The women have stifled their cries.

The reverend clears his throat. "Let us pray."

The screen flashes and bursts with light. I hear a hiss from the corners of the ceiling, and the room begins to fill with smoke. From behind the screen, I hear a clicking sound, like the reels that are used at the theaters I am accustomed to attending. Reverend Blackwell speaks carefully, drawing out each of his words.

"Oh, spirits of the afterlife . . . heed my words. Show yourselves as I call you forth."

The smoke begins to waft slowly through the room, and from behind the screen, I hear the small tinny notes of a music box. My attention is drawn to the screen, where a large black blotch of shadow appears in the center, morphing and dancing with the light.

"I call you forth, Ophelia, daughter of *Madame* Cauchy. You were taken from us in your youth. Before you had a chance to truly live."

The shadow on the screen splits into two, and the blotches swirl around each other. I hear a gasp from one of the women.

The shapes move like leaves after a long rain, circling as if they were being pulled down a slow drain. The shadow of the reverend's arm cuts across the screen, and the shadows catch, bunching into swirls and patterns: a kaleidoscope of black and white, a slow, rich drip of darkness on a canvas of white. I squint at the screen, and the smudges of shadow and light appear as a cheek, the border of a face . . . and the distinct, pear-like shape of an ear. A shriek breaks across the plink of the music box.

"Ophelia!" one of the women chokes out. "Oh, Ophelia! I love you, *ma chèrie*. I love you! Your *maman* loves you."

As quickly as the shadows have come together, they disperse, a flurry of wisps, like snakes, scattering in all directions across the screen.

"No!" The woman rises, stretching her arm desperately toward the screen, "No! Ophelia! Come back to me!"

"Now, now, *Madame* Cauchy, be seated. Ophelia is a timid spirit," Reverend Blackwell croons. "She was a timid girl, was she not?"

Madame Cauchy nods tearfully.

"Don't despair, *Madame*. Come back next week, and she may grow braver."

Despite the reverend's words, *Madame* Cauchy is inconsolable, and the other two women she is nestled between put their arms around her, smoothing her back to calm her sobs. When this fails, they lead *Madame* Cauchy out of the theater.

All who remain are *Maman*, my *papa*, and myself.

"Well, well!" the reverend bellows from behind his screen. "Theodore! Helena! And Larkin . . . oh, little Larkin! What a distinct honor it is to have you at one of my services. I expect you have come because of Lucinda?"

My *papa* clears his throat. "We're here because my wife is a fool. She is so addled with grief, she is willing to believe anything . . . including this little charade of yours, *Reverend*. I'm here to show her it is pure fantasy. You're nothing more than a scoundrel, preying on the hopes of grieving women to fill your appetite for attention."

"Theodore," Reverend Blackwell's voice carries a whisker of sarcasm at its tip. "That is no way for a gentleman to speak."

My *papa* crosses his arms and leans back in his seat. "Get on with your charade."

The theater falls to silence; neither the tinny pluck of the music box nor the reverend's booming voice fill the space. I look at the screen, and it is white, pure white, like a pond on a winter's day. I hear a shuffling, a rattling of a reel, and the reverend's footsteps. His shadow fills the screen again, his lantern fusing with his arms and legs, transforming him into a grotesque creature.

"Very well," he says quietly. "*Madame, Monsieur*, and *mon petit Monsieur* . . . I present to thee, Lucinda."

The light of his lantern pierces the screen, blazing through like the glimmer of a diamond in the sun. I hear the clatter of the lantern's reel—no music box—and only a small hiss of smoke. The room grows cold. So cold, and the hairs on my arms and legs stand on end, even beneath my shirt. I shiver, pressing my arms against my chest.

So cold. So cold.

On the screen, an image appears: wisps of ice, like sewing needles, piling on each other. My teeth begin to chatter. So cold. So cold. I tighten my arms around my chest, but the chill penetrates my skin. I look to my mother, and she sits in comfort. I turn to my *papa*; he is unmoved, slouched, glaring at the reverend through the screen.

I hear another hiss, but it is not that of smoke. It is different. The hiss grows louder, and it is followed by a low, throaty sound . . . an old tongue moving after a long slumber.

"Bring . . . him . . ."

I jump up and cry out, and my mother turns to me. "Larkin!"

"Sit down!" my *papa* bellows.

My legs are shaking as I take my seat, my teeth still chattering. The wrought-iron bench sends a shiver through my spine.

"Bring . . . the one . . . with the guilt in his eyes."

I watch the screen in a trance. As the veins of white and shadow merge and pull apart, it is *Maman's* scream I hear.

"Reverend!"

A ghoulish creature comes together in pieces, a fragment of an arm, a smear of a neck. A long, ruined veil, masking half a face in shadow. The face is not that of a human—it is either angel or demon—no eyes, only darkness and light—no nose or cheek—darkness and light, darkness and light.

My *papa* shudders in distaste and, perhaps, half in fear. He reaches across me and grips *Maman's* arm, and she turns to him, sobbing.

"Reverend, we are leaving!" my *papa* cries. "I have had enough of your tricks and illusions!" My *papa* releases *Maman* and yanks my arm, pulling me from my seat. He drags me across the room, and we spill back out into the alleyway amid smoke. *Maman* sinks to the ground.

"Theodore, oh, Theodore!" She blinks once, twice, and stares straight ahead, looking past us. "Was that truly Lucinda?"

My *papa* shakes his head. "No, *ma femme*," he says. "That is the invention of a disturbed man."

I climb into bed alone, unable to shake the image from my mind. The apparition continues to haunt me, long after we've returned from Reverend Blackwell's service. Long after *Maman* locked herself downstairs in her bedchamber. Long after my *papa* settled in the main room to drink from his collection of bottles.

So cold. So cold. Her words were a breath of ice.

"Bring . . . the one . . . with the guilt in his eyes."

Her message haunts me on through the morning, while I sit at the breakfast table and eat my porridge, and into midday, when I walk in the park.

Lucinda. *Was it truly her?*

The sun shines brightly, and families are gathered on the grass, blankets and baskets sprawled across the park, but I shudder.

She has come back for me.

I turn to head home, but my legs urge me in the other direction, down past *l'école*, past *la bibliothèque*. I follow the same path I took that night—that horrible, frigid night—when my *papa* lay sprawled in a bottle-induced stupor across the couch, my mother locked tightly in her bedchamber.

I continue past *le marché* and *la boulangerie*, until I arrive at the steps of a small home made of timber and stone. I look at the flowerbeds and expect to find them full of colorful blooms, but they are barren. In my childhood, they flourished with petunias— Lucinda's favorite flower. The last time I came to this home and laid eyes on this flowerbed, it was as empty as it is now—the first snow of the season having arrived.

Six months ago.

I cannot believe it has been so long since I've been to this place or have seen my sister's lovely brown curls and kissed her soft cheek.

She was two days away from her eighteenth birthday at the time of her passing.

We had long been victims of my *papa*'s hand when his glass was empty and my mother had irked him—the dishes not having been washed, or his pipe being out of place. During those nights, Lucinda would take me by the hand and guide me up the stairs. She would place me into bed and squeeze a pillow around my ears. We would pretend not to hear my *papa*'s bellows or the crash of his fist against the table.

"We are not in our bedroom," Lucinda would say. "You are a *cuisinier*, and I am a *hôtesse*. We have opened a restaurant deep under the ocean. We serve the finest trout to the mermaids, and they pay us in pearls."

Pearls. Oh, Lucinda. Sweet Lucinda. She had loved pearls.

The night of her passing, she had worn pearls around her neck.

"Larkin, listen to me closely," she said. A row of pearls peeked from her collar as she bundled me in my heaviest coat. "We are old enough now to make our own decisions, to live our own lives. Don't you think?"

I nodded.

"*Papa* is very cruel. Do you remember when he roared at me for bringing home the books from the library?

I nodded. "The ghost books."

"Spirits, Larkin. Spirits. We are not heathens. *Papa* says ghosts are the work of the Devil. Do remember this?"

I nodded.

"He believes me to be possessed, and he's ordered that I be sent to the ward. Do you remember what happened to my friend Sophie when she went to the ward?"

I shook my head.

"She came back . . . different. She was never the same."

Lucinda's words taper into nothingness, and she twirls a lock of her dark hair. "Anyway, Larkin, I do not believe we should be subject to his whims any longer. Don't you agree?"

I nodded.

"Then it's settled." Lucinda gave my jacket a playful jerk. "We are going to live with *oncle* Christophe."

"What?"

She smiled at me. "I have already spoken to *Maman*. She will come and visit us often. But we must go now; we must go tonight."

She took me by the glove, and we slipped down the stairs, holding our breath as we passed our *papa*'s sleeping shadow. Lucinda cracked the door open, barely wide enough for both of us to fit through in our thick jackets. We hurried down the street, her legs carrying her much more quickly than mine could carry me, past *l'école*, past *la bibliothèque*, past *le marché* and *la boulangerie*. We took a sharp turn, and Lucinda released my hand. She whirled around beneath a streetlamp, twirling like the falling snow.

"We are free, Larkin! Free to live our own lives! No more whispering or sneaking around the house—no more lectures and no more talk of . . . the ward!"

She patted a ball of snow between her gloves and hurled it at me. It hit my jacket with a quiet pat, and Lucinda tossed her head back, a peal of her sweet laughter filling the air.

I returned her smile and gathered snow between my hands. We chased each other, the night filled with snowballs and laughter, until we approached my *oncle*'s neighborhood, small clusters of identical half-timbered homes lining the street.

"*Oncle* Christophe is waiting for us," Lucinda said. "We may stay up and read books with him and eat tarts past bedtime . . ."

My eyes lit up with excitement, and I rushed up the steps to knock on the door. Lucinda caught my hand.

"Wait. Before we go . . . I must tell you something, Larkin."

"What is it, Lucinda?"

"There is a condition to our staying with *oncle* Christophe."

"Is it you, Larkin?"

I am shaken from my stupor, noting that the door to my *oncle*'s home stands open, his long entry corridor stretching before me. He stands tall, towering over me in a loose but finely pressed shirt. His face is pale, as though he has not seen the sunlight, and his once meticulously trimmed beard has grown wild. My eyes shift to the white collar at his neck.

"Reverend Blackwell."

The reverend frowns and shakes his head, as if he were disappointed. Rays of sunlight reflect off his brown hair, peppering it with silver, like tinsel. "I'd like it if you still called me '*oncle*,' Larkin."

My lip juts out in disgust, and I wrinkle my nose. "You are no longer my *oncle*. Not after what you did to Lucinda."

The reverend's frown deepens, and his brow falls. "I suppose that's why you're here."

I feel a sting in the back of my throat, and my arms begin to quiver. I tuck my hands into my pockets to disguise their shaking. "She would still be alive, were it not for you!"

"Larkin, we must talk . . ." Reverend Blackwell reaches for me, and I snarl, pulling away from him.

"Keep your hands off me! It's your fault! It's all your fault!"

"It isn't what you think. I was only trying to protect Lucinda. And you."

A sob forms in my throat, and before I can stop them, cold tears slide down my cheeks. Colder than the air, colder than snow.

Colder than death.

I wipe my sleeve against my face and clear my throat. "It's your fault, Reverend."

Despite the sun hanging high above us, a winter wind bites through my clothes, and I struggle to hold back more tears. My teeth chatter, and Reverend Blackwell places a gaunt hand on my shoulder.

"Come inside, Larkin. Have some tea. We need to talk about what happened that night." He takes a deep breath and closes his eyes. In my mind, I can almost hear him pondering, searching for words. "We need to talk about what happened at last night's service, as well."

I wish to run away, to snap at Reverend Blackwell, to hurl ugly words and truths at him—until he confesses. It's his fault! It's all his fault my sister is dead! Her icy image floats across my mind, and I shudder.

So cold. So cold.

I bite my lip and blink away my tears. Was the shadow I saw truly Lucinda, or is my *papa* correct? Was it just one of the reverend's tricks? He tricked Lucinda—why should I believe that what I saw was anything more than smoke and lights?

I play *Maman*'s cries in my head, recalling the chill that shrouded me when the phantom's shadow spread across the room. *Maman* and Lucinda were very close. Did she feel her presence too?

Though I am afraid, I must know if it was her. If Lucinda is looking for me . . .

I clear my throat and nod at Reverend Blackwell, following him into his home.

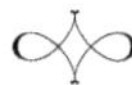

I sit by the fireplace, a blanket draped over my shoulders and back, and I sip at the cup of tea that the reverend has handed me. His house is small and tidy; every item has a specific place in which it belongs. The throw pillows on his loveseat are plump and well-tended. The walls are lined with bookshelves: encyclopedias stacked neatly in order of volumes, and I see many titles in Latin with leather-bound covers that appear very old. The wall above his hearth is lined with clocks of all shapes and sizes, minute hands and seconds set at different times of day. In the past, I had been to this home many times and sat in this very room, but the clocks are a new addition—a chaotic touch to an otherwise immaculate room. The tick-tick-tick of the Reverend Blackwell's many clocks is maddening, and I wonder how he can stay in this home with a constant cacophony of times and ticks.

The blanket warms my body, and my hands are warm cupping the tea. The reverend sits across from me and sips at his own cup of tea.

"Are you feeling better, Larkin?"

"Yes, Reverend."

He frowns, undoubtedly at the title, but takes a silent sip of his tea. "Let's talk about the night Lucinda passed."

I rub my eyes and sigh deeply, allowing the memories to flood back to me.

"A condition? What condition?" I turned to face Lucinda, and she smiled at me, twirling her pearls between her fingers.

"Did you know that *oncle* Christophe bought me this necklace, Larkin?"

"You always loved pearls."

"It's beautiful. One of my favorites." Lucinda knelt in front of me, placing her hands on my cheeks. "Larkin. You must understand. *Oncle* Christophe cares deeply for us. But we are just children, and we are not his."

"What does that have to do with your necklace?"

"Nothing," Lucinda said. "And everything. *Oncle* Christophe can care for us in a way that *Maman* and *Papa* never could. He is a Blackwell—he has the same wealth as *Papa*—but he is kind and caring. He would never send me to the ward for treatment."

Lucinda paused and stroked my cheek. "Larkin, if our *papa* comes looking for us, he could take us away and we would be forced to come home with him. And *oncle* Christophe—he would go to prison for kidnapping us. Can you imagine the wrath we would face from *Papa*?"

I shivered at the thought of my *papa* raising his voice, bellowing while Lucinda and I hid under her bed.

Lucinda smoothed her hand over my forehead, pushing my hair back. "Do not worry, Larkin. I have found a way to protect us. *Papa* cannot come for us . . . if I am married."

"Married?" I blinked and scrunched my nose. "What do you mean? Married to *oncle* Christophe?"

"It would only be in name."

My lips folded back and my face soured—Lucinda, married to our *oncle*? The idea made my stomach turn. My mind reeled, and the ground felt shaky beneath me. I could not think straight, and of all the thoughts and protests that churned in my head, I blurted out the first one that came to my mouth: "You are too young!"

"Hush, Larkin! No one knows my age but you. We would be wed tonight—and in two days, it would not matter. I'll be eighteen and can do as I please."

"Lucinda, no!" I pushed her hands away from me. "He's our *oncle*! It's disgusting! And wrong!"

Lucinda lowered her voice. "No one would know this but you. And like I said—it would only be in name."

I shook my head hard, my hair whipping across my forehead. "It's a trick, Lucinda! We must go home. We can wait until your birthday and run away together!"

"We have nothing on our own, Larkin. We would be reduced to begging on the streets or thieving. And *oncle* Christophe . . . he will provide us with a home and take us far away from Chantilly. I will wed him tonight, and then the three of us will leave tomorrow for his vacation home in—"

"No!" I shouted. "No, no! I won't let you do this! I'm going home!"

I turned to run, and Lucinda reached for me, grabbing me by the sleeve.

⸙

"Larkin!"

I blink rapidly and jump at the Reverend Blackwell's voice.

"Are you listening?"

"I—ah . . . yes, Reverend." I turn away from him, lift my tea, and stir it furiously to hide my embarrassment.

"Lucinda only wanted to protect you. And so did I. We meant you no harm. You must believe me when I say this."

I tap the edge of my spoon loudly against my porcelain cup.

"I was heartbroken, finding her . . . in that state. I should have never made her come to me. I should have retrieved both of you from your *papa*'s house myself."

I clank the cup against the table. "But you didn't."

He sighs and sets his own cup down. "I loved your sister, so much that I was willing to become a pariah for her. Do you know what that is, Larkin?"

I press my chin between my hands. "I don't care."

"It's an outcast. A reject. I was willing to become the man known for wedding his own niece. If it would save you, and her, from your *papa*'s temper . . ."

I glare at the reverend. "I don't believe you."

"Do you know why I became Reverend Blackwell?"

I sigh and slump forward in my seat. The blanket falls from my lap.

"It was right after Lucinda died. She had a fascination with apparitions and the afterlife. You must have known this. She was a voracious reader, and she brought my books home often. Your *papa*, it seems, did not approve of her interest. She came to me with her troubles."

"You mean the ghost books belonged to you?"

"Yes, Larkin." Reverend Blackwell rises and walks to his books. He removes a leather-bound book from a shelf and places it in front of me. The words on the cover read *La Lanterne Magique*. "This one was her favorite."

I trace the grooves of the words, running my hand over the coarse texture of the book.

"Yes, she loved the idea of communicating with spirits. When she died, I sought out a *lanterne magique* and began a deep study of the occult. I learned how to use it. I attended services . . . like the one you came to last night."

Reverend Blackwell takes the book from me and cracks it open. The spine creaks as he flips through the pages. "I am hardly a writer, Larkin, but I was so vexed by Lucinda's death, I tried my hand at poetry." He pulls a thin sheet of paper from his book. "I scrawled a few lines and placed them in this book." He holds the paper to me, and I read his handwriting:

> *Oh, the folly of winter and ice:*
> *Your death leaves me in jealousy's vice*

The reverend purses his lips, and I see him swallow. "It is hardly a masterpiece, only the ramblings of a mourning heart. But it was enough—enough for Lucinda to come through." His fingers trembling, Reverend Blackwell unfolds the paper, revealing a wisp of ink below his writing, so subtle it is barely visible on the page.

Bring the one with the guilt in his eyes

Lucinda.

The words are the very same as those she spoke to me.

"Reverend Blackwell!"

"I know, Larkin." He folds the paper and tucks it back between the pages. The book closes with a thump. "I think it's time you spoke with her. It seems she has been waiting for you."

⌖

We walk quickly down the street, past *la boulangerie,* past *le marché,* and past *la bibliothèque* and *l'école.* Reverend Blackwell carries his *lanterne magique* like a suitcase, drawing stares from the *mesdames et messieurs* we pass on our journey. We arrive finally at the alley behind *Bistro Éclairé,* and the reverend opens the door at the back, leading me into his makeshift theater. We are the only two in attendance, and even in the early afternoon, the room appears as dark as it did on the night of the show.

"Come, Larkin." The reverend motions for me to follow him behind the screen. I watch him open the lantern and lift a pipe to a piece of stone inside; the pipe hisses, a flame roars from its end, and the stone alights, illuminating the room and casting the reverend's shadow across the screen, my own beside it. He shuffles a pair of plates, slides one inside the lantern and adjusts it, and then closes the lantern tightly. He waves me to the other side of the screen; with my shadow now absent, a young woman's face appears, waxing and waning in shadow and light.

"Lucinda!"

I hear Reverend Blackwell's voice from behind the screen. "Yes, it is her image. I had it painted on a plate. But she has not arrived yet." The reverend's shadow raises its arms to the ceiling. "Let us pray."

I shudder as a wave of cold hits me. The shadows on the screen morph into thin, needle-like spines over the woman's face.

"Oh, Lucinda, sweet child," Reverend Blackwell moans. "Come forth and rise—I have brought you the one with the guilt in his eyes."

The needle-like shadows begin to move faster, gathering in greater numbers on top of the face, and she fades in and out of view. The spines quickly plummet toward the bottom of the screen.

A blast of frigid air hits me.

So cold.

I hold my arms to my chest and gasp. I do not believe my own eyes. The shadows—they have come alive—they gather in bunches, hanging as icicles, dripping from the edge of the screen.

"Reverend!" I scream and run behind the screen, grasping for him. He turns to me, a look of terror painted on his face—and it is the last image I see. I hear a flicker—and the room is suddenly dark.

"The lantern! It's out!" Reverend Blackwell pulls free from my grasp, and I hear him fumbling with the lantern.

A chill rides up my neck, and I hug my arms tighter against my body. I hear clinks and scrapes. The temperature in the room plummets. I am shivering furiously—my hands, my knees, my teeth shaking against my will. I feel a hand press down on my shoulder, and I sigh. The reverend has reached out to comfort me. Soon the light will return, the air will grow warm again, and the shadows will be gone.

I wait, but chills continue to rack me, penetrating me to the bone. A wisp of icy air tickles the back of my ear. My spine straightens, and the hairs on my neck stand on edge.

The hand. It does not belong to the reverend.

I am paralyzed with fear.

✤

"Let go of me, Lucinda! Let go!"

"Larkin, please! It will all work out! Please, stop!" Lucinda pulled at my coat to stop me, but I tore myself away from her.

"No! I'm going home! I won't be part of this!" I dashed down the stairs quickly, my foot slipping upon ice on the last step. I steadied myself and hopped to the ground.

"Wait, Larkin!"

Lucinda turned to come after me, but I ran down the street as fast as my legs would carry me. Midsprint, I glanced back to see Lucinda's boot catch on the step that had nearly caused me to slip. She spread her arms wide to catch her balance, but it was too late— she tumbled backward, a terrible crack ringing through the air as she landed.

I exhaled sharply, relief washing over me. With the fall slowing her, she would not catch up to me. I rounded the street corner, eager to crawl into my bed and sleep—and wake to find the whole night a dream.

✤

"Larkin . . ." An icy hiss dances in my ear. *"Mon frère. The one who carries guilt in his eyes . . ."*

My teeth chatter, and cold tears stream down my cheeks. "I'm sorry, Lucinda! I didn't mean to leave you! I thought you would be all right, and I would wake up and see you the next morning—"

"Hush, Larkin. Listen to me."

I feel the weight of her hand on my hair, like a heavy fall of snow. I want to run, but my legs are planted firmly in place. Lucinda's breath chills my ear.

150

"Oh, the folly of winter and ice:
My death grips you in jealousy's vice.
Two men carry such guilt in their eyes;
Mourn me no more, 'tis no fault of thine."

I feel the weight of her hand come off me, the chill on my ear and neck beginning to subside.

"I-I don't understand!" I cry. "You're forgiving me? But I left you behind! You would still be alive if I had only come back for you—"

"It is not your fault, Larkin. Think no more of the night of my death. Promise me this, Larkin." Her voice is faint and melodic, like the plink of a music box. *"You must release your guilt for my spirit to pass from this world.* Oncle *Christophe must do the same."*

A sob catches in my throat. The cold is leaving my body, and I stretch my fingers out into the darkness. "I promise, Lucinda. I promise."

"Take care of oncle *Christophe,"* she whispers. *"He must let me go too."*

"Lucinda . . ."

The room erupts into light, and I shield my eyes. My arms and legs tingle, warmth rushing back into them.

"Larkin!" Reverend Blackwell says. "I do not know what happened. The light in the lantern . . . it's never done that before."

The reverend moves quickly toward me, and I feel the weight of his hand on my back. I flinch from the gesture, but remembering Lucinda's words, I do not pull away.

Realizing his action, he pulls back from me suddenly and clears his throat. His brow is folded, his lips twisted with worry.

"Did you see her, Larkin? Lucinda? Shall we summon her again?"

I smile at him softly and reach for his hand, threading my fingers through his. "No, *oncle* Christophe. Let us summon her only through our memories."

Ɛlysium in the Ꮪnow

Celosia Crane

I turned up my coat collar, burrowing as far into my scarf as I possibly could. An icy wind was howling down the street from the harbor, bringing with it the scent of snow and ice.

Up ahead on the street corner, a young girl bravely sang carols, holding her hands out for whatever change those who passed along the streets would give.

Adjusting my shopping basket on my arm, I pulled out my small purse to fish out a few coins. As I approached, I held her gaze for a few seconds and swallowed hard. It was her eyes that grabbed me. Haunted, in her narrow, pinched face.

How long had it been since I stood there in her place? How old was she? Eight? Nine?

"I don't have much, but you need it more than I do." Dropping the coins into her hands, I watched her face light up. "Go buy yourself something warm to eat."

Smiling, she bobbed a slight curtsy. "Thank you, miss."

Her skin was a shade of gray that I was all too familiar with. It was the color of neglect, of not having enough to eat, and of always being too cold.

Unwinding my scarf, I wrapped it around her thin shoulders. "Please, take this."

She clutched my hand for a moment. It was a small claw, icy with cold.

Swallowing the tears that welled in my throat, I met her gaze and saw reflected there the same broken soul I knew could be seen in mine in quieter moments.

"Are you sure, miss?" Her voice trembled, even as her hand released mine to burrow into the warmth of the wool scarf.

Gently touching her head, I smiled. "Stay out of trouble, little one." Clutching my collar more closely about my neck, I continued down the street. Glancing back over my shoulder, I was glad to see the little girl wrapping the scarf about her freezing hands.

The memories were never far away at this time of year. Always cold, always hungry. Never enough clothes to keep warm. The orphanage had been underfunded and never gave us enough to eat, so I had often escaped into the city in hopes of begging enough money to buy something.

Shivering as the wind snaked down my collar, I walked on.

All around me, the shop windows were brightly decorated, filled with gaudy red-and-white toy soldiers, gaily painted dolls in real silk dresses, and other things that delighted small children. Even the jeweler on the corner had made his display more festive, adding brightly colored glass balls and silver tinsel.

That alone was not enough to send me down the path of my childhood memories, but the groups moving up and down the street were: Mothers and fathers holding their children by the hands. Grandparents bearing away their triumphant purchases. Shouts of laughter and belonging cut just as deeply into my soul as the wind cut into my body.

I stepped inside the grocers as the frigid wind picked up again. Taking my list out of my pocket, I scanned the items: butter, flour, milk, and eggs.

Even here, great cheer abounded. Mounds of beautifully bright fruit were piled in their stands, while gaily wrapper crackers and chocolates tempted those who could afford them. But while I was beginning to get some good, reputable trade, rent was still tricky some months. There was no extra money this time of year for trifles.

After purchasing my items, I stepped back outside and began to hurry toward home, thankful that the wind was blowing against my back as I moved away from the harbor.

I'd moved recently into the apartment over my studio. The small one-bedroom flat was large enough that I had set up a small studio for my private works in the parlor, leaving the kitchen and bedroom for living in. Most importantly of all, the space was mine. I did not have to share it with anyone, unless I wished to.

Reaching the door, I lifted the key ring hanging from my chatelaine. Unlocking the door and relocking it behind me, I climbed the narrow flight of stairs on the other side and set my shopping basket down in the warmth of the kitchen.

Removing my hatpin, I laid my hat on the stand and stared at my reflection in the only mirror I owned. Reaching out, I touched the glass. Even now, I sometimes expected my reflection to flinch away.

The cold wind had brought a pale pink flush to my cheeks, but otherwise my skin remained alabaster white. I could trace faint blue vessels beneath the skin of my eyelids and at my temples. Such a change from the warm, sun-kissed complexion I had once taken for granted.

My eyebrows and eyelashes were only a few shades darker than my skin, making my brown eyes seem black in comparison. My hair, which had once been a pretty fawn brown, now lay atop my head in silvery platinum coils. The only things that remained the same were beneath the skin, and even now I barely recognized myself.

I looked like a ghost.

And on many days, I felt like one. The attack was never far from my memory, especially any time I stared into a mirror. The depths of the shadows haunted me: The diaphanous forms of men shifting as streetlamps extinguished, one by one. The last of the gas streetlamps catching the sharp edge of a knife before it guttered and went out.

The knife had glittered in the the fading light as I screamed.

Then he had appeared. A solid avenger. Thanatos, my midnight savior.

Turning back to the table, I began unpacking my shopping. The scrape of metal sounded from the door as a key turned in the lock, drawing my attention as much as the cold draft of air that snuck up the stairs with the door's opening. I heard the rustle of fabric as Thanatos took off his great coat, and then his smoky voice cut through the silence.

"You were gone longer than I had anticipated."

Turning slowly, I felt the sense of security that his presence always brought slowly filling me. It warmed the last of the cold places in my chest.

Before the night of the attack, I had seen few men who even came close to his description. And those had been sailors down at the wharves, unloading cargo from distant lands.

It was no wonder I hadn't noticed him, that night. His skin was the darkest blue-black ebony. His eyes were a brown so deep, they often seemed to reflect the night. Port Apollo was a diverse city, but very few men lived here with skin as dark as his. Black as midnight.

He had been there when I woke after the attack. Now we were trying to figure out who those men were, why they had attacked me, and even more importantly, why they were killing so many people throughout the city.

Shrugging, I knew my smile was halfhearted. "Shopping this time of year always seems to take longer. I feel like there are more people on the streets and clogging the shops."

Moving to the stove, I opened the door before adding another log and poking the embers to stir them back to life. "Would you like some tea?"

The scrape of wood on wood sounded behind me as he pulled a chair away from the simple table. "Yes, that would be lovely. The wind is bone-chilling today."

Closing my eyes, I drew in a breath as fatigue and frustration that didn't belong to me washed through my body and mind. Placing the kettle on the stove, I turned and sank down into the chair opposite him. "Every year, I think the same thing."

He leaned forward, his hands clasped casually about his knee. His ebony skin stood out against the gray of his trouser legs. His dark eyes flashed in the light from the kerosene lamp on the table. "And what is that?"

"That I wish I knew who they were." Clearing my throat, I blinked rapidly against the tears that blurred my vision.

"Your parents?" His voice was soft and kind, breaking the tension I could feel settling in between my shoulder blades.

In truth, I had not known him long. Yet Thanatos was the first person outside the orphanage whom I was comfortable sharing these thoughts with. He had stayed by me when I woke, dazed and confused, faint from blood loss. He hadn't abandoned me as I fought the fever that accompanied the sharp cut to my upper arm.

But it was more than that.

The attack had brought us together and bound us in ways neither of us could explain. Without trying, I knew when he was near. I could feel his strong emotions, almost as though they were my own. The connection forged between us that night was strange, yet strangely comfortable. Almost familiar.

The kettle on the stove sang its cheerful tune, bringing me back from my remembrances. I set down two mugs, along with the bottle of milk. "I'm sorry, but I don't have any sugar right now."

Thanatos flashed me his white smile. "Do not worry, Makaria. I like it better without."

After a few minutes, Thanatos broke the silence. "I see you painted her again." He'd turned his head toward my studio, where on the easel sat the portrait of a beautifully exotic woman.

Rich brown hair gleamed in the light from the bay windows. Golden skin reflected the sun's bounty, while a mischievous smile played about the painted lips.

I set my cup down on the table. "I don't know who she is, but she keeps coming to me in my dreams." I could feel a frown tightening my forehead as I stared at the canvas. "I feel like I should know her. That she is familiar to me somehow. But I have never seen her before."

Thanatos set his mug down on the table, the ceramic cup colliding with a faint clink. "How many times now, Makaria?"

I stared across the table at him, and our gazes connected and held.

This man, Thanatos, had come into my life like a whirlwind. Now, as I stared into his dark eyes, my heart began to pound, and I struggled to draw a normal breath.

With an effort, I drew in a slow breath. "How many times has she walked my dreams?" Swallowing hard against the lump in my throat, I could feel my chest tightening. A hard knot seemed to live within my breast these days, as though someone were squeezing my heart, tightly. "Since I was old enough to realize there is a difference between dreams and reality. And that some children had mothers and fathers and nice homes to live in." My vision blurred. Blinking rapidly, I fought this fresh onslaught of tears.

Thanatos stretched a hand out toward me across the table. For a moment, I stared at it. Then I set my hand in his. Warmth seeped into my hand from his as his fingers curled around mine, holding them close. My hand, lying in his now, looked pearlescent in contrast.

There we were, opposite sides of the spectrum held together in an intangible way that neither of us could explain. I squeezed his hand gently before letting go.

"How does she appear to you?"

"She is kind and loving, nurturing and gentle." Lifting my mug, I took another drink of my cooling tea to fight off more tears.

"Could you have a faint memory of this woman? Maybe from before you were placed in the orphanage?"

I stood up and walked across the room to the easel. I stared into eyes that were as familiar to me as my own. "I don't know how that could be, but maybe. I don't remember anything from that time. Only the cold and hunger of those early years."

Wrapping his arms around me, Thanatos placed his chin on my

shoulder and stared into the face of a woman I had painted hundreds of times now.

"How have your dreams been lately?" His voice was soothing, his presence comforting in the middle of this strangeness. With his chest against my back, I could feel his voice as it rumbled out of his body.

Shivering, I leaned more strongly into his embrace. "Stronger and more vivid than I ever remember."

"And you are still writing them down?"

Nodding, I found it hard to break away from the portrait's gaze. "Yes. I keep hoping I'll learn something useful." I couldn't shake the feeling that she was trying to tell me something.

Warm breath gusted against my cheek, his words slow as though he were thinking. "This is a bad time of year for both of us. We are both mourning something."

I nodded, unwilling to speak. Thanatos pulled back slightly, turning me slowly until I faced him. His hand brushed my chin, lifting my head so I met his gaze.

"You, the family you never knew. Me, the sister who was twisted and torn from me." Leaning forward, he pressed his forehead against mine. "But, Makaria, you aren't alone anymore. Remember that."

The warmth and certainty of his words washed through me. Blinking, I felt tears spill over onto my cheeks. The warmth of his affection filled the cold emptiness in my chest and slowly spread through me. I smiled, even though my lips were trembling.

"No, I'm not."

Burying my face in his frock coat, I breathed in the scent of him. The warmth of his hand cupping the back of my head added another layer of security to his words. Together, they helped fight back the cold, nebulous thoughts that came whenever I tried to envision the future.

"Whatever this is that's connecting us, Makaria, we'll figure it out. We'll figure it all out. I promise." I felt his hand flutter over my arm, where the grisly scar reminded me of that terrifying evening.

Pulling back, I met his gaze. "All of it?" The dreams? The secret society that he believed was behind these attacks? Our mysterious connection? My mysterious transformation?

There had been nothing but confusion in our lives these last two weeks. Suddenly, I wanted everything to be normal and boring again. Except for Thanatos—I still wanted him in my life.

He nodded seriously. "Yes, all of it."

Closing my eyes, I listened to the beat of his heart and the sounds of people passing in the streets below. Fighting back a new fear, I held him tightly, breathing in his scent to steady myself.

After a while, Thanatos pulled back. "I will be out tonight." He gently brushed at my forehead. "Will you be all right?"

I bit my lip. "Have you found any more clues?"

He shook his head, then cocked it to the side. "There have been no new leads. I know that if I could just find the knife they use, that would give us so much more to work with. But until then . . ." He shrugged. "I still have to try." His gaze remained holding mine, waiting for my answer.

Turning, I faced the stove. "I'll be fine, Thanatos. The new locks are strong. The new spring-loaded system works amazingly well."

"I'm glad."

Smiling, I squared my shoulders and turned to watch him pull his great coat back on again. "Perhaps I'll have a new dream for you to read when you return."

Holding his hat in his hands, he looked at me, his forehead drawn into a slight frown. "The intensity of your dreams has me a little worried, Makaria. I can feel them, and your struggle, even while you sleep." Shaking his head, Thanatos walked back to me, pressing a kiss to the center of my forehead. "Be careful, Makaria."

The evening had changed to night by the time he left. Wrapping a blanket around myself, I curled up in the oversized armchair that lived in the corner of the kitchen. I leaned my head back against the chair, allowing the warmth of the stove to make me drowsy. The kitchen was the warmest room in the apartment, and tonight the sound of the logs crackling inside the stove was a comforting symphony. Closing my eyes, I drifted toward sleep.

The dream reached out to me, even before my eyes were entirely closed. It wrapped around me like tendrils of fog from the sea, enveloping me and drawing me in.

"Makaria! There you are!" The melodious voice chides me gently as though I've been hiding for a long time. I turn around slowly. I already know who it will be.

She is just as beautiful as I remember. Long, curling mahogany hair, skin that glows with the health and life of summertime. But it's her eyes—the way the light shifts in them, dappled green one moment, brown the next—that always catches me off guard.

This time, she is wearing an elaborate ballgown in the current fashion. The rich crimson satin rustles as she moves and glows in the light from a gold-and-crystal chandelier. Deep rubies, the color of pomegranate seeds, circle her neck and hang from her ears. She holds out a black-gloved hand toward me. "The ball cannot begin without you."

I glance down and find that I am dressed in a pale silver gown covered in gray lace and sparkling with diamante. I place my hand in hers, my white silk glove standing out against her black.

I am back. And a small part of me rejoices.

The darkly gorgeous gothic mansion of my dream world is no less impressive tonight. All the wall sconces are lit, illuminating the rich silk wallpaper and the deep, luxurious carpets. Indeed, black, gray, and deep, rich crimson seem to be the prevailing colors here.

The trains of our dresses rustle behind us, cascading down off our bustles as we slowly descend the stairs toward the ballroom.

And then, there he is.

He waits at the bottom, his face lifted and flushed with joy. Tall with broad shoulders, he's dressed impeccably in a black frock coat, with a glowing white satin vest and a bright chain of office about his shoulders. His hessian boots gleam as brightly as obsidian.

"Where have you been hiding yourselves away?" Smiling, he holds open his arms. "Come to me, my blessing."

Releasing the woman's hand, I pick up my skirts and run forward into the outstretched arms. Arms of a man who feels so familiar to me, and yet so strange.

"Makaria, wake up." A warm hand shaking me by the shoulder tore me away from the glittering ballroom, where couples had spun across the floor to the sound of an orchestra.

An orchestra the likes of which I had never heard before.

"Thanatos?" Blinking, my vision cleared. Tears tightened my throat as I came awake. In my chest, the tightness made it hard to breathe normally, as the reality of my small kitchen surrounded me once again.

"You were dreaming again."

I closed my eyes, leaning my head back against the chair. It was a statement, not a question. I could feel his concern washing through me as he crouched before my chair.

"Yes," I replied. His hand cupped my cheek. Opening my eyes, I met his gaze. "Thanatos, there are times I don't want to wake up." The tears filling my eyes spilled over onto my cheeks. "I want to stay in the dream, with them. Why is this happening to me?"

"I felt the dream, Makaria." His thumb brushed across my cheek. "For some reason, these dreams are coming across our connection more and more strongly." Picking up my hand, he kissed the back of it. "I hate that this is happening to you too." Standing, he held out both hands. "Come to bed, Makaria. I don't have any answers for you tonight."

I let him pull me to my feet. Standing, we faced each other in the silent kitchen, and I stepped forward, burying my face in his chest as the tears escaped. His arms wrapped around me, pulling me close. He pressed his cheek against the top of my head and just held me. No, we had no answers tonight. But we did have each other.

Carolers sang on the street corners as the sea whipped itself into a great icy inferno. Most of the shoppers had disappeared as the weather continued to worsen. In my downstairs studio, the life-size portrait I'd been working on was almost complete. It had to be finished and dry in time for the lady to present it as a gift to her husband for Christmas.

She was tall and coldly regal, and not even a tightly laced corset had been much help in defining her waist. This made my job even more difficult, for it was often the way, to flatter one's patrons with unrealistic paintings. Sighing, I set my brush down in a container of linseed oil and stepped back, taking in the whole work. I had managed, without lying too much, to enhance her shape beyond what it truly was. Now she stood before me, a regal woman in her late forties.

Brushing my hands across my smock, I nodded, satisfied. "Finally finished."

I rubbed the back of my neck. Today, it felt like a marble pillar. The tightness in my muscles only reminded me of my dreams.

Closing my eyes and letting silence wrap around me, I felt warmth rush across the connection in my mind. "Thanatos. My midnight savior." A flush rushed up my throat and into my cheeks as I jumped, having spoken out loud. The murmured words almost bounced off the walls in the stillness of the studio. The new gramophone I had been able to purchase a few months ago had finished playing its engraved disk over an hour ago, and I hadn't changed it, too focused had I been on finishing the portrait.

Not much else lived in my studio space. I had rented it for the large glass windows at the front, which let in a beautiful amount of light and the high ceilings. Perfect for the kind of portraits I had been receiving an increasing number of commissions for.

In the remaining space, a settee, a few wingback chairs, and a chaise lounge provided my subjects places to rest while they were not posing for their portraits, as well as a place for me to talk business with my clients.

All that was left on this particular commission was to place my signature in the bottom corner. Raising the easel, I dipped a tiny brush into a small pot of gold paint and began to form the illuminated letter I had taken as my artist's signature.

The silence was often a blessing, as I could shut out the world while I worked. But more and more frequently, the dream world slipped into my thoughts throughout the day. So did Thanatos, for that matter, and the Cleste society—the secret society of men who had attacked me that fateful night.

Shaking my head, I finished my signature and replaced the lid on the expensive gold paint. Walking over to the door, I looked out at the brave souls who dared traverse the city streets. We were in for an epic storm, but Christmas was Christmas.

Turning the key in the lock, I flipped the sign to *Closed* before turning and staring back at my coldly elegant painted companion. I was done for the day and ready to curl up by the stove in my kitchen with a cup of tea. Already, the afternoon shadows were turning dark and the storm sent down sheets of icy rain to turn the pavements into dangerous ice rinks. The wind shrieked and howled as it tore down the streets and alleyways, taking me back again. Back to a time when I thought I would never be warm again.

Walking slowly up to my apartment, I unlocked the door and stoked the fire, then sank down into the chair, covering my face with my hands. The memories clung to me: typhus breaking out, children dying all around me. I had survived, but why? Surely there had to be a reason.

"Who am I? Where did I come from? Why am I still here?" As I cried out, the words seemed to echo around my head in the quiet of the space.

Behind my closed lids, winking gems the color of pomegranate dazzled my eyes. Warm hands and happy smiles taunted me.

Every night, visions of a happy family haunted me. Of beautiful, loving parents.

"But you're not real!" The tears came hard and fast. "You haunt me and tease the corners of my mind every night. But I always wake up in the end. I always come back here." I shook, and my nose dripped almost as fast as the tears that fell from my eyes. "It isn't fair!"

Pulling my legs up onto the chair, I buried my face in my skirts and sobbed. My tears slowed as the dream reached out for me. More forcefully this time, the tendrils wrapped around my limbs, pulling me toward the shadowy forms awaiting me.

"Makaria, my love, will you bring me the music box from my dressing table?" She sits on the edge of a gorgeously dressed four-poster bed. Red and gold brocade curtains hang about it, tied back by twisted golden ropes.

I walk to the equally stunning dressing table and pick up the item. It is a small gold creation in the shape of a four-petal flower. It carries inlaid rubies, garnets, and pearls on its surfaces, depicting a luscious pomegranate fruit.

Taking it to her, I watch as she takes a key from around her neck, where it hangs on a delicate gold chain, and winds the music box slowly. A gently haunting melody fills the air. After a moment, she begins to sing along with the tune.

I close my eyes as the music wraps around me. Her hand pulls me down onto the bed beside her.

"Makaria, why are you so sad?"

Her words catch me off guard. Opening my eyes, I blink back tears. "Because I'm only dreaming." The words come out low and hoarse. "You're not really here." A sob catches in my throat. "And I really want you to be here."

Her soft hand brushes my cheek. "Am I not?" Her face echoes a similar sadness. "Do you have any idea how long your father and I have been searching for you?" Her voice throbs in the stillness, and I realize we are alone in her chambers.

I shake my head. "No, you don't understand. I'm an orphan. I don't have parents."

Her other hand cups my cheek, turning my face to meet her

gaze. "Don't you?" She brushes my platinum hair back off my forehead. "Listen to your heart, Makaria."

She lays her hand directly over the scar from the cursed Cleste knife. The very wound that has changed my life irrevocably. It throbs beneath her touch.

"What is happening to me?" The cry bursts from my lips before I can stop it.

"Oh, my darling," She pulls me into her embrace. "You are awakening. And your father and I are so happy. He has missed you dreadfully."

Pulling back, I meet her gaze, fighting my confusion. "What do you mean, awakening?"

Her smiling face begins to fade, even as she opens her mouth to explain.

◇

"No!" Jumping out of my chair, I paced the kitchen. "You were just about to tell me! Please, please! I need to know what is going on."

Footsteps pounded up the stairs, and Thanatos burst through the door. "Makaria, are you all right?"

He paused in the doorway for a second, then strode across the room, wrapping his arms around me. "I'm here. We'll figure this out." I felt him press a kiss to my hair. "I promise."

"I dreamed of her again, Thanatos. She was about to tell me what is going on. Then—" I hiccupped. "I woke up."

I pulled back, swiping angrily at my cheeks. "She said I was awakening. What is that supposed to mean?"

His ebony forehead crinkled in confusion. "I'm not entirely certain, but I do think we are getting closer to finding out."

I turned to him. "You found something out?"

He nodded, taking my hand and leading me into the cold parlor. "Yes, I'm learning things." Shaking his head, he turned to look out the window at the winter sunset that stain the sky crimson. "Oh, Makaria, it's a very tangled web. The conspiracy goes much deeper than either of us initially thought."

I gripped his hand. "We'll find our way. We have to."

Turning back from the window, he faced me. A slow smile crossed his face as he raised a hand to brush at my cheek. "Yes, together we will find a way."

Two days remained before Christmas. Citywide curfew was still being strictly enforced. Thankfully though, only a small handful of new deaths had been announced over the last few weeks. It appeared that the cold was slowing them down just as much as everyone else.

The newspapers still clung to their sensational headlines, claiming vampires walked among us. But most people had ceased to believe that. Now, all thoughts were turned toward family and home.

I still had occasional nightmares about them, as they had come at me that night. Their forms had been diaphanous. How they had appeared to break apart like smoke, gusting across the pavement as they attacked me with that accursed blade!

Thanatos was busy during the evenings, more often than not. His search was beginning to turn up answers. And while my dreams were becoming stronger, I was not afraid of them.

We both had our reasons for searching for answers to what had happened in the past. And neither of us could explain, still, how the bond between us had formed. It had become such a tether of safety for me. This presence, even when he was not physically with me—I clung to it. For the first time in many years, I delighted in the closeness it brought.

I feared the day we both had the answers we sought. The day he left me. Would the connection remain once we found our answers?

That night, as I made a cup of chamomile tea before heading to bed, I felt him. Satisfaction and relief washed across the connection so strongly that my knees nearly buckled beneath my weight.

Picking up my tea, I returned to the bedroom. I lay down and curled up with my feet on the blanket-wrapped stone I had heated in the oven.

Facing the prospect of the dreams' return, I welcomed it. As I drank my tea, its warmth coursed down my throat, filling my stomach. Lying back against the pillows, I closed my eyes.

And the dream was there.

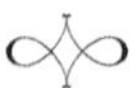

A series of elaborate glass houses stand before me. And there she is, walking out of one to greet me. "Come, you must see my latest success!"

She pulls me into the beautiful greenhouse, which is filled with plants of various kinds. She pulls me all the way to the back of the room, her excitement palpable. There, on a table in a simple terracotta pot, a single rosebush blooms. The delicate white flowers are covered with deep burgundy splotches, like blood on fallen snow.

"Isn't it beautiful?" Her voice is hushed as she reaches out a glowing golden finger to brush the delicate petals. "Just like you are." Turning, she brushes the same hand across my cheek. "My delicate rose." Leaning forward, she brushes a kiss across my forehead. "You are stronger than you realize."

Laughing, she grabs my hand again. "Come along. Your father is getting impatient." It's hard not to become excited, her delight is so infectious.

Stepping out of the greenhouse, I see him waiting for us. His eyes zero in on me. I study him as we slowly approach—this man she calls my father.

He has an oval face with a strong jaw and cheekbones. A fine straight nose is centered between equally strong black eyebrows. He is a study of contrasts. His face appears stern and cold, but his dark eyes glow with warmth as his lips curl into a smile of delight.

"Look at my beautiful girls."

I stop a few steps away from him and hold his gaze as he continues speaking.

"You were stolen away and hidden from us. We have searched for you for what feels like ages." He shakes his head, and I can see tears gathering in his eyes. "Not even Zeus was able to give his assistance."

I blink but remain quiet.

He swallows, and when he speaks again, his voice is deep in the stillness. "Then something must have happened because you began appearing to us."

I nod. "I was attacked by a secret society and wounded by a ritualistic knife."

He turns his head to meet her gaze, where she stands beside me, his face suddenly shadowed. "I see I should be paying more attention to what is going on in the human realm."

For a long moment, the silence stretches out between us. Finally, she touches my arm. "Is that when you began to see us?" Her voice is soft and low.

I nod slowly, processing the new idea. "I've always seen you in my dreams, but the colors weren't always so bright. It was as though you were just beyond my vision. Now when I sleep, I dream of you. Of being here. Wherever here is." Looking around, I see the exterior of a massive gothic mansion behind us. Beyond that, there are no landmarks to give me any clues.

"You were so young when they stole you from us," he says.

She touches my arm again, turning me to face her. "Just know, Makaria. This is more than a dream." She lifts her hand and touches my face. "Your dreams are just how you are getting here right now."

Around us, snow begins to fall, slowly and gently. I stare back and forth between them. "But where are we? Why don't I recognize anything? Why can't I see beyond the walls of the house?"

He chuckles. "Shadows like to play tricks on the eye, down here."

"Down here?" I rub my hand over my face. "Why are you always talking in riddles? Can you please just tell me what is going on?"

Sighing, he reaches out a hand and brushes my cheek. "Oh, my blessed one, I wish I could. But the time is not right yet. You are not ready."

I close my eyes, leaning into the touch. His deep voice seems to flow around me. "Just know, Makaria, that you will see us often in your dreams. We will help you as much as we are allowed. Even here, there are restrictions to our power."

I open my eyes and meet his dark gaze. "I still don't understand."

He smiles, squeezing my hand. "I know, but you will someday."

All around us, the ground is now covered in a light blanket of snow, but none has accumulated on any of our clothing.

As I watch, he reaches inside his jacket and pulls out a small package. "We are able to give you this." He holds out the present. "Remember, Makaria."

"Remember . . ."

∝⟩○

I opened my eyes to see dawn's light breaking through my window. Beside me, Thanatos lay breathing evenly. Lifting the blanket carefully, I slipped out of bed and walked into the kitchen.

Adding wood to the fire, I stirred up the coals and ashes from last night and shivered as I waited for the fire to catch and the heat to begin radiating through the small room. Filling the tea kettle, I wrapped myself in a blanket, content to wait. I loved the stillness of early morning, curled up in my chair drinking tea before the city woke to the hustle and bustle.

A short while later, as I sipped the hot tea, my gaze caught on a small package lying on the table. It was identical in shape and paper to the one given to me in my dream the evening before.

My breath catching in my chest, I picked it up and turned it over in my hands hesitantly. There was my name, written in her beautiful handwriting. I knew each loop and curve as well as if it were my own.

Untying the ribbon, I carefully unfolded the paper. A deep-red box glowed in the early morning light. I lifted the lid and set it aside.

Staring at the contents, I forced myself to draw in a breath. "How is this possible?" My whisper seemed like a shout in the stillness.

In my hand was a small gold music box. It looked identical in shape and design to the one she had played for me in my dream. Taking the key, I wound it slowly, already sure of the tune it would play.

As the familiar notes began to waft through the still air, I found I remembered the words as well. Sinking down into my chair, I held the beautiful, delicate music box and sang:

Our child sleeps, as pale as snow.
My love, please guard her, here below.
I cannot stay.

A mother's grief, a world in pain.
A father's order. I can't remain.
I don't want to go.

The time is near, the hour has come.
For my return up above.
I cannot stay.
I don't want to go.
My love, please guard her, here below.

Tears slipped down my face. For the first time, her pain echoed to me through the words of a song I now understood she had written and composed herself. The music box continued to play its haunting melody.

As I stared down at it, a new awareness began to expand within me.

A sound at the doorway made me look up. Thanatos stood there. Silently, he came over to where I was sitting and perched on the arm of the chair. I leaned against him as his arm wrapped around my shoulders.

"Do you think it snows in hell?" I looked up at him solemnly, my tears still wet on my cheeks.

His face echoed mine, a glimmer of tears in his own eyes. "I believe Hades can make it do whatever he wishes. It is his realm."

I nodded, turning the key to hear the haunting melody once more. Thanatos began to run his hand over my hair. "Where did you get that?"

I gave a choking laugh. "You wouldn't believe me if I told you."

"You are learning more, aren't you?" His voice was calm, his touch soothing. His voice was suddenly knowing.

"I'm beginning to believe, if that's what you're asking."

He looked at me curiously. "Believe what?"

"Why the Cleste weapon did not kill me as it has everyone else." Even as I spoke the words, the certainty of it expanded within my mind. "Because it could not."

He smiled, leaning down to press a soft kiss to my lips. "No, it couldn't. I came to that conclusion myself last night. In a while, I will share with you what I uncovered." His smile is tender. "But for now, let's just be."

Outside, the sounds of people moving up and down the street began: street vendors hawking their wares and the bustle of the final days before Christmas. The storm had blown itself out the night before. Now the sounds filtered in through the windows as we sat together in the kitchen. Leaning my head against his shoulder, I felt his arm wrap around me.

Here in the warm haven of my kitchen, we could just be. And the knowledge of who we were did not matter. This morning, it was enough to lean my head against him and feel his arm around me.

In a short period of time, we would have much to do. Much to set right. Many to bring to justice. But this morning, we sat together drinking tea and talking in low tones. Certainty began to fill me as I watched Thanatos move around the kitchen.

I would never be alone again.

Missing in a Yuletide Blizzard

K. N. Gemme

Chapter 1 (Diana)

I stood staring out the family room window, watching the snow softly fall as I sipped a cup of hot chocolate. Most liked the bitter taste of coffee, but I preferred the dark bittersweet blend that came from the cocoa bean.

I took another sip of the dark drink. I almost spit it out when I saw a rugged man, almost seven feet tall with a Viking build and a thick black beard, chasing after a small blonde-haired girl with rosy cheeks and mischief in her mismatched gray eyes. She was trying very hard to reach the forest at the edge of the clearing, but no matter how fast she ran, her small legs would never outrun his longer stride. He moved with the grace and speed of a wild beast.

Sure enough, within a few short strides, the man scooped her up into his arms. He caught a small white-and-gray bundle as it fell out of the girl's hood. As the little creature climbed back into the hood, the girl's face lit up with giggles that could not be heard through the window. Warmth filled my soul.

"So this is what Mother Nature does when she's not messing with the weather," said a soft feminine voice from behind me.

"Shh, do not tell anyone. I have a reputation to uphold," I whispered back, as if I were hiding a big secret.

"You fool no one, Diana," she argued.

I turned to smile at her innocently.

Elaina was a beautiful and elegant woman. Tall and lean, she had pale skin and a knowing smile. Most would think that her lavender hair or kind amethyst eyes would be her most striking features, but in fact it was the soft shimmer of light that always surrounded her. It marked her as not human.

The truth was, none of us were human. We belonged to the races that came from the Unknown. Some could shift into other creatures, some had power over the elements, while others could see into a being's very soul. Like the many different birds that graced the Earth, just as varied were the races of the Unknown.

"I love watching them together. When Alec is with her, he's not the Alpha. He's just a loving father of a wild little girl who loves to laugh."

"He is a good father," Elaina stated, watching as they played in the snow. "I see it started snowing last night. That must mean the storm is ready. Will the guests have time to get here before the blizzard truly hits?"

My eyes shifted to look at the thin layer of white already covering the ground. When I had first come to this planet through the Veil, it had been nothing more than a deserted rock. It had taken many, many years and a lot of magic to nurture and tie the seasons into its natural cycle. Over time, it was able to maintain the seasons on its own, with only minimal help from me and my Elemental Guardians to keep them balanced within each rotation.

For example, this year. The creatures of summer had had a little too much fun, which had caused a warmer-than-usual autumn. This, in turn, had caused those who lived in winter to have difficulty waking up. So I had to step in and craft a storm meant to rejuvenate everything winter.

This blizzard had taken me weeks to craft, and now the clouds were so full, they were starting to overflow. "The storm will start tonight when we light the Yule Log. Most of the guests are already here: you, Myst, and the other Guardians, the Shadows and their mates. The last few should be here within the next couple hours."

"Oh, good. Are they all staying through the storm?" she asked.

"All those who cannot move through the Dark or create magical doors home are," I said, teasing her. "They wish not to risk the storm."

Elaina was a spirit. She could return to her home at any time with merely a thought. She could also create portals to anywhere she wished, using the Unknown as a bridge. All she needed was two doors to use as anchors. Aside from the Guardians, I was the only other being who had this gift. Elaina usually only created doorways for her sister, Myst, who was unable to travel at will.

"This is true. I forget sometimes." Humor filled her words, but I could hear the sadness just underneath. It wasn't always easy for her, living alongside a world she could see and hear but never touch.

"Is there much left to do?" I asked, trying to change the subject. She had reminded me that I should be doing something productive to get ready, anyway.

"No, but Calder could use your help in the kitchen. I believe he and Drake are arguing over dinner."

I sighed. "That won't end well. I should go mediate." Fire and water never mixed well. With a final reluctant look at the merry fun outside, I turned and walked away from the window.

Chapter 2 (Diana)

The last bit of preparations did not take as long as I had expected. All that was left was to finish decorating the tree, and there was one little girl who I knew would want to help.

Seeing they were no longer outside, I went in search of my mate and daughter.

I found them in the family room, getting warm by the large fireplace. Alec's large frame was stretched out on the floor in front of it, placing himself between it and Evanna as she played with a small white-and-gray, leopard-spotted kitten. The kitten was the little bundle I had watched fall out of Evanna's hood earlier. Poor Ebony—Evanna was always getting her into trouble.

"There you are," I said, walking into the room. I caught Ebony looking from Alec to Evanna, then back again . . .

Then again, that kitten was more a partner in crime than a victim.

Ebony gave a small innocent meow when she caught me staring.

"Hello, Ebony," I greeted.

Looking up, Evanna placed her small finger over her lips. "Shh, Papa is sleeping."

I looked over at the prone body, just in time to see Alec's lip twitch. Then I felt his humor and affection brush my mind.

Alec was currently on his back, one arm under his head and the other resting across his chest. His eyes were closed, and he was breathing evenly. It didn't surprise me that Evanna thought he was sleeping; anyone who walked in would think so. However, as long as our daughter was in his presence, I knew he was aware of every movement.

"Is that so? Then we must not disturb him." Playing along, I crouched down in front of her and quietly asked, "Would you like to help me finish decorating the tree?"

"Yes!" she squealed excitedly and jumped up, only to cover her mouth and look over at her father.

When he didn't move, she leaned in close to whisper in my ear. "Yes."

I took advantage of her closeness to steal a hug. She still smelled like fresh snow from her time outside. When she started to wiggle, wanting to be let go, I placed a raspberry-like kiss on her cheek. I laughed when she finally escaped my arms with a "Mama, stop it!"

"I'm sorry. I won't do it again," I lied. Contentment filled my mind, which continued to betray that Alec was awake.

"Mama, before we decorate the inside tree, we need to go for a walk in the outside trees." Evanna pointed toward the forest.

"Maybe after the storm—"

"But it might be too late by then," she whined, flopping her arm down with all the frustration a six-year-old could have.

"I'm sorry, but it will have to wait. We have guests, and we need to finish the tree before the rest of them arrive." Then, trying to distract her by changing the subject, I asked, "Did you and Ebony have fun outside with Papa today?"

"Yes! Papa made a snow angel! It was *huge*, Mama." She giggled, taking the bait and relaxing as she stretched her arms wide in a failed attempt to show me how big her father's snow angel was.

"Compared to you, my little snowflake, I'm sure it was. Did you make one?"

"Yes! I made it right on top of Papa's. It almost fit in his belly!" She giggled again, clearly picturing the funny scene, before turning toward the door. "Do you want to go see? We can go for a walk in the trees after."

Just at that moment, the man in question opened his eyes and sat up. "Anna, your mother said not today, and I told you the same outside."

"But—" she started with a stubbornness she had gotten from both her father and me.

"No," he said sternly.

I expected her to continue whining or to put up a fight, but instead she stayed quiet. There was a determined look on her young face that I couldn't quite decipher. Before I had a chance to really examine it, Alec shifted, catching my attention. "Hello, love."

His voice was like the grinding of dark chocolate, gravelly and rich, with a smooth bittersweet finish that I would never get tired of. I looked into his steel-gray eyes, and for just a moment, I forgot where we were. In all my years, I'd never seen a shade like it, and they pulled me into their depths every time. I couldn't stop myself from leaning in to give him a soft kiss.

"Gross!"

I looked over to see Evanna covering Ebony's eyes with one hand and her own with the other. "One day, my little snowflake, you will know this feeling."

Her eyes grew wide in a look of pure horror. "No, I won't!"

I heard a deep rumble next to me as Alec tried to hide a laugh.

"Since you're awake, would you like to help us finish decorating the tree?" I asked him, trying unsuccessfully to hide my own laughter at our daughter's horror.

"I should check in with the Shadows, make sure the cabin is secure for tonight," he said as he got to his feet, easily picking his small daughter up as he rose.

"Oh, please, Papa! Help me reach the top? *Please?*" she pleaded, grabbing his face with her small hands to get his attention.

I saw in his eyes the moment he gave in. *"You are so wrapped around her little finger."*

The corner of his mouth jerked, showing he had heard my silent comment but refused to acknowledge it, which only made my smile widen.

Holding Evanna with one arm, he reached down with the other to help me to my feet. "All right, I'll help you with the top, then I must check the grounds."

Once I was on my feet again, Alec turned toward the door.

"Don't forget Ebony!" Evanna cried out before he managed to take two steps. She was pointing at the tiny kitten, who was currently attacking a pinecone.

"I've got her." I reached down to pick up the small kitten. She clutched the pinecone in her small claws, still chewing on it aggressively.

"Now where did you manage to find that?" I asked her, attempting to take it from her.

"Mine," a small, squeaky feline voice growled in my head as little claws latched on tighter.

"Well, look who's finally found her voice." Surprised, I lifted her in front of my face to get a better look at her. At first glance, she looked like a typical fluffball of a kitten, with nothing to mark her as unusual. Only her mismatched eyes proclaimed she was special.

Her left eye was a dark steel gray, the same shade as Alec's eyes, while her right eye was a striking silver gray. Evanna had the exact same mismatched eyes. The unique similarity proved that they were familiar and charge.

"Mama, she's always been able to talk. Duh." Evanna giggled, clearly thinking my comment was silly.

Technically, she was correct; all familiars could communicate with mindspeech, and Ebony was no different. Only when they were older and stronger could they communicate with anyone beyond the person they were bonded to.

"You are correct, snowflake, but she wasn't old enough to project her voice and talk to the rest of us yet. It looks like that has changed." I scratched the kitten under her neck, making her purr and finally drop the pinecone. "It's nice to finally hear your voice, Ebony."

Even though she looked like a tiny kitten, Ebony had been born the same day as Evanna. Unlike normal cats, Ebony would grow at the same rate Evanna did. The familiar bond would make sure they reached maturity together in their early thirties. At that point, they would stop aging physically, and their powers would begin to grow beyond what they could do now. As her powers grew, Ebony, like all familiars, would learn to keep her charge grounded and protect her from holding onto too much magic. Without one's familiar, one risked getting lost in the magic. In that way, Liealia, my familiar, had saved my life many times.

"Mama."

I looked over to find Evanna content in her father's arms while holding out her own, silently asking me to give her Ebony. Their obvious desire to always be near one another meant their bond was strong. Eventually, they wouldn't need to be so close all the time. Prime example, Liealia was currently lounging in the kitchen, hoping Drake or Calder would give her a bite of whatever they were cooking.

When I handed her over, Ebony climbed into her usual spot, tucked into Evanna's hood. I could just see her nose poking out from beyond her hair.

"Okay, let's go decorate this tree!" I said.

Chapter 3 (Diana)

Since the birth of our daughter, the Alpha in Alec had been very selective about whom he allowed near our home. It wasn't often that so many stayed at our cabin, but with the storm, he had agreed to let them as long as he could choose who came.

Due to the Earth's large size and the need to patrol all of it, Alec had created smaller packs run by alphas and had given them territories to control. He himself had gathered a few of the strongest, ones with no desire to lead, and created a personal pack of his own, known as his Shadows. They would forever be tied to his soul in a Shadow Bond.

These five men had arrived over the last two days: Kage, with his mate, Lucina; Ozul, with his mate, Natela; Tirich, with his mate, Photine; and the brothers Draven and Druvish. Though their own homes were scattered within a five-minute run from our cabin, they had decided it was safer for everyone to stay for the duration of the storm.

Elaina and Myst had arrived earlier in the day with the four other Elemental Guardians: Drake, Mason, Raiden, and Calder. Unlike the rest of the guests, they would be leaving tonight. They didn't want to leave the island they lived on and the secrets they protected unguarded for long.

Aside from these trusted men and women, there were only a handful of other pack members from the surrounding territories whom Alec had invited to stay. Most I had met but interacted with very little. One in particular was an interesting addition to the invite list: the young Marcus.

Although I'd met him a few times and Alec had mentioned him more frequently in the last few months, this was first time he'd been invited to one of our holiday gatherings. It was also the first time Evanna had met him, and she seemed fascinated with him.

Interesting.

When all the guests had finally arrived, the cabin filled with laughter and joyous conversation. Sadly, none of them had children of their own, so Evanna was the only child among a sea of adults. Not that that seemed to bother her. She was used to the Guardians and Shadows being around, so she was content with telling her adventures to whichever one would listen.

Dinner was served, and the Yule Log was lit. Evanna found it quite exciting when I allowed her to attempt to light it with her magic. She wasn't quite strong enough to do it on her own, but with my help, she managed. As it started to burn, I unleashed a final burst of magic, releasing the blizzard.

We all watched it for a time before wandering off into groups. I found myself sitting by the fire with Lucina, Natela, and Photine, chatting about our mates, when Evanna came running over.

"Mama, Mama! Look what Uncle Drake gave me!" she squealed. She bounced on her feet, unable to contain her excitement, and held out her hands.

A deep-rustic-red dragon scale was cupped between her two small hands. "Wow, that was very nice of him. Did you say thank you?"

"Yes! It's so warm." She hugged it close.

"Do you know why it's warm?"

"Because Uncle Drake breathed fire into it," she said, giving me a proud smile. "Like when Uncle Calder makes the blue scales cold."

"That's one way to explain it," I agreed, trying not to laugh. She was so smart for her age yet was still so full of innocence. One day, she would understand the Guardians, but that could wait until she was older. Right now, I wanted her to keep the joy in the magic.

"I'm going to go add it to the other ones. I think this one is the reddest." She ran off to her room, where she kept all her little treasures. She had gained quite a few new ones tonight.

"Make it quick!" I hollered after her. "It's almost time for bed, and you need to say good night to everyone." My words fell on deaf ears; she was too excited to listen.

"If Drake keeps giving her scales, he's not going to have any left." Alec wrapped his strong arms around me from behind, placing a kiss on my cheek.

"He knows they keep her warm during the cold nights. Just like Calder fills her room with scales in the summer to keep her cool. Mason has little stone statues everywhere keeping an eye out for danger. Do you know Raiden is determined to bottle a primary feather for her? What she could possibly do with it, I have no idea, but it's only a matter of time before he figures it out." I laughed, placing my arms over his and giving them a light squeeze.

"Why am I not surprised? They spoil her." I felt him shake his head. His emotions told me he was at ease knowing so many looked after and cared for his little girl.

"Can you blame them? She will be a child for such a short time. Before long, she will be all grown up and her innocence will be forgotten." I couldn't stop a hint of sadness from creeping into my words at the thought.

I felt his love within my mind as his arms tightened around me.

"She will grow up to do great things. Find comfort in knowing she will never face them alone," Elaina said, gliding over to join us. Her words did not surprise me. As a spirit, and the most powerful of them, she always seemed to know things others were blind to. Her next words proved it. "Alec, Marcus may be young, but his soul is strong and pure. Listen to your instincts; they lead you true."

Alec straightened, and I lost the warmth of his arms. "How did you . . . ?"

"It's Elaina," I said as explanation and turned to look at him. "Why is she telling you to follow your instincts?"

His eyes shifted toward the man in question, who stood on the other side of the room. "I'm thinking I might ask him to become a member of my Shadows in a few years. He still has much to learn, but I think he would be a great asset."

I looked over to where Marcus stood talking with Kage, Alec's second. Although he was tall and muscular like all his kind were, he wasn't as filled out as the rest of them, which betrayed his youth. Yet there was a strength in him that went beyond the physical. My gut agreed with Elaina, and I told them so.

"I'm surprised. You said no to the last two I suggested." He watched me with narrowed eyes and a soft brush of curiosity across my mind.

"He sat and listened as Evanna told him the same story three times, while Ebony curled up in his lap. The two before wouldn't even look at her. But beyond that, like Elaina, I can see his heart is true."

"I will think on it. Thank you both." An odd look crossed his face as he glanced from Marcus to the stairs where Evanna had gone.

We continued to chat for some time, catching up on recent events, until Raiden, coming from the kitchen, interrupted the conversation.

"Diana, where's Evanna?"

"In her room. You better not be giving her sweets this late," I scolded, pointing my finger at him and narrowing my eyes.

"She's not there. I just looked." Then he smiled devilishly and added, "I would never."

"Liar." I laughed as I made my way to the stairs that led to the bedrooms.

When I reached hers and looked in, I saw a small bed with a thick quilt of blended forest colors, tossed aside and left rumpled from her nap. Toys were neatly lined up, except for a bunch of scales, stones, and feathers scattered across the floor. There was space in the center of the mess that was just big enough for a child to sit in.

A spot that was currently vacant.

Chapter 4 (Diana)

"Evanna?"

She didn't respond.

"Evanna!" I called louder, thinking she might have wandered into another room. But there was still no answer. Alec must have felt my panic through our mated bond because he was standing at the top of the stairs when I turned toward them.

"She's not in her room, and she won't answer my call."

"Anna, can you come here please?" Alec hollered, knowing his voice would carry farther than mine and drawing the attention of the others. I could hear their footsteps on the stairs.

"What's going on?" Kage asked. He was the first to reach the top and stood directly behind Alec.

"Evanna's not in her room and isn't answering us," I told him.

"Could she have fallen asleep somewhere? Maybe one of the other rooms?" Marcus asked, unfamiliar with her habits.

"She has before. I think we've all found her in our rooms at one time or another," Natela said, to the agreement of the others.

She was right. Evanna did use their rooms as extensions of her own since they stayed in the main cabin so seldom. They never complained about the toys she left in them or when they found her napping on their beds. They would just pick her up and put her back in her own bed.

Without waiting to be asked, guest after guest walked down the long hall to search their rooms.

"She's not in one of ours," said Raiden moments later after he and the other Guardians had checked their rooms.

"Nor in ours," said Tirich, as he and Photine walked out of their room.

Before long, all the rooms had been searched with no sign of her.

"Where could she be?" I asked no one in particular, trying to think of every possible hiding place.

"Diana," Elaina said, drawing everyone's attention with the haunted tone in her voice. "I don't sense her in the house."

"What!" I said, louder than I meant to as my heart skipped a beat.

"Diana, there are no dragon scales here," Drake said from Evanna's room. He was staring at the mess of trinkets she had left on the floor.

"Why would she remove the dragon scales?" I wondered out loud. Before anyone could answer, a thought occurred to me and I turned to Alec. "She wouldn't . . ."

I saw his eyes widen in understanding. We were both running for the back door before we finished our next breath.

I could hear the others following but paid no attention to them as I silently chanted, *Please don't be there. Please don't be there.*

It didn't take us long to get through the house to the back door. It was closed, and for a moment, I thought maybe my fears were unwarranted. Surely Elaina was wrong and Evanna was somewhere in the cabin we had not checked. Then I saw a small puddle of water at the base of the door, and my heart sank. Someone had opened it.

"Has anyone opened this door?" I asked quickly, placing my hand on the door handle.

There was a collective murmuring of noes.

I closed my eyes and opened the door. I felt the biting cold of snow on my face. *Please don't be there.*

I opened my eyes and looked down. Tiny footprints were slowly disappearing as they headed out into the storm.

I don't remember ever running faster than I did as I followed the tiny tracks that weaved their way through the yard and disappeared into the forest.

"Alec, why didn't I take her for a quick walk?" Fear like I'd never known turned my blood cold. I had stopped just beyond the trees, knowing it wasn't smart to blindly follow the tracks into the forest. This storm was one even we could get lost in if we weren't careful.

"We couldn't have known she would run off. She's never done this before." He'd raised his voice to be heard above the raging weather. Otherwise, he sounded calm, but I could feel his emotions riding him like the angry storm we were standing in. "Can you stop it?"

"No." I looked into his dark steel-gray eyes. "I don't have the strength. I've spent weeks crafting this blizzard, and tonight I pushed a lot of power into releasing it. Once I set it loose, it was not meant to stop. It was meant to run its course . . . but I might be able to slow it down."

"What about a tracking spell?" Drake asked, coming up to join us. Snow evaporated as it touched his heated body, evidenced by the steam rising from his skin. It was the only outward sign he would give that he was upset about Evanna being missing.

"It's one or the other. Slow the storm or track her. I can't do both." Helplessness settled in the pit of my stomach. "I'll need the help of you and the rest of the Guardians as it is."

"Stall the storm. I will find her my way," Alec said with a controlled roll of his shoulders, as if loosening his muscles. "How long can you give me?"

"An hour, maybe two."

"Then I better get going. The Shadows will stay to guard you while you and the Guardians are vulnerable."

"Take someone with you."

Our gazes locked. I thought he would argue with me, but to my surprise, he simply nodded. That told me just how worried the Alpha was for his daughter.

"Kage and . . . Marcus, come with me. Draven, you're in charge. Keep my mate safe."

Without a word, Kage and Marcus stripped and shifted into their beast forms. Standing on two legs, they grew to the size of Kodiak bears. They even gained similar bone structures, though their bodies were leaner, more like those of jungle cats, for swift mobility.

As they dropped to all fours to better shake out their fur, I spotted their heads, which were more wolflike, with pointed ears and longer muzzles. Their teeth were long and sharp and their pelts dark as the night, but like all those that came from the Unknown, it was their eyes that marked them as something else. They glowed an eerie red, visible even in the darkest of nights.

"Why Marcus?" I asked Alec silently so no one else would hear as the two beasts disappeared into the forest on powerful legs.

"He's a skilled tracker."

"So is Ozul."

"Yes, but I will only be able to concentrate knowing you are well protected."

He wrapped his arms around me for a hug I knew he needed just as much as I did. *"I only take Kage and Marcus because you asked. I do not need them to find our daughter."*

I gave an understanding nod as I whispered into his chest, "Bring her home."

"I promise." He laid a quick kiss on my lips before he himself shifted into a beast, not needing to remove his clothes as the others had.

I was tall for a woman at just shy of six feet. Without looking down, I stared into eyes that were not red like the rest of his kind but the most striking silver. They matched the shade of Evanna's right eye.

That wasn't the only difference between him and the rest of his kind. Instead of dark fur meant to blend in with the shadows, his was as white as untouched snow. The White Alpha was easily the most beautiful of his kind, and the most feared.

These were the beasts that brought nightmares to the most dangerous creatures of the Unknown, yet I trusted no one more to bring my baby home.

Turning away from my mate as he disappeared, joining Kage and Marcus, I addressed the Guardians. "Elaina, I need you to link the other Guardians to me. Let's stall this storm."

Chapter 5 (Alec)

"Alec, the footprints lead north." Kage's deep voice rumbled through my head. Mindspeech was the only way we could communicate in our beast forms, as our muzzles were not meant for speaking. *"Toward the Hourglass."*

The Hourglass was where the river narrowed to six feet wide. After Anna was born, with the help of Mason the Earth Guardian and Calder the Water Guardian, Diana had shifted rocks and logs to make a rough bridge for easier crossing. It was one of Anna's favorite spots to sit and watch the fish swim by.

I found Kage and Marcus waiting for me at the water's edge. The snow was falling thick and heavy. Even with our advanced sight, it was hard to see more than a few feet in front of us.

"She's going to end up lost in a snowdrift at this rate," Kage commented as he tried to shake off the excess snow clinging to his fur. It was accumulating fast.

"What in the world possessed her to come out in this?" asked Marcus, his voice more gravelly than Kage's.

I joined them at the water's edge near the bridge. *"I do not know, but the faster we find her, the faster we can get out of this mess."*

"Do you think she crossed?" Marcus asked, looking at the rocks and logs. His eyes shifted toward the other bank, searching for tracks, but the snow was too thick to see clearly.

A jolt of fear made my tail twitch. *"She's crossed many times, so I'm sure she would think this time was no different."* It was hard to tell if the darkened stones and logs were just wet from the river or if there was ice. Either way, there was no way to tell if she had fallen in.

"Kage, head downriver and see if there are any signs of her. Marcus and I will cross. If we pick up her tracks, I will call out to you, and if you find anything . . ."

I couldn't bring myself to say it.

"I will call," Kage finished with a nod of his massive head. He turned and slowly made his way down river. I saw him stop every few steps to sniff the ground and look out over the moving water.

Marcus and I jumped over the narrow section, easily clearing the six feet to the other side. Anna would have had to hop the stones and logs in order to cross.

We found no sign of her. The wind had carried away not only her scent but also the layer of snow along the river's edge that would have held her footprints. I found myself looking at the moving water again, silently chanting words similar to what Diana had used a short time ago: *Please don't find her.* Anna would not have survived a fall into the river, even if she had managed to climb out and curl up with the dragon scales. Her tiny body would have frozen.

Pushing away the thought, I tried to reach out with my mind, but I received no response. Which meant either she was unconscious or someone was preventing her from answering. The last thought made my hackles rise, and a growl slipped out.

All of a sudden, the blizzard stopped. I looked up to see the clouds shifting and rolling angrily, but only flurries fell.

"Thank you, love," I projected to Diana, knowing she could still hear me, even from a great distance. No verbal response came, yet I felt her confidence and love like a caress across my senses, letting me know she had heard me.

That confidence spurred me forward. I slowly made my way northwest, while Marcus slowly walked northeast, both of us looking for any signs of Anna.

It felt like hours, but it could not have been more than ten minutes before Marcus bellowed, *"There!"*

That single word made my heart leap. Anna had made it safely across the river!

Her tracks headed northeast toward the darkest part of the forest. What could she possibly want there? I let Kage know we had found Anna's tracks so he could end his search downriver and help us continue ours farther into the forest.

"Be right there," he responded. As one of my Shadows, he would be able to find me through the Shadow Bond, so I did not wait for him as Marcus and I kept pushing forward.

"Alpha," said Marcus. *"Look at her footprints and the surrounding foliage. I don't see snapped twigs, stumble marks, or wayward tracks. These show a quick, steady pace, heading in one direction. Only veering for difficult terrain. There's no panic in her movements."*

"It's as if she knows where she's going," I agreed.

"She can't be that far ahead," Kage said, catching up to us, looking at the footprints and Evanna's path. *"She didn't have that long of a head start."*

"Which makes her lack of response to my calls all the more worrisome. Fan out. It looks like she is still heading northeast. I will stay on the track; you two go about twelve feet to either side of me and see if you can find clues."

It had been about a half hour, and still nothing. No sign of her. It made no sense. We should have found her by now.

"Can you sense her?" Marcus asked for the third time.

"No!" I snapped with a frustrated growl as I bared my teeth at him. Instantly, both of my men lowered themselves to the ground and tilted their heads, exposing their necks.

I stared at them both for a moment, then shook my head slightly and let my whole body relax, letting them both know the danger had passed. It wasn't Marcus's fault we had not found my daughter yet.

"No," I said again, more calmly. *"It's as if she were just gone, but every instinct in me tells me she is here. We must keep looking."*

The snow was starting to pick up speed. Instead of flurries, it was now lightly snowing. I could sense Diana's exhaustion through our bond. She would not last much longer. We had to hurry.

I let out a loud howl, knowing the sound would travel and hoping Anna would call out when she heard it. I had been doing this every five minutes, but so far, there had been no answer.

"What is that?" Kage suddenly asked. He was to the left of me, examining something in front of him.

I followed his line of sight to see a dark spot under a tree, barely visible in the snow about a hundred yards ahead.

I felt my heart rate increase as I stared at it. The distinct shade of red stood out against the bright white snow. With a deep breath through my nose, I caught just a trace of the sent on the air.

It was blood.

Chapter 6 (Alec)

For a moment, I couldn't move for fear of what I would do if it turned out to be Anna's blood. Then, not completely sure how I had reached it, I found myself staring down at the blood-coated snow.

There were footprints everywhere. Some were the size of a small child's, which I was confident belonged to Anna, while the tiny feline paw prints had to belong to Ebony. It was the larger ones that gave me pause.

They also looked feline, about the paw size of a lynx, an animal that wasn't unheard of within these woods. What made me pause and doubt it was a lynx were the two distinct drag marks on either side of the prints.

I wasn't sure what could have caused those, but I could tell the blood was from whatever had made them. The blood droplets followed the tracks as the animal stumbled its way to this tree, where it had finally fallen.

"It's not her blood," I told my men. I felt such a rush of relief that I sat down in the snow and looked up at the trees for a moment.

Both Kage and Marcus bumped into me, letting me know they had both heard and showing their support. Then the snow crunched as they moved away to investigate the surrounding area, while I interpreted the impressions.

After a deep breath, I lowered my head and looked down at the scene. Following Anna's tracks backward, I could see she had slowly approached. At a few points, I found a left and right footprint next to one another, which told me she had stopped. When she had finally reached the animal, there was evidence she had knelt down next to it.

The animal must have been lying there for a while, by the size of the blood pool. I had hoped to get an impression of it, but it must have moved around at some point. I was unable to get a clear image, except that its size appeared to be consistent with a lynx. Which made the mystery of those drag marks more curious. What could cause them?

That's when I saw something in a melted patch of snow next to the impressions.

"It's a dragon scale," I told Marcus and Kage.

"That confirms it was her, but why did she leave it and where did she go from here?" Marcus asked.

"Good question," I said.

"Found some tracks heading this way," Kage said from about fifty

yards to the right. *"They're moving away from the blood, and they're heading south."*

"How many sets?" I asked.

"Just the cat with the drag marks," Kage said.

"Any blood?" Marcus asked.

"No," Kage said, his mindspeech turning curious. *"But, Alec, I think she's riding it."*

"What?" Marcus and I said at the same time, making our way over to him.

"Come look at the prints," Kage said. *"You can see where the animal is walking along. Then the animal stopped and someone small—I'm guessing Evanna—landed here. She searched in the snow—for what, I can't tell, but she must have found it because I don't see anything. Then the animal walks on, only leaving its own tracks. Meaning Evanna must have climbed back on."*

I stared at the tracks, not doubting his assessment. All the evidence was in front of me, but I could not process it. Clearly, whoever or whatever this creature was, it had everything to do with why Anna had snuck out. I just could not understand why.

If only I could figure out what it was . . .

"Well, well, well. What do we have here? The mighty Alpha . . ." A voice of silk with a chilly edge came from behind me. My whole body whipped around; I did not like having that voice at my back. "Shouldn't you be tucked inside your nice warm home with your sweet little family?"

I was shocked to see the woman who stood next to the pile of bloody snow, curiously staring at it. She had pale skin and long white hair that blended in with the snow falling heavily around us. The woman had sharp, beautiful features, as if she had been chiseled from ice. She wore a gown of blue and silver, which should have appeared unusual within the forest, but she somehow made it seem natural.

She reached down toward the dragon scale that still rested where I had found it, but she quickly pulled her hand away as if she had just been burned.

I used her moment of distraction to shift into human form so I could speak to her. I was one of the lucky ones who could retain my clothing through the shift. A blessing, since I had no desire to stand naked in this woman's presence.

Marcus and Kage quickly took up positions on either side of me, watchful of our surroundings. This woman was rarely alone.

"Snow Queen," I said, calling her by her preferred title. The crystalized crown of diamonds and sapphires, arranged to look like snowflakes, gave her away. "You're far from your castle." Normally, she stayed in her domain way up in the northern mountains, where it was always her preferred frigid temperature and always snowing.

"I came to enjoy the delightful storm your lovely mate worked so hard to create for us winter folk. It seemed a pity to miss it. A shame it seems to have ended before it began. Your mate is losing her touch." She didn't bother concealing the petty insult.

A long time ago, Diana and the Snow Queen had been friends. I wasn't sure what had happened. Diana refused to talk about it, but clearly the Snow Queen was still bitter.

Yet even bitter, she was not stupid, and insulting Diana was a stupid move. So why would she?

"Careful," I told her in an even tone. I would not take the bait, but I could not ignore it, either.

She shrugged her shoulders. "Apologies. I meant no disrespect. I'm merely disappointed."

"The storm will continue soon." I knew in my heart it was true. With every minute that passed, the storm grew more intense; at the same rate, I could feel Diana tiring. We were running out of time.

"So it's being delayed?" She tapped her chin in an annoying way that told me she knew exactly why. "What could possibly cause Mother Nature to delay a storm she had already started and her mate to leave the comfort of his home and family?"

I crossed my arms, staying silent even as my blood began to boil.

"Ahh . . ." She stopped the chin tapping to point up at the sky. "Now that I think of it, this wouldn't happen to have anything to do with a little blonde girl? About yay big, with mismatched gray eyes? Looks a lot like her mother?"

"Stop playing games, Eira!" I snapped, tired enough of her

feigned ignorance to drop her title. It was obvious she knew something.

"All right. No need to get so snippy. The snow whispers to me." She raised her hands as if she were caressing the very snow that fell, before looking down at the blood-soaked snow. "It told me where to find her. So I followed the whispers, and there she was."

"Where did she go?" I asked through clenched teeth, unable to stop a growl. Marcus and Kage had similar sounds slipping through their teeth.

Yet she didn't answer right away. Instead, she looked back down at the bloody snow. "You have a very powerful little girl, Alec the Death Bringer. If I had not seen it with my own eyes, I would not have believed it . . ."

Suddenly, she looked up and said in a rush, "I will tell you where she is for a future favor. That is my price. Do you agree?"

Before I could give the Snow Queen my answer, the air pressure shifted and we were all hit with the full force of Mother Nature's blizzard.

Diana had finally lost her hold, and Anna was still missing . . .

Chapter 7 (Diana)

"Where are they?" I asked for what had to be the hundredth time. I paced back and forth in front of the window, occasionally looking toward the door.

"Diana, you need to come sit down," Elaina said. "You're exhausted. You used a lot of energy holding off the blizzard."

"I should have held the storm longer," I snapped, angrier with myself than anyone else.

"You held it off as long as you could." The loving voice gliding through my mind like smooth, rich honey was one I'd heard since birth, but it was not the voice I longed to hear. *"Alec will find her."*

It had been over an hour since I lost my hold on the storm— and almost as long since my mate bond with Alec went quiet. It was still intact, so I knew he was alive. But something was causing static, so I couldn't get a clear read on his emotions or hear him if he had tried to speak.

"I'm Mother Nature. I should have the power to stop it," I responded out loud, looking at Liealia.

She was currently perched on the back of an empty chair in the form of a great horned owl. *Even you have your limits, and you know it.*

Next to her perched what appeared to be a beautiful harpy eagle with fiery blue feathers. Myst, Elaina's sister, was a blue phoenix stuck in bird form. She was part of why Liealia spent so much time as an owl. She provided Myst with a friend who understood her need to fly.

I wasn't surprised when she spoke up.

Listen to Liealia and Elaina. Alec will be here soon enough. Her voice was very similar to Elaina's, but it lacked her sister's softness. The result of dying over and over, only to be reborn again and again. *Now drink your tea.*

"What tea?" I asked.

At that moment, Mason's large frame walked into the room. He was over seven feet tall, with a strong handsome face, and he looked like he could take down a brick house with his bare hands. To be honest, he probably could. It was almost funny seeing him with a fragile teacup in his large hand.

"You're almost as scary as your sister," I told Myst, taking the cup from Mason. It smelled like chamomile. "Thank you."

I felt Myst smile, though her beak wouldn't allow such movements. *I know.*

Mason continued to stare at me until I sat down and took a sip. With a nod, he headed back toward the kitchen, where Raiden, Ozul, and Natela were putting together some food for when Alec and the others returned.

I looked around the room. Those who weren't in the kitchen or patrolling the grounds were all gathered here. Some had fallen asleep, while others chatted softly. There wasn't much any of us could do but sit and wait. Which was not easy for a group of individuals who were used to action. I caught Lucina staring at the door. I wasn't the only one worried; Kage had gone silent too.

It felt like a lifetime had passed by the time I finally took the last sip of tea and carefully placed the cup on the side table. I stood up and began pacing the floor again, rubbing my arms. I felt cold, even with a fire blazing. Drake had made sure it stayed lit and warm, but I couldn't feel it. Even the warmth from the tea was fading from my bones.

I stopped in front of a window. The same window that, only hours before, I had stared out of, watching as Alec and Evanna played in the lightly falling snow. I would give anything to go back to that moment and take Evanna for the walk she had asked for.

"Elaina—"

I couldn't finish the question as I felt a sudden pull on my heart. It was weak but familiar. I knew what it meant. They were coming!

I raced to the door and flung it open. There was nothing but a dark abyss filled with falling snow.

"Diana, what are you doing?" someone called from behind me.

"They're here," was all I could say as I watched a familiar shape make his way through the thick snow. I couldn't move until, at last, he was close enough that I could see he was carrying a small bundle within his arms.

Then I heard it.

"Mama!"

Chapter 8 (Diana)

I don't remember moving, but she was in my arms and I was crying. Every emotion—anger, relief, love, happiness—ran through me as I sobbed into thick blonde hair that smelled like fresh snow.

Alec managed to usher us into the warm cabin. I could hear cheering within the room while everyone crowded around, but it was all a blur. All my mind could process was that I had my baby in my arms and she was safe.

I couldn't stop crying, even as I felt strong arms wrap around both of us and heard my mate's reassuring whispers. "She's okay. We're okay."

It was a long time before I could bring myself to loosen my hold. Evanna started to wiggle, wanting to be put down, but I couldn't let her go. As an excuse, I began to look for wounds.

"Mama, stop it. I don't have any hurts," she said, pushing my hand away from her face for the third time.

"Evanna, what were you thinking? I told you I would take you into the forest after the storm."

"I didn't mean to scare you, Mama. He was hurt and lost," she said, sounding more grown-up than she should have at such a young age. "I had to find him."

"Find who?" I asked, ignoring her dismissal as I continued to search for wounds.

"Him," she said, pointing behind me.

That's when I finally noticed all the shocked faces. They were all staring at something that cowered by the door. When I got a good look at him, I forgot about my search and stared, dumbfounded, at the creature, just like everyone else.

When I finally found my voice, I couldn't bring myself to say it. "Is that a . . . ?"

"Yup," Alec said. "He's why Anna left tonight."

He was about the size of a large dog. He had a feline body, resembling a juvenile lion's, with white fur and reddish-brown spots. At its shoulders, the fur transitioned into brown feathers, which continued up the neck. There, they finally reached a hawk's head with a strong golden beak that hooked down at the end. Growing out of each shoulder was a white-and-brown spotted wing.

"Mama, he's a gryphon!" Evanna hollered excitedly. "I'm going to call him Gawain."

I just stared from Evanna to the gryphon. *A gryphon?*

"How did you . . . ?" I couldn't find words. They were supposed to be extinct. And I was Mother Nature, I would know.

She shrugged. "I felt him."

"Where did . . . ?" I really needed to work on my words. I looked to Alec. Luckily, he and I had been together long enough that he knew how my brain was processing the situation and how to answer my unfinished question.

"The Snow Queen," he said, a touch of frustration entering his tone. Then he explained everything that had happened. How they had tracked Evanna across the river and found the blood that they learned was Gawain's. His kind could mindspeak, but he either couldn't or wouldn't speak to anyone, so how one so young had acquired a wound that bled so badly would stay a mystery.

"Evanna healed him," Kage said. He and Marcus were standing by the fire. They were both wrapped in blankets and drinking something hot. Lucina was tucked under Kage's arm, holding him close.

"Evanna, honey. How did you heal him?" I asked my daughter. My head was spinning.

She shrugged. "I don't know, but he's now mine." She tapped the side of her head before pointing to her heart.

"I don't understand." I looked at Alec.

"I can't explain it, but it looks like she claimed him. Like I claimed my Shadows," he said. "Gawain's been Shadow Bound."

"How is that possible? She's too young, and he's not one of your kind."

"I can't explain it, but it's true. As Alpha, I can feel the claim that connects them."

I sat there staring at him.

"I can't . . ." I rubbed my hands down my face before asking, "What happened next?"

"We found some tracks heading south, but before we could follow them, the Snow Queen showed up. She knew where Anna was and offered to take us to her. The full force of the blizzard hit, so I took her up on her offer."

"Alec, she cannot be trusted."

"I know, but we do not need to concern ourselves with it now. What matters is that she was able to lead us to Anna. That's when we found her, or technically Gawain. He was curled up, using his wings as cover. When we finally convinced him we were not a threat, he unfurled his wings, and we found Anna and Ebony curled up underneath, content with a dragon scale for warmth. He's the reason it took us so long to find her. His magic kept her hidden. He's young, barely a juvenile, and he didn't understand what he was doing. Or at least, that's what Anna told us."

"It's true. He can't control it," Anna said, looking up as she stuffed more of the pastry someone had brought from the kitchen into her mouth. I watched as she gave a leftover piece to first Ebony and then Gawain. "But it's okay. He's mine, so I'll teach him."

I stared at her as she fed the gryphon. *"Teach him?"*

"It's instinctual," Liealia said. She stared at Gawain with her head slightly tilted, as if looking at him at an angle would answer her questions and satisfy her curiosity. *"Like with Ebony."*

"Alec, what does this mean?" I asked so only he could hear.

"It means she's more like me than we thought."

The next hour passed quickly, as food was brought out and the events of the night were shared. When Evanna finally fell asleep curled up on Alec's lap, everyone said good night and found their rooms. The Guardians left for the island with a promise to return in the morning to continue the Yule celebration as originally planned.

Evanna never stirred as Alec and I tucked her into bed or as Ebony walked across her to curl up in her usual spot at the nape of Evanna's neck. I was surprised when Gawain hesitantly climbed onto the bed and lay across the foot of it and then carefully stretched out his right wing, just enough to touch Evanna. It was as if he needed to make sure she was still there.

"I never want to feel this way again, Alec," I whispered as I watched them sleep.

"I can't promise you won't, but I—we—will keep her safe as long as we can. Ebony, and now Gawain, will have to watch out for her when we cannot," he whispered back, taking me by the hand.

I knew he was right. Ebony was a Fae leopard and Gawain a gryphon. She couldn't have better protectors. With a final look at the sleeping child, I gave a slow nod and let Alec pull me from the room, down the hall, and into our own.

That night, I would sleep with Alec's love and strength wrapped around me. The next day, I would enjoy the Yuletide celebration with those I considered family.

The rest I would save for another day.

About the Authors

M. Rose Callahan's interest in the paranormal and all things spooky gives her insights into the terror lurking beneath the ordinary and innocent. An author of short and flash fiction pieces, she twists fright and fate into dread-filled tales, providing readers with a supernatural experience in the well-lit room of their choice. Her tales include "Toss of a Coin" and "The Color of Fear." Follow her haunts on Twitter @MRoseCallahan.

Kelly Lynn Colby is a professional volunteer who lives in the suburbs of Houston with a menagerie of two-legged and four-legged family members. She's an avid believer in community and promotes the writing one wherever she goes. Her BS in biology hangs above her desk looking important while she writes about magic and dragons. To find out more about her and her other publications, visit her website at www.KellyLynnColby.com.

Celosia Crane is a vintage maven by day and a romance / spec fic author by night. She is a whiskey-loving lady with a passion for classic American muscle cars and a penchant for hair flowers, crinolines, and lipstick. Weaving together themes of connection and second chances, her works include "The Ranger and the Greenwitch," featured in the bestselling spec fic / romance anthology *Rogues and Wild Fire*, "Cardinals in the Snow," a novella, and *Whiskey Punch: A Vintage Hearts Novel*, which is published as a serial at www.patreon.com/CelosiaCrane. You can follow her antics on www.facebook.com/CelosiaCraneAuthor and on Twitter and Instagram at @CelosiaCrane.

H. M. Forrest is an experienced writer and editor who lives in sunny Arizona with her son and exotic pets. She has been published under various pen names in Chicken Soup for the Soul books and through winning short story fiction contests. She loves all things elves and has completed numerous short stories about the wondrous world of elves and their adventures, with full-length novels for young adults in progress. You can see her works and updates at www.facebook.com/H.M.ForrestAuthor.

K.A. Fox is a proud military brat who has lived all over the world but now calls the Midwest home. She uses her psychological training to facilitate successful negotiations at work and to convince her husband and three sons that she's always right.

When not writing, she can usually be found hiding somewhere with a book and a bit of chocolate or chasing after her adorable super-sized Yorkie.

You can find her online at www.imkafox.com.

Kimberly Gail grew up in Kansas but has neither lived on a farm nor been swept away to a magical land by a tornado. She does, however, craft magical worlds in her mind that she lovingly transforms into words through her writing.

She is a mother of three: two newly minted adults and one highly opinionated preteen whom she is currently homeschooling.

You can find Kimberly at kimberlygail.com, where she shares about writing, life, parenthood, spirituality, and homeschooling. You can also find her on Instagram at kimberly_gail_writers_life, as well as on Facebook.

K. N. Gemme is a city girl with a country soul. Born and raised in Massachusetts, she didn't start out with a love of books. In fact, she actively avoided them. It wasn't until her fourth-grade teacher recognized her struggle, and a kind woman volunteered to help her, that K. N. finally saw the magic of the written word.

It took years, a simple idea she couldn't let go, and the love and support of her family and friends for K. N. to realize she could be more than just a book snake ("bookworm" is too small a creature to describe her reading habit). So she became a writer herself. Nowadays, once K. N. finishes her time in the real world, you can often find her stepping into the pages of her own work, writing urban fantasy.

K. N. Gemme can't wait to share more of her story with you, so check out her website at kngemme.com.

Ynes Malakova holds a deep reverence for the beauty found in darkness. With intense imagery and lyrical prose, she celebrates life, death, and the specterlike boundary between them. Her debut novel, *The Viper Within*, is quickly nearing completion. Ynes is known for her gothic elegance and has a closet full of sugar skulls, roses, and lace. Follow her on Twitter at @YnesMalakova.

Allorianna Matsourani grew up on the East Coast of the United States and has been a writer at heart since she wrote her first fantasy short story at age twelve. She attended journalism school at the University of Maryland and has directed her writing efforts toward nonfiction articles for newspapers and magazines. Most recently, Allorianna was the editor of a business-to-business magazine for the oil and gas industry.

An avid reader and fan of science fiction, fantasy, and mystery novels, Allorianna has spent the past several years refocusing her writing on fiction. "Ghost Lights" is her first short story to appear in an anthology.

Logos Peregrin grew up in southern US suburbs. Preferring adventures of stories to the tedium of the real world, Logos wanted to be a writer from the age of five. Only her twin sister, an avid reader herself, kindled within Logos any kind of interest in the world around her.

Then, when the Peregrin twins turned eight, life handed Logos the perfect story. By handing her sister the perfect book.

Suddenly, this world didn't seem real. It was overlaid with a strange, new truth. A multiday disappearance and a near-death experience led to the discovery of a power inherent within names and language. A power the Peregrin twins learned both to avoid and to harness. A power that shapes Logos's writings as surely as it shapes the lives of both her and her sister.

You can follow her on Facebook at facebook.me/LogosPeregrinAuthor and on Twitter at @LogosPeregrin.

About the Authors

Emily Van Engen tells people often and proudly: "Middle schoolers are my people." Teenagers in general, with their awkwardness and angst, are exactly the type of people she wants to get trapped in a room with. (Well, maybe not trapped, unless there are an abundant supply of snacks and deodorant.) She writes YA fiction to show her students that they can achieve anything if they work hard. Though she spent her childhood as a proud Virginian, Emily happily embraces her life as a Michigander, including the three seasons of winter. When she isn't teaching her "kids" at school or writing about the ones that occupy her mind, she's at home reading or being lazy with her husband and dog, Cloud (@cloudpups). Her first novel, *Turn*, a young adult suspense, debuted in September 2018. Join her on a journey of creative and educational hijinks at emilvanengen.com or on Instagram @emilyvanengen.